A. M. DASSU

FIGHT BACK

STANDING TOGETHER

Tu Books

An Imprint of LEE & LOW BOOKS, Inc.

New York

BOOKS BY A. M. DASSU

Boy, Everywhere
The Story of Banker of the People Muhammad Yunus

TU BOOKS, an imprint of LEE & LOW BOOKS Inc., 95 Madison Avenue, New York, NY 10016
leeandlow.com

Manufactured in the United States of America
Printed on paper from responsible sources
Edited by Stacy Whitman
Book design by Sheila Smallwood
Typesetting by ElfElm Publishing
Book production by The Kids at Our House
The text is set in Hoefler

10 9 8 7 6 5 4 3 2 1
First Edition

Library of Congress Cataloging-in-Publication Data

Names: Dassu, A. M., author. Title: Fight back / A.M
Dassu. Description: First edition. | New York : Tu Books,
an imprint of Lee & Low Books Inc., [2022] | Audience:
Ages 10-14. | Audience: Grades 7-9. | Summary: Thirteen-year-
old Aaliyah is inspired to stand up to a rise in Islamophobia
after a terrorist attack at a concert, and searches for ways
she and her friends can combat racism. Identifiers: LCCN
2022017532 | ISBN 9781643795881 (hardcover) | ISBN
9781643795911 (ebk) Subjects: CYAC: Identity—Fiction.
| Racism—Fiction. | Muslims—England—Fiction. |
LCGFT: Novels. Classification: LCC PZ7.1.D33556 Fi
2022 | DDC [Fic]—dc23

LC record available at https://lccn.loc.gov/2022017532

MIX
Paper | Supporting
responsible forestry
FSC® C103098
www.fsc.org

For everyone who felt they didn't belong and couldn't express themselves the way they wanted

CHAPTER
1

MATHS—we had a substitute teacher in. And he was SO boring. I could barely keep my eyes open as he droned on about ratios. We'd covered this last week but I don't think the teacher knew, so I looked out of the window at the tiny Year Sevens squealing and shouting as they played cricket on the sunlit field.

Someone prodded my shoulder from behind and I jumped. "Aaliyah!"

When I turned, Sukhi handed me a folded note. Huh? She didn't do this kind of thing.

She shrugged and mouthed, "Jayden."

A note from Jayden? Bad boy from the back of the class to *me* at the front? Weird. I glanced at the teacher—he wasn't watching, so I dropped it in my lap.

Aleeyar

He had totally misspelled my name. Ignoramus. I unfolded the paper slowly to make sure nothing fell out; you never knew what Jayden and his gang were going to do. But there was just a black scrawl in the middle.

I felt another nudge on my shoulder. Sukhi splayed her hands, asking me what it said. Three tables behind, Jayden's blue eyes pierced into me. He was grinning, his two goofball mates mirroring him. I don't know how they got into the top set in maths.

"One sec," I whispered to Sukhi before turning to read it.

Is the London attacker one of your uncles? I heard your dad got the weapons from Pakistan for him.

Heat rose in my cheeks. My chest tightened. He was blaming *my* family for the terrorist incident in London flashing all over the news this morning. As if we were all related.

Ugh. I hate him, I hate him, HATE HIM.

I didn't want to give Jayden the satisfaction of seeing he'd got to me. I scrunched up the note and shoved it in my bag, picked up my pen, and tried to focus on what the teacher was saying.

Ignore them, I told myself. *Their brains are full of snot. They haven't got a clue about anything.*

"So, what'd it say?" Sukhi caught up with me as I pushed through the door, trying to race out of class before Jayden got a chance to say anything else. "Did he ask you out?"

"NO!" I shouted a lot louder than I'd intended, my voice carrying over the rabble of kids in the tiled corridor.

"All right! Calm down! What *did* it say, then?" She rubbed her hands together. Sukhi was always cold, even in the middle of May.

"I don't wanna talk about it, Sukhi. Not here."

"Okay, okay. But you have to show me later." She adjusted her backpack strap and linked her arm in mine. "Have you done your biology homework? Bet it took you, like, five minutes."

"'Course. Would be pretty embarrassing for a future doctor not to know how to label an eye, right?"

"Don't you start with your gory eye stories. Bleurgh." Sukhi rolled her own eyes dramatically and pushed her glasses up the bridge of her nose.

"Ha! I've got a new one, but I'll save it till lunch!"

"Great! So much to look forward to." She raised her neatly shaped brows.

"What you got now?" I asked.

"I've got art. You've got drama with Lisa, right?"

"Yeah." I turned my head to check Jayden wasn't around. "That's kinda an appropriate statement right now. Plenty of drama in *my* life!" I said, singing the last of my words as if I was in an opera.

"Meet you in the hall at lunch, yeah? I so wanna know what he wrote!" Sukhi unlinked my arm and headed toward the stairs.

"I've got library duty today."

"Oh, yeah. See you after that, then!" she shouted as the swarm of kids carried her away.

Books. The comforting smell of books. The calm and quiet library was the best room in the whole school. A safe space for kids like me, a place no Jayden or Mark or Rikesh would ever willingly enter.

Half an hour had already flown by when Mrs. Patel came through the door with her steaming cup of tea and smiled. "Thanks, Aaliyah. Any issues today?"

"No, miss." I finished shelving the copy of *Romeo and Juliet* that one of the Year Ten girls had left on a table and rushed back to the desk to pick up a piece of notepaper. I handed it to Mrs. Patel as she came into the wooden booth. "Mrs. Smithers asked me to give you this list. She said she needs the books ordered in before the end of the month."

"Thanks, I'll take a look later."

"Okay, bye." I grabbed my bag and went to join Lisa and Sukhi, who were waiting for me at the door.

"Hiiii!" I said as Lisa linked one arm and Sukhi my other before we walked down the corridor together. I was now complete, all the different parts of me re-attached. It never felt right being at school when the three of us weren't together.

"How come you were at your holy place so late on a school night?" Lisa was asking Sukhi about the pic she'd posted on Snappo yesterday.

"Oh, the gurdwara?"

"Yeah."

"We had a big langar meal last night for the Bhai Saab Ji who passed away," said Sukhi.

"Oh, right, sorry." It was obvious from Lisa's expression that she had no idea who Bhai Saab Ji was or what it meant.

"He was the guy in charge of the gurdwara, so we all had to go," Sukhi said as she squeezed into me to let a kid from Year Nine pass with his cello.

"When's your Diwali, then?" asked Lisa, eyeing a colorful Hinduism display as she pushed through the door into the empty English block.

"In October, same time as everyone else." Sukhi unlinked my arm and followed me through the door. It was always strange to be in school at lunchtime when it was warm and barely anyone was inside.

"You gonna wear a sari this year?" I smirked, knowing what Sukhi's answer would be.

"Err, no way, not after last time! Couldn't walk in one if I tried." Sukhi laughed and waddled as if she was wearing a mermaid's tail.

"I'd SO love to try one," said Lisa.

"My mum's got some," I said. "Try one on when you come over. You're almost as tall as her—her underskirts should fit you."

"That'd be fab! Yay!" Lisa nudged my shoulder with hers.

We walked into our citizenship class and slid into our seats—Sukhi to my right, and Lisa to my left. The tables were set in a square, so we could all see each other. I got out my exercise book and started doodling with the pencil I'd left inside it.

Lisa rolled the ends of her glossy blonde hair, which still looked freshly straightened, between her fingers. "I'm soo tired," she said.

"Why? Were you on YouTube again all night?" Sukhi bent down to get in her bag.

"Nooo, I wish!" said Lisa. "Darren got home late. He was drunk and shouting soo much."

"Why?" I asked, leaning closer to hear her answer over the chatter and shoes shuffling into class.

"That stupid terrorist attack in London. He was *fuming*."

"Yeah, but that's in London. Like a hundred miles away. What's it got to do with your brother?" said Sukhi.

"Did he have friends there?" I asked.

"Nah. He thinks we're not safe."

"Yeah, I get that. I'm scared to go to London now." I felt around the bottom of my backpack for my pencil case.

Sukhi whacked her citizenship book on the table. "Yeah, I know! Can you imagine living somewhere that's, like, a target? Must be hard," she said.

"Yeah." I put my pencil case in front of me.

"Anyway, I'm tired 'cause he couldn't get over it. He was so angry that innocent people died on a night out. That's all he talks about with his new mates at the Hare and Hound, ever since his friend's dad died in that bombing in London last year. He went on and on for hours, and I had to listen to it all 'cause Mum and Dad were at work. It was like he was ready to kill someone."

I remembered how laid-back Lisa's older brother was when we started Year Seven and first met him. He used to be so much fun, but now he hunched his shoulders and screwed his face at us if he ever opened the door at their house.

"He needs to get a life," Lisa went on. "My mum was really annoyed with him too when he started ranting first thing. Anyway—did you see Jo Mumford's post on Snappo this morning?" Her face lit up. "Can't believe she managed to get NINE extra tickets for 3W from her cousin who works at Montfort Hall! We're going, right?"

"Errr, yeah!" Sukhi chimed in. She rolled her left shoulder back twice and then her right, like Won in the "Wreck" video.

"Obviously!" I said, my insides squealing with excitement. "I thought they were all sold out! Will you ask Jo to save some for us?" I didn't really know Jo Mumford, but Lisa and Jo sat together in history so she would hopefully get Jo to save tickets for us. "I'm gonna beg my mum tonight!"

"Me too!" Lisa and Sukhi said together. We all laughed and then straightened our faces as Mr. Wilkinson emerged in front of our table.

"Okay. Today, we're going to talk about current affairs." Mr. Wilkinson swiftly turned on his heels and paced toward the front of the class just as the last chair scraped under a table. His long arms stretched across the whiteboard as he scribbled something.

TERRORISM

Oh, great. I kept my head down and tried not to look bothered.

"Yes, Jayden," said Mr. Wilkinson.

I looked up. Jayden had his hand in the air. He was grinning and staring right at me from across the room.

"Sir, we've got an expert in here. Just ask *her* all about it," he said, nodding at me.

A few people laughed. As if Jayden was actually funny. I clenched my jaw and started clicking the button on my pen.

"Jayden! I'm warning you!" said Mr. Wilkinson.

Sukhi put her hand up. "Err, sir, maybe we could discuss bullying next week, we've got an expert on that here." She made a face at Jayden and his smirk became a frown as the class whooped.

"Right, ENOUGH!" shouted Mr. Wilkinson, sweeping his blond hair across his forehead. "We've got a lot to get through. Turn over your sheets and read the newspaper article. I'll give you three minutes before we start discussing it."

I kept my head down and flipped the yellow sheet over, hoping Mr. Wilkinson wouldn't let Jayden speak for the rest of the lesson. Sukhi elbowed me and mouthed, "Ignore the idiot."

It was easy for her to say. Jayden didn't send her a note saying she was related to a terrorist, and Sukhi never got bullied for her skin color or her religion. Most people didn't even know Sukhi was Indian when they met her. And it wasn't like anyone who called themselves Sikh was going around bombing places.

Even though I knew the attack had nothing to do with me, I couldn't help letting Jayden's words get to me. He'd always been nasty, but until recently I'd somehow managed to avoid being his target.

Tell him we're not all like that. Maybe it'd shut him up if I didn't stay quiet when he dissed me.

Next time, I told myself. *Next time I have to speak up.*

CHAPTER 2

"I<small>T'S JUST A QUICK SHOP</small>!" said Mum after school as she grabbed a flowery reusable carrier bag and closed the boot. The car next to us beeped and its headlights flashed as its owner approached it.

"I thought we were going straight home! I've got homework!" I squinted in the late afternoon sun as I followed her through the parked cars toward Sainsbury's double doors.

"I know, and I'm so happy you're joining me." She stopped and tucked the loose hair blowing across my face behind my ear.

She was far too cheerful today. Then a thought struck me. Maybe I could make the most of her good mood and ask her to let me go and see 3W with Lisa and Sukhi? Jo had told Lisa in history that she had a couple of different blocks of tickets, and we'd agreed we were more likely to get our parents to say yes if we went for the cheaper ones.

"Mum?" I said, trying to sound completely normal.

"Yeeeeessss, Aaliyah?"

Wow, she *was* in a good mood.

"How come you're so happy today?"

"What do you mean? I'm always happy!" She frowned.

"No, I mean—more than usual!" Good recovery, Ali!

"Well, your abu got the promotion he applied for. He's going to be Head of Science at Judgefield Secondary School! Yay!" She grinned, adjusting her beige scarf to cover the tiny strands of silky brown hair slipping across her forehead.

"Oh, cool!" He'd been asking us to pray he'd get this position since he first went for an interview months ago!

"I just want to pick up some cake ingredients, that's all. You can help me make it, if you want?"

"Errr, I've got work to do, Mum . . . but I'll help you eat it." I grinned back at her.

"Ha! Bet you will!" She smiled, picking up a basket as we stepped through the automatic sliding doors.

"SO," I said, glancing at her, and hesitating before I went on. "You know . . . to celebrate Dad's promotion . . ." I dodged an elderly woman trying to keep control of her overflowing trolley.

"Yes?"

"Could I go and see 3W with Sukhi and Lisa?"

She was quiet.

"Mum?" The temperature dropped as we entered the chilled aisle filled with yoghurt and milk.

"Hmmm . . . not sure how that's celebrating with your family. Your dad wouldn't enjoy it. Anyway, who is this—3W?"

"It's a K-pop band. You know that, Mum! I've only been talking about them for a whole year!" I stopped and passed her a tub of double cream. "They're so big right now, and I can't believe they're coming to perform HERE of all places. It'll never happen again—it's a total one-off."

"You do know that the Rolling Stones played in Lambert too? Your naana actually went to it in his wild days! We're not that far off the map." She swapped the cream for a larger tub.

"Oh, okay . . ." I said. That must've been a big deal for Granddad. Apparently he was a super-fan when he was young. "Well, Jo Mumford at school managed to get some extra tickets because her cousin works at Montfort Hall."

She walked ahead of me and I tried to keep up, weaving between people and their annoying trollies.

"Mum! Listen. If I go to the concert here, then you don't have to take me far, to Manchester or London, see? It's a win-win," I said, taking in the yeasty smell of warm bread from the bakery as we passed it. "PLUS it could be my early birthday present! You don't have to get me anything else. PLEEEEASE?"

"Hmmm. I'm not sure, Aaliyah. You're very young. I'll have to talk to your abu first."

"Ohhhh, Mum!"

Mum blinked hard and sighed. "Okay, look. If it's local and in a proper venue, we can *think* about it—as a one-off experience." She stopped by the flour and viewed me. "You'll need a chaperone, of course."

"Why?" It just came out.

"Because you're thirteen, Aaliyah, and I'm not sending you to a concert on your own."

"Sukhi's big sister will take us. She's twenty-one," I blurted out. Harpreet probably wouldn't want to come with us, but Sukhi had said we should say she would, to convince our parents to let us go.

"Okay, well, let's see." She smiled, putting some icing sugar into the basket. "Right, all done. Let's get you back home to do your work."

I took that as a yes, even if she hadn't said it. "Yay!" I squealed and hugged her tight.

I marched toward the car, grappling with the heavy carrier bag, trying to get there before I dropped it.

I sped past a toddler running all over the tarmac, his mum's trolley rattling as she tried to keep up. Mum followed close behind me.

With no cloud cover and the sun too bright, I had to squint to figure out where our car was parked. Someone bellowed. I stopped mid-step, thinking they were warning me a car was pulling out, but there was no car. And then I heard another shout from behind.

An old bald man stood about a meter away from Mum, inching closer. He pointed his finger at her, his flamingo-pink face sneering.

"AND TAKE THAT THING OFF, IT DON'T BELONG 'ERE."

Mum scurried away from his finger, her shoulders curled over her chest, her head down.

"Mum!"

My gaze darted around the car park, looking for witnesses or someone to help, but the woman with the toddler had grabbed her son's hand and dashed off. *How dare you?* I thought, but the words wouldn't come out.

Mum grabbed my elbow as she rushed away from the man, forcing me to turn with her.

I looked back to check if he was following us, my heart racing. The man stormed off, still shouting.

I swallowed. "Mum. You okay?"

"I'm fine," she said, clearly fighting back tears.

"What happened?"

She was quiet.

"Mum?"

"NOTHING, Aaliyah. Just a rotten old racist man."

"Did he *actually* tell you to take your scarf off?"

She pulled out the key from her handbag, her hand shaking as she unlocked the car. "Get in. Quickly," she said, frantically looking around the car park.

"Mum!"

"Aaliyah, stop annoying me and just get in." She chucked her bag into the car boot. She eyed me as if *I* was the one who had attacked her.

I hung my shoulders and walked over to hand her the heavy carrier bag before climbing into the front seat. I took a deep breath. *Why would he shout at someone who was just minding their own business?* He had no right to do that.

Mum bashed the steering wheel as we parked in our driveway. I looked up from my half-typed message to Lisa about having maybe convinced Mum to let us go to the concert. Mum's brows were wrinkled and her jaw was clenched. She had frowned the whole way home, and I didn't say a word in case she got annoyed with me again.

Mum noticed me looking at her and sighed. "I should have told him where to go," she said finally. I think she was explaining why she was so frustrated. "But I didn't want to make a scene in the car park."

"But Mum, even if you did, everyone would've understood." Even though there weren't many Muslims or even brown people in this area, I couldn't imagine anyone supporting a nasty, aggressive man like that. The woman with the toddler had looked panicked too. As if she was afraid of him and didn't want to get involved in case he attacked her as well.

"Aaliyah, when you wear a hijab, no one understands."

"Has this happened to you before?"

Mum sighed. "No, not like this. Never. I've had looks of disapproval—you get used to that—but until today no one has shouted at me and told me to take it off. Stupid man. People are getting more and more vocal—"

"How old were you when you first put it on?" I cut in. We'd never really talked about it before. It was just such a normal thing. I'd been tugging on it since I was a baby, and before we moved to the suburbs so many women around me wore it, there was nothing to discuss.

Mum looked surprised. "My hijab? Oh, just after I graduated at university . . . after 9/11 happened in

America." She sighed deeply. "After all our lives changed forever."

"What's 9/11 got to do with your hijab?" I asked, slipping my phone into my blazer pocket. I'd send my message to Lisa later.

"Well, weirdly, when women were taking their hijab off for fear of being attacked, I thought it was the right time to put it on. And it *was* the right time for me." Mum pulled the car key out. "All we saw on the news was this link between Islam and terrorism, as if we're all taught to blow people up, and so people started hating us and becoming suspicious of us, and one day I just decided I was going to wear one, even though no one in our family did at the time." She unclipped her seat belt. "I had this strong desire to visibly show my identity as a Muslim and go out to work and remind people that what they saw on the news wasn't really representing all of us . . . Didn't work, though, did it? Muslims are still getting the same abuse as twenty years ago." She raised her eyebrows and pulled her car door open to step out.

It was weird; I'd always imagined Mum had started wearing it after she got married, but she had only been eight years older than I was now. I wondered what it felt like to cover your hair all the time and for your hijab to be the first thing people noticed about you. It was probably really hard. And I was glad I didn't wear it yet.

As we stepped into our shaded porch, Mum said, "Go and do your work. *Ja*. Go."

"I'll help you make the cake," I said, sliding off my school shoes before wandering into the hallway, hoping that might cheer her up.

"I don't feel like making it right now . . . I have a bit of a headache," she said not too convincingly. "Make sure you pray your zuhr before you start."

"Okay," I said, slipping off my school blazer and hanging it on the coat stand, unsure what to say. She was obviously still upset about what had happened. I wished I'd said something to the man. But it was too late now.

CHAPTER 3

W*OOHYUN, ALSO KNOWN AS WILL*—*the boy of my dreams,* I thought as I watched him backflip across the stage on my laptop. I loved his floppy hair, his smooth skin, his cute smile, everything about him. And I was going to see him in the flesh. Tomorrow! My skin tingled just thinking about it.

My first concert—it was going to be *epic*. I don't know how I'd got through the last two weeks waiting for it. When Dad *finally* agreed to buy me a ticket as a super-early birthday present because I'd moped around for days, I'd hugged him so hard, he shoved me off because he couldn't breathe. Ha!

We weren't the only ones who had jumped at the chance to buy tickets from Jo, so we were happy we'd managed to get the last four. At first Mum had said I could only go if she came as our "chaperone" because we were too young, but Sukhi's mum—also Mum's best friend—insisted that we wouldn't enjoy ourselves as much with a parent there, and after a few conversations Mum eventually agreed that Harpreet, Sukhi's older sister, could take us.

My phone pinged on my bed. I spun round in my desk chair and grabbed it. Lisa had messaged us on our group chat.

So I'm thinking of wearing this

She followed with a photo of herself in the short sparkly pink dress she'd worn at her roller-skating birthday party. Well, there was no way in hell my mum and dad would let me go out in anything like that.

I jumped off my bed and yanked open my wardrobe doors. What could I wear? Jeans and my favorite silver sequined Converse—obviously. But which top? I couldn't go in my favorite hoodie—that would look too laid-back and, anyway, it was too warm for it.

A couple of seconds later, Sukhi sent us a pic of a heavily embroidered lehenga hanging in her wardrobe with her other skirts followed by five laughing emojis.

I laughed out loud and sent them a pic of a yellow and green kurta my mum had made me wear to my cousin's wedding last year—proper fluorescent and gross.

Ummm. Maybe a bit much for a concert? Lisa messaged back with a thinking face emoji.

Ha ha! I was thinking of wearing my jeans! I messaged back.

Actually — I'm gonna wear my denim skirt with my 3W T-shirt tucked in. Sukhi messaged.

My shoulders dropped. So I'd be the only one looking different with my legs covered, as usual. If Sukhi had blonde hair, she and Lisa could've looked like cousins. Ah, well, I didn't want to wear a short skirt anyway. Even when Mum had said I could wear the mid-length school skirt with leggings, I'd gone for the longer one.

Oh, yeah! I'll wear mine as well! Lisa messaged.

Eeek! I'll wear my Will one! Can't wait! I typed.

You would! Sukhi messaged with a laughing emoji.

What? He's gonna fall for me the minute he sees me. Watch! I typed back, grinning.

"Aaliyah! Yusuf!" Mum hollered from downstairs. "Dinner's ready!"

"Coming!" I shouted, closing my laptop.

Dad sat at the glass dining table in the kitchen, his brow furrowed, reading the newspaper. Mum was grinding something in the food processor.

"What's up, Abu?" I asked, pulling out my chair.

"Huh? Nothing." He straightened and put on a smile that looked totally fake. I peeked over his shoulder and saw the headline:

AIRPORT BOMB. TERRORIST THREAT LEVEL RAISED

Oh, great. As if one attack wasn't enough. My stomach churned. I'd have to somehow get through next week without anyone asking me how I felt about the incident. Like it had anything to do with me.

"So how's your new job?" I said, trying to distract myself and Dad.

"Oh, I won't be in that position till after the summer holidays." He put his plate over the newspaper headline on the table, and his face cleared and brightened. "But thanks for asking . . . Your brother's home," he said.

"Hmmm . . ." I said, pursing my lips. "He's gonna hog the TV. Bye-bye, my shows," I added.

"Don't be like that," said Mum, putting a steaming plate of rice on my placemat. "I've missed my boy."

I inhaled the smell of cardamom, cloves and lamb. My stomach moaned.

"Mum! He was only gone one day! Bet he was having way too much fun to miss us," I said, picking up my fork. "Can't believe you let Yusuf go on a mini-holiday with his mates!"

"It wasn't a holiday. He went to sort out his university accommodation. It's not his fault the halls had double booked his room." Mum tutted.

"He's eighteen, Aaliyah. Don't compare," said Dad. "He needs everything sorted before September."

"Yeah, whatever." I shoved a forkful of rice into my mouth. It wasn't fair. Yusuf could do so much more than me just because he was older.

Yusuf stepped into the kitchen, his hair wet and his towel draped around his neck.

"Put that out to dry or in the laundry basket, Yusuf. You're not having dinner with a towel around your neck." Mum put a plate of food on Yusuf's placemat.

Yusuf dumped his towel on the back of his chair and sat down.

"So — what did you get up to on holiday?" I asked, knowing it would annoy him.

"What d'you think I got up to? I went to check out my flat that's about *two miles* from my uni," he said, narrowing his eyes at me.

"Hmmm, really?" I said, snapping off half of the papadum on his side plate and taking it.

"Shurrup, squirt!" he said, snatching the papadum back. We both watched it crumble on to the glass table. "Now look what you've done!"

Uh oh.

"Aaliyah, stop it. Leave him alone," said Mum.

I picked up the broken pieces and put them back on his plate, trying to look sorry. Yusuf grabbed a piece and popped it in his mouth. He turned to Mum.

"You've gone viral, Mum. You've got a thousand likes and counting. What happened?"

Mum rolled her eyes. "Why are you stalking my Twitter account?"

"I'm not!" said Yusuf picking up his fork. "My mate liked your tweet from two weeks ago and so it came up on my feed. Anyway, where was this? You want me to go back and find him?"

Dad looked up, chewing his food. "What happened?"

I pulled out my phone and searched Google for Mum's Twitter handle @hijabilawyer. Her top tweet had 1.1k likes and said:

> Not safe from abuse anywhere, it seems. Not even in a supermarket car park where I was minding my own business. Of course a man felt the need to tell me what I should wear and that my hijab doesn't belong here ☹

Mum sat next to Dad with her plate of food. "Remember, I told you about that man in the car park? I was annoyed, so I mentioned it on Twitter. I didn't realize it would resonate so much with people." Mum poured fresh orange juice into her glass.

I was about to ask what people were saying about her tweet when she looked at me and said, "So what time do I have to drop you to this concert?" She obviously wanted to change the subject.

"Mum, I told you, Lisa's mum is taking us. She said there's no point trying to find parking for two cars." I smiled, remembering I only had one more sleep till I was dancing away to 3W songs LIVE.

It was *finally* Saturday 4th June and I was ready for the biggest night of my life. I'd been counting down the hours on our group chat all day:

2 hrs to go!
1 hour! AARGH!
30 minutes!!! EEK!!!

We met at Sukhi's house half an hour before Lisa's mum finished her shift at the hospital. Sukhi had her 3W playlist on, and we were doing two things: dance routines and falling over laughing.

Sukhi's mum had come in once already, asking us to calm down before she went out to visit a relative, but it was impossible. I couldn't stop giggling.

We only got serious around 5:15 P.M.

"Where *is* she?" Lisa paced back and forth between Sukhi's and her sister's beds while glaring at her phone.

"The doors open in forty-five minutes!"

"Still not here," I said, staring out of the window.

Sukhi switched the music off. "Mum and Dad aren't gonna be back from my aunty's till at least seven — do you think we should start walking and see if we can get a bus?"

"Maybe." Lisa turned to us. "Jo said our tickets aren't the same as her special fansign ones. Ours are the cheap unreserved ones so I can't even ask her to save us a space because she'll be backstage somewhere. And if we get there late, *we* might not even get to be together!"

My insides churned. This was supposed to be an amazing experience, and it was already going wrong. What if we were all split up? It wouldn't be the same — it would be awful.

PING!

Lisa swiped her phone to read the incoming message. "Oh, PHEW! Mum's left. She said she had to stay because of an emergency, but she's on her way."

Sukhi jumped off her bed and I followed. We all stood in the middle of her bedroom in a tight circle, jumping up and down and squealing.

"STOP IT!" Sukhi's sister Harpreet yelled from downstairs. "YOU'RE GONNA COME THROUGH THE CEILING!" We looked at each other and fell about laughing again.

The line for the concert snaked all the way around the corner of Montfort Hall. Everyone in the queue looked tiny next to the tall gray building. It was going to take *ages* to get in. It was a warm sunny evening with barely any clouds, just blue sky. We all looked the same in our 3W T-shirts, as if we were in uniform—everyone chatting, people playing 3W songs on their phones, giddy with excitement. Some people held signs declaring their bias—their favorite band member—and others held glow lights that they'd use in fan chants during the concert. I was glad I'd worn my Will T-shirt—other girls were giving me thumbs ups and smiling when they spotted it.

Lisa stood behind a tall man and his young daughter. Lisa's arms were folded and she had her back to her mum. Lisa's mum, who was still in her nurse's uniform, insisted on staying with us until we got to the door, and I felt bad that Lisa was being rude. It wasn't her mum's fault she hadn't been able to leave a sick patient and then had got stuck in traffic.

"Yeah, I'll send it when I get off . . . Love you too," I said to Mum and ended our call. I took a short video of the long line and the venue and sent it to Mum. My battery was already low from putting on my 3W playlist on the way here, and sending the video drained it further. After scrolling quickly past the K-pop and running videos, and the medical stories on my Snappo feed, I slipped my phone into my pocket so I'd have enough battery to take some photos when we got inside. Sukhi was engrossed in messaging someone. To pass time, I focused on my sparkly Converse and moved them around to catch the evening sun on the silver sequins. They were multipurpose—shoes and entertainment.

A phone rang and I looked around to see whose it was.

Sukhi put her phone to her ear. "Yes, we're fine, Mum." She looked at me and rolled her eyes. "We're in the queue waiting to get in, but it's moving now . . . Yeah, Harpreet's here and Lisa's mum is still with us." Sukhi looked at Lisa's mum and smiled.

Sukhi's older sister Harpreet was staring at her phone. At first she'd refused to come with us, but when Sukhi's mum had sat her down and explained that she was the best person to chaperone us at a concert full of young people and if she did, she could go to a concert in London later this summer, she'd agreed. She was making it really obvious how much she didn't want to be here, though. She stood behind all of us and tutted every time a young girl squealed. And she was still wearing the joggers and plain black T-shirt she usually lounged around in at home.

I put my chin on Lisa's shoulder and she cupped my cheek. "It's going to be amazing when we get inside," I told her. "Let's make the most of it, yeah?"

Lisa turned around. "Yeah, it is, you're right."

"Let's figure out how many people are in front of us," I said, peering around at the queue and the man hand-selling glow sticks. Lisa linked my arm and started counting with me.

When we were only five people away from the entrance doors, Lisa's mum kissed Lisa on the cheek. "See you girls later. Have a great time! Make sure you call Sukhi's mum as soon as the concert finishes so she can pick you up. And wait inside until she's here, okay?"

"We will." I grinned. "Thank yoooou!" I couldn't contain my excitement. I was five minutes from seeing Will!

Inside the man at the counter scanned our tickets. Then he checked them over again. I bit my lip. Lisa and Sukhi looked as worried as I felt. Even Harpreet tensed up. What if the tickets were fakes? What if we weren't going to get in?

The man went on to his computer, his face stern, and I was sure he was going to tell us to leave. Sukhi tapped her foot, and Lisa looked close to tears. It felt like we'd been waiting for five minutes when he finally spoke. He broke into a smile and told us there were some extra seats in Block 212 in the upper tier, and if we wanted to stay together we should go there. He pointed us to the right entrance inside, where we were stopped by a security guard. He let Lisa pass, but stopped Sukhi, asking to check her bag. She lifted the flap of her crossover bag, and he glanced at it before letting her through. I smiled at him nervously like I did at the security guards at the airport. "I don't have a bag," I said.

He nodded and let me pass, asking Harpreet to step forward. Phew!

Another usher pointed us to a staircase, and I raced up the stairs two at a time to the hall, Lisa and Sukhi following and Harpreet trailing behind. We had to climb a gazillion steps to get to the upper tier. The bass was thumping in the dimly lit stairwell, and everyone around us was in a rush to get inside the concert hall.

"Hey! Sukhi! Aaliyah, Lisa! Stop!" Harpreet called.

I stopped mid-step. What now?

"Let's buy some drinks so we don't have to leave the hall once we're inside."

"Oh, yeah!" Sukhi said, running back down a few steps to the entrance of the middle tier. I didn't want to stop, but I guessed she was right. Harpreet had been to concerts before so she knew what she was doing, and Lisa and Sukhi were already lining up.

Once we'd got our drinks, I tried not to spill my Coke as I hurried higher up the building, my thighs burning from the exercise. *Maybe I shouldn't have dropped out of running club*, I thought.

The lighting was low when we got to the door to the hall. My heart raced wondering how much we'd missed and if I'd get to see Will close up.

When we got through the door, we heard "You" playing on the speakers, and I soon realized there was no chance of seeing the band properly. Our seats were the furthest from the stage at the top, like in a massive theater.

"This is so far back!" Lisa said, tramping down the steps.

The hall was HUGE and we were right at the top of the gradient.

I held on to the handrail, keeping my eye on the luminescent strips on each step as I stepped down looking for our aisle. It was impossible to see any seats because of all the people standing and dancing to the thumping music.

We moved along our aisle, which was three rows from the exit at the back, squeezing past people standing in front of their folded seats just like in a cinema. I stood in front of my seat and took in the huge stage and the strong whiff of perfume, hair spray and sweat. The song started fading out and the video on the big screen to the left of the stage went blank. The hall went dark and Sukhi and Lisa grabbed my hands. I think we'd just made it!

The screen flashed on and I SAW WILL'S FACE! Loads of people screamed with me. Then came Won's face, and Sukhi hollered with the other people who loved him, then Wolf's face showed up and Lisa whooped with all the rest. When all three were on-screen together, the whole hall screamed. I felt as if I might burst and I hadn't even seen them in person yet! And we did this again and again with each face, each pose till they started walking down some steps. I couldn't tell if the steps were on the stage here or if this was pre-recorded.

Some flames went up in front of the stage and we all screamed louder. The stage lit up and 3W stepped to the front. I jumped and clapped, my arms high above my head.

We couldn't see 3W properly, only close up on a big screen. But it really didn't matter that we were so far back. This was amazing. The atmosphere was electric. Everyone was singing and cheering and dancing. *Everyone* was happy. Sukhi and Lisa looked at me, and we all squealed. Even Harpreet smiled.

I. AM. HERE. BEST CONCERT EVER!
#3WConcert

I thumbed my phone keypad in the dark, pressing Send to tell all the saddos on Snappo that they were missing the BEST. CONCERT. EVER. They didn't need to know it was the only one I'd ever been to and had nothing to compare it to. I wanted the world to know I was actually here, in the same room as 3W. Okay, a very big room, but we were breathing. The. Same. Air.

The music was pumping. Bass travelled in my ears and flowed through my veins. Everyone jumped to the beat of "Take Me Back," the seventh song of the night, shouting the lyrics in unison and trying to copy the dance moves. Some girls around me were recording the music and 3W on the stage, the light from their phones illuminating the dark hall, but I was happy just reveling in the vibes.

"DRAMA. DRAMA. DRAMA," we all screamed as they sang.

3W looked like tiny action figures on the brightly lit stage, jumping to the beat, a sea of arms waving in front of them. They were wearing white T-shirts and denim, just like us, and it was incredible to hear them sing all the songs we knew live. Sukhi and Lisa screamed the words as if 3W might hear them. I took another swig of my warm, watery Coke—all the ice had melted.

Harpreet was texting someone. The girl next to me swayed with the beat and we smiled at each other as she hollered at the stage. Even though the air was hot and stuffy and I'd hardly slept the night before because of my excitement, I was ultra-awake, my face aching from being stretched into a smile for so long.

The strobe lighting pulsed over the stage. I raised both my arms and sang loudly along to the last line of the chorus with everyone else.

"THANK YOU!" shouted Will as they finished the song. My stomach fluttered. Won and Wolf turned to drink some water, and the whole arena burst into whooping and applause. Will called up an interpreter, who told us Will was really happy to be in the UK tonight and thanks for the biggest welcome.

Life equals awesome, I thought. I don't think I'd ever felt happier. I sighed and put my arms around Lisa and Sukhi, squeezing them both tight. They squealed and hugged me back.

BANG!

The boom echoed around the hall. The room shook and flashed with light in the lower gallery. Everyone stopped and there was silence for a second. We parted from our group hug and whooped. It must've been fireworks to start off the next section of the show, *or* maybe 3W was releasing a new song, right here, just for us!

Then screaming echoed through the hall, but it didn't sound like before. Smoke rose in the far corner near the stage and drifted up the gallery. Onstage, we could see the silhouettes of the band and crew running past the huge speakers to get off the stage.

This wasn't part of the concert.

Lisa, Sukhi, and I shared a look, the whites of their panicked eyes freaking me out in the dark. Harpreet put her hand on Sukhi's shoulder.

What was going on?

And then we saw hundreds of girls and their parents stampeding in our direction.

I gasped and searched my best friends' faces. A split second later I knew what we had to do, and yelled, "RUN!"

CHAPTER
4

PANIC SWELLED THROUGH ME. My heart pumped a hundred times faster than it should. All the people who had been in front of us during the concert were scrambling for the exit stairs—toward us. I grabbed the back of Sukhi's T-shirt and we followed Lisa and Harpreet out of our row, pushing into the heaving crowd on the walkway. Around us, panicked fans jumped over seats, trying to get to the exit quicker.

Lisa tripped on a seat that hadn't been pushed back and fell head first as she entered the horde of people. I tugged on Sukhi's T-shirt and bag strap to stop her from falling on Lisa. Sukhi screamed, "HARPREET!" who turned and yanked Lisa by the arm as if she were a toddler. Lisa got up and put her arms out to feel for Harpreet's back as she entered the walkway. Sukhi clutched Lisa's T-shirt and I clung to Sukhi's.

The pressure of the crowd made it hard to keep my

balance. Each person that shoved past me trod on my toes. We had to keep moving—the throng of people surging in our direction would trample us if we didn't. An elbow jabbed me in the lip and I tasted blood.

I gripped a railing to stay upright. Suddenly, the hall lights came on. Lisa's face was red and streaked with tears. Sukhi prodded Lisa to move forward, her determined gaze on the exit doors where Harpreet was heading. They seemed so far away, even though we were only meters from them.

My body burned and my chest was tight. Screams enveloped us. The hall was becoming cloudy with dust and smoke, and I could smell burning. We had to get out, and with all the pressure building from all sides, I wasn't sure we were going to.

Finally, we surged through the doors into the large foyer, and Harpreet, Lisa and Sukhi spread out. I gulped. It was filled with people from the other exits. We were *still* so far from the main entrance. Here, though, it was quieter, except for a girl sobbing somewhere close by.

"Stay together," Harpreet ordered, grabbing Sukhi's hand. I held Lisa and Sukhi's hands either side of me, and we stepped down onto the staircase.

In silence.

Step after step after step. In time with the heartbeat booming in my ears.

Focused on the backs of concertgoers ahead, I stepped onto the ground floor after what felt like half an hour. I stumbled over something and let go of Sukhi's hand to steady myself by holding on to the damp shirt of the man in front of me. That's when I noticed all the shoes and bags strewn over the floor, abandoned in panic. My stomach lunged.

"KATY!" Someone grabbed my T-shirt from behind. My breathing was so fast I wondered if this was what it felt like to have a heart attack. Gripping Lisa and Sukhi's hands tighter so I wouldn't lose them, I turned around.

A woman with a shaved head pressed against my arm. She pushed between me and Sukhi, leaving the scent of her strong perfume behind as she plunged forward, sweat trickling down her tattooed neck. There was blood splattered over her 3W T-shirt—a previously pristine white one just like mine. Oh god.

"KATY!" The woman lunged through the row in front of us and tapped a girl with a brown ponytail. But when the girl turned, it obviously wasn't who she was looking for, and the woman pushed past her, still calling for Katy.

I wiped the snot and tears rolling off my chin with my shoulder. Sukhi clasped my wrist and squeezed it. I looked out at the sea of white T-shirts and took a breath, thankful I hadn't lost Sukhi and Lisa and Harpreet.

I fixed my eyes on the man in front of me as our bodies knocked into each other in the crush, and I took each step praying we'd make it out. That we wouldn't all get crushed in here somehow. I repeated Allah's name in my head, begging him to help us. The scent of vomit rose up my nostrils, and I prayed I hadn't stepped in any. There was no way I was going to stop and check.

Streetlights. I blinked as we finally made it into the humid night through the main doors, thrust forward by all the people behind us. It wasn't the same calm street we'd been on a few hours earlier. It was mayhem. People screamed names over the sound of distant sirens, searching for their friends or parents. Adults cried into their phones. Kids much younger than us stood alone in their stained and creased 3W T-shirts, tearful. They'd probably lost their parents in the crush. A woman with dust-covered hair pushed past us back into the crowd, followed by a guy with a deep gash above his eyebrow who was coughing violently, blood dripping down his face. People were rushing from another exit toward the one we'd come out of, looking for their loved ones. The knots in my stomach tightened. I had to call my mum. I let go of Sukhi's hand and tapped my jeans pocket. Thankfully, my phone was still there.

"GET OUT OF THE WAY! MOVE!" A skinny

bearded man in a black backstage T-shirt and trousers that were split open jostled past me. He looked as if he'd been in a war zone. Behind him came two dust-covered men carrying a woman lying flat across their arms. Her eyes were closed.

Every single hair on my body stood on end. I turned to Sukhi, whose face was pale; Harpreet looked panicked and was breathing heavily; and Lisa's eyes brimmed with tears. I swallowed. What had *happened* in there?

We spilled onto the pavement and the crowd loosened.

I gulped air and let go of Lisa's clammy hand. "You okay?" I asked.

"I think I hurt my arm, and my head's killing." She rubbed her temple. Her cheeks were so flushed they were almost scarlet. "What just happened?"

"I think it was a bomb or something," said Harpreet, her eyes watery.

A bomb? My stomach twisted in knots. I couldn't speak. Those were words we heard on the news, not in real life.

"We have to get away from here," said Sukhi in a panic, eyes darting around.

"Let's go and sit on that wall," Harpreet said, pointing at the Holiday Inn.

We crossed the car-blocked road and sat on the

hard brick wall beside the hotel. I wasn't cold, but I couldn't stop shivering.

Where had the bomb gone off? 3W had thankfully run off the stage and everyone else seemed to have run out in the same direction we did, so who were they trying to bomb?

My toes curled. I didn't want to think about it. "How's your arm?" I asked Lisa. She circled it around slowly—it seemed to move okay so it wasn't broken.

I scanned Lisa, Harpreet and Sukhi's clothes, and then mine, for blood and dust—from the outside we looked almost the same as when we'd arrived, but it was obvious we weren't the same on the inside. Lisa and Sukhi looked as shaken as I felt. Harpreet had tears streaming down her face as she messaged someone.

"Oh my god, Darren's called me about ten times," Lisa said, staring at her phone as I pulled out mine to call my mum. Sukhi was already calling hers.

"I can't get through!" Sukhi said, glaring at her screen. "I think the network's jammed 'cause everyone's using their phones at the same time. Can that happen?" She stared at me. Her black hair stuck to her forehead with sweat.

"I don't know," I said. "Gah, mine isn't connecting either and the battery's about to die."

"I'm gonna try and get hold of Mum. Stay here." Harpreet got off the wall, her phone to her ear, and walked a little further down the road.

"LISA!" someone bellowed. I glanced up and saw the road crammed with police cars. Officers had left their car doors wide open as they ran toward the hall. Paramedics in green uniforms with huge backpacks pushed through the crowds still pouring out of the exit doors.

"LISE! LISA!"

We all sat up and searched for the voice. Ahead, I saw Darren, Lisa's brother, in a gray hooded top and joggers. He stood at the edge of the crowd, put both his hands to his mouth and screamed. "LISA!"

"DARREN!" Lisa stood and shouted back.

I let out a breath. It was good to see someone familiar. He'd take us home.

Sukhi and I joined in yelling his name, and Darren spun toward us, his face gaunt. He ran across the road.

"Lisa! Thank god!" When he reached us, Darren leaned down and pulled his sister into his arms. He closed his eyes and rested his cheek on her hair. "I'm so glad you're safe," he said.

Sukhi glimpsed at me, both our eyes filled with tears.

"How did you know something happened?" Lisa spluttered in between sobs.

"I was drinking outside a bar round the corner. I saw ambulances and police cars racing this way. I knew it was a bomb. I just knew it. This is what they do. I checked Twitter and people in the hall were tweeting about it, so I ran over to find ya."

Lisa cried into his chest.

"Shhh, it's all right. I'm here. I'm gonna sort it." Darren raised his head to look around. And that's when his eyes fell on me. His face hardened and his mouth twisted.

Why was he looking at me like that?

I stepped back as he released Lisa and moved forward, his legs wide, his hands fisted, his eyes narrow and cold.

"This is all your fault!" he spat.

"Leave her alone, Darren!" screamed Lisa, grabbing his arm.

He snatched it away and pushed her back. "You Muslims need to go back to your own country. Bomb your own people. The less of YOU the better!" His finger almost touched the tip of my nose.

I froze. My heart felt like it'd stopped beating. My mouth went dry. I tried to speak, but no sound came out.

I didn't know what to think.

He wasn't going to help us get home?

He was blaming the bombing on *me*?

Sukhi dragged me back by my arm. "Come on!" she yelled, while Lisa tried to push Darren back.

"You'll get what's coming to ya! You watch!" he shouted after us.

CHAPTER
5

AS SOON AS I got around the corner and couldn't see Darren any more, I was sick down the hotel wall. The Coke I'd drunk, the chips I'd eaten, splatted on the floor. Tears soaked my face. Sukhi pulled a tissue from her bag, handed it to me and rubbed my arm.

I wiped my mouth, then tugged at Sukhi's arm, but she wasn't budging. "Come on! We have to go!" I yelled at her.

"Ali, my mum's picking us up. Harpreet will be looking for us. We can't leave!"

"Did you see his face? I can't stay and wait!" I turned and started walking fast up the steep road. I had to get away.

"Where you going? We have to wait *here* for my mum and Harpreet!" she called.

"I need to go!" I said, breaking into a run.

"Ali!" she screamed. "Just wait!"

But I knew I couldn't risk Darren coming back.

I'd passed two buildings when Sukhi shouted, "Call me when you're home, Ali!"

I put my thumb up, not looking back. I had to get away from Darren. He didn't hate Sukhi. He didn't say anything to her because he knew she wasn't Muslim. He hated *me*.

I sprinted as if I was in a hundred-meter race, my feet pounding the pavement, trying to block out the sirens and honking horns in the streets around me, tears streaming down my face. The indigo sky, without a star in sight, seemed to stretch on forever. I passed row after row of tall office buildings closed for the weekend. The road was empty, a complete contrast to how it was in the day. A black cab drove by, and I wondered if I should chase after it and ask the driver to take me home. Mum or Dad could pay the fare. But it sped toward the concert hall and out of sight.

I didn't know where I was going until I got to the top of the hill and saw a bus stop for the number 53, which went down Lancaster Road. Uncle Aziz's house! Dad's eldest brother and his wife lived that way, through the park. I'd be there in a few minutes. I pulled out my mobile and tried to call our house phone. It still wasn't connecting. Then it switched off in my hand and died.

Oh god. I'd have to call Mum and Dad from there. I had to make it to Uncle Aziz's house. I'd be safe once I got there.

It wasn't long before I reached the big wrought-iron park gates. I stopped outside them, near a bin that smelled like it needed emptying. It seemed too dangerous to go through the park alone at night. I focused on my breathing to slow it down. My insides lurched as I tried to figure out another way to get to their house. If I followed the pavement up to the main road, I'd be able to get around the park. It would take longer, but at least I'd be under the streetlights, where it felt safer.

Still, I looked over my shoulder every few seconds to check no one was following me. I tried to reassure myself that no one would know I was Muslim. I didn't wear a hijab. They couldn't know—Darren only knew because of Lisa.

Please, Allah, don't let the bomber be a Muslim. Please don't let them be Muslim, I prayed. I wanted to prove Darren wrong. I needed to prove everyone wrong.

The main road was eerily quiet because it'd been closed off. There were cone barriers on the intersections. The police were probably all at the concert. I don't know how long it took, but it felt like forever. It felt as if my chest had a weight on it and I was running through sand.

When I finally made it to the townhouse-lined street, I stopped to catch my breath. *What if they're not in?* It was a Saturday night. What if they'd gone out to eat? I was probably safer nearer the concert hall. I shouldn't have left. But now that I'd made it all this way, I had to at least check if they were in.

I knocked on their brass doorknocker five times and rang the doorbell, to make sure they heard me. If they were home. The upstairs landing light was on, but they could've left that on for security.

The hairs on my neck stood up. *Oh, no, what an idiot!*

I ran down their front steps to check if I could see any movement through the windows. I couldn't.

Hanging my head, I pulled open their wooden gate and stepped onto the pavement. I had no money, a dead phone, and the concert hall was miles away. I didn't even know how I'd run that far. What if Darren found me as I walked back? My stomach rolled at the thought.

"Hello?"

I did a sharp turn and breathed out.

Uncle Aziz stood at the door in his night-robe, gazing out.

"As-salaamu alaikum, Bareh Abu!" I cried as I rushed back through the gate into his small front garden.

He squinted to see me more clearly.

"It's Aaliyah!" I said, as I got up the stone steps.

"Aaliyah? Baitay, what are you doing here at this time? We were just going to bed. Where's your dad?" he asked, searching for our car on the road, his forehead creased with concern.

"Umm . . . He's not here. It's just me. My phone's not working, I need to call my mum and dad."

"Come, come in," he said, stepping back and ushering me inside.

Aunty Rashida came down the stairs in her night-time kaftan and stood in the narrow, dimly lit hallway.

"Aaliyah? Are you okay? What's happened?" She looked as baffled as Uncle Aziz.

Her warm, motherly face made me burst into tears. I couldn't help it.

"Aaliyah?" asked Uncle Aziz. "Has someone hurt you?" He put his hand on my shoulder. "Come in, we'll call the police," he said, leading me into their front room.

"No, please," I said, wiping my face as I bent down to pull my laces apart and take my Converse off. They were grimy from being trampled on, not the sparkly shoes I'd left my house in. "You don't need to," I added, following him. Aunty Rashida came in after me and shut the door.

I stood awkwardly in front of the blue velvet sofa facing their marble fireplace as they both sat on the matching armchairs either side of the room. My cousin's football trophies were pride of place across the mantelpiece, even though he'd moved out years ago. I was safe, yet I didn't feel any relief.

"Sit, Aaliyah, sit down," said Aunty Rashida, waving her hand toward the sofa behind me.

I flumped at the edge of the sofa, the side closest to the door, trying my best not to inhale the lingering smell of incense. It would only make my headache worse.

"I-I need to call my mum and dad. My phone's not working." I rubbed my eyes and stared at the smudged eyeliner on my fingers.

"Where have you been all alone at this time of night? It's half past ten," said Uncle Aziz, glancing at the wall clock.

"I was . . . I was at Montfort Hall . . . at a . . . erm . . . with my friends . . . erm . . . my friend's big sister and mum," I said, wondering what they'd say if I told them I was at a concert on my own at night. "A . . . I think . . . a bomb went off in there."

"Ya Allah!" said Aunty Rashida, putting her hand over her mouth.

"What do you mean, a bomb?" said Uncle Aziz, leaning forward, his arms on his knees. "A bomb in Lambert? Are you hurt? Are you okay?" He cast his eyes over me.

"Yeah. I'm fine . . . I wasn't near it, thank God."

"Praise be to Allah," Aunty Rashida put her hand to her chest. "Alhamdulillah."

"Allah willing, it won't be another stupid idiot-fool calling himself a Muslim," said Uncle Aziz, his brow furrowed deeper than I'd ever seen it. "We have enough problems, without things like this."

"I'll go and call your mum," said Aunty Rashida, taking the house phone off the cradle and heading to the door.

Uncle Aziz got up to switch on the big flat-screen TV that sat on a wooden stand in the corner of the bay window.

And there it was. All over the news. Spelled out right in front of me:

**MULTIPLE INJURIES IN LAMBERT TERROR ATTACK.
POLICE RESPOND TO MONTFORT HALL BLAST REPORTS.**

"Breaking news from the Midlands," the reporter said. "Police are responding to a serious incident in Lambert after an explosion during a 3W pop concert. Eyewitness reports say they heard a loud bang. Police are refusing to confirm whether it was a bomb at this early stage."

The screen shifted to mobile footage taken by someone at the concert. Panicked fans were running down the stairs. Jumping over barriers and seats. Screaming in fear.

My heart raced. My breathing sped up. It was as if I was back in the concert hall, going through it all again, the same panic coursing through my veins.

"Aaliyah? Aaliyah!"

CHAPTER 6

Uncle Aziz's hand was on my shoulder. His brow furrowed with worry.

"Here, have some chai." Aunty Rashida handed me one of her posh flowery china mugs.

"Thanks, Bari Ammi, but I don't drink tea," I said.

She looked at me as if I was extraterrestrial. "Okay, I'll get you some water. Don't cry, beti." She stroked the top of my head before leaving the room again.

Would Mum and Dad be angry with me for persuading them to let me go to the concert? I acted as if I was all grown up and could handle myself. But what did I know? We were so lucky to have got away uninjured. What if we'd had better seats at the front? I shuddered and rubbed my arms.

I needed to message Sukhi and Lisa, to check if they were okay. But it felt awkward to ask for a charger right now. What if Sukhi and Harpreet were *still* waiting for their mum? I closed my eyes to block the thought.

"It's a good thing you came here," Aunty Rashida said as she entered the room again. "All the roads around the concert hall have been closed, so your ammi and abu wouldn't have been able to get to you." She handed me a tall glass of water.

"Thank you," I said, taking a sip, watching Uncle Aziz glued to the news. He ran his hand over his bald head.

"I've just spoken to them. They're on their way." Aunty Rashida stood in the middle of the room, observing me. "They'll park somewhere and walk here."

My poor mum and dad. And then the thought struck me that someone might attack Mum because of her hijab.

"I'll go to them. Tell them not to come," I said, getting up from the sofa.

"No, no. You can't go out there, Aaliyah," said Uncle Aziz, still facing the TV screen. "They will come here and get you."

"As-salaamu alaikum. Where is she?"

It was Mum. She was crying.

I put my glass of water on the mantelpiece and rushed out of the door. "Mum!"

"Oh, Aaliyah!" She pushed past Aunty Rashida in the front doorway and wrapped her arms around me, burrowing her face into my head. I don't think I'd ever been happier to see her.

"Aaliyah, my baby." It was Dad. His arms wrapped around me and Mum. I was safe. "Allah shukar. Well done for making it here . . ." His voice broke. He sounded like he'd been crying.

Inside the front room, Mum and Dad sat on either side of me on the three-seater sofa.

"I was going out of my mind," said Mum, squeezing my hand tightly. "I couldn't connect to your phone or Sukhi's mum's. The police didn't have any information. We thought we'd lost you." She broke into tears again.

"I tried to call you," I said. "But the network was down and I couldn't get through, then my phone died." I rested my head on her shoulder and closed my eyes, taking in the sweet, floral scent of her perfume.

"How did you get here?" Mum asked. "Have the girls gone home?"

My stomach rolled. "Uhhh . . . I ran here in a panic . . . They're still at the—"

"Were they with you the whole time? No one got separated or injured?"

My tear splashed on to Mum's hand. I'd left Sukhi

and Lisa. Even though Harpreet was technically an adult, I really shouldn't have.

"Shhh . . . it's okay." Mum stroked my face. "I texted Lisa's and Sukhi's mums, but they haven't got my messages. I'll try them again once the lines clear. Thankfully Rashida Baji got through to the house phone soon after, otherwise I'd have had a heart attack worrying about you."

"My phone's dead. Can I try and send Sukhi and Lisa a message from yours?" I asked Mum.

"Yes, yes—check they're okay." Mum unlocked her phone and handed it to me. I went into Messages and then realized I didn't know Sukhi's or Lisa's numbers by heart. Ugh. What if Darren had got angry at Lisa for being my friend after I left? Why did I run off without checking Sukhi had found Harpreet? I closed my eyes and dropped my chin to my chest, the shame rising inside me. I'd been so stupid.

I looked around for Uncle Aziz's phone and saw it was newer than mine. I couldn't even ask for a charger because it wouldn't work on my phone.

The room grew silent, the clock ticking the only sound.

"So was it a Muslim?" said Dad out of nowhere.

I sat up straight. Dad looked small tucked into the sofa next to me, repeatedly rubbing his thighs, lines across his forehead.

"No one knows yet, but they're already speculating. It's only a matter of time," said Uncle Aziz. His recliner clanked open.

"God willing, it won't be," said Mum.

"Of course it will be! It always is nowadays!" said Dad. "A bomb at a concert full of little kids? It's going to be some nutjob claiming he's doing it for ISIS or Al Qaeda or some other sick group." He rubbed his forehead with two fingers as if he had a headache.

My heart plummeted. If he was right, it would give people like Darren more "proof" that all Muslims were bad.

The doorbell rang at 11:45 P.M. We jolted in our seats. Aunty Rashida left the room. What if it was the police, looking for witnesses or something?

"Where is she?" It sounded like Yusuf.

"Oh, Yusuf!" Mum cried as he came through the door and released my hand to jump up and hug him.

"As-salaamu alaikum," he said to everyone in the room. "All right, everyone? Dad." Yusuf nodded at Dad.

"You all right, squirt?" he asked, bending down to rub and mess up my hair. He always did that even though he knew it annoyed me.

"Gerroff," I said, shoving his hand off and pushing into Mum's shoulder, forcing a tearful smile. It was so good to see him.

He sat on the beige carpet in front of the fireplace, his head down, pulling on the carpet pile. He shifted and looked at me on the sofa. "Seriously, you all right?"

A lump formed in my throat. His protective-brother face reminded me of the time he'd had words with Luke Branstan in Year Three when he kept running off with my woolly hat. He would've sorted Darren out. He'd never have let him scream at me.

"Yeah," I said, as a fat tear rolled off my lip. And suddenly I couldn't stop crying again.

CHAPTER
7

I PLUGGED MY DEAD PHONE into the charger on my desk as soon as I got home and looked around my room, taking it in—my bed next to the window, my small desk and the shelves above it full of books, my wardrobe filled with clothes opposite the door. The piles of laundry on the floor. All of it gave me some relief. I was lucky I was home and not in a hospital. My phone came on after a few minutes and I stood waiting for it to upload my notifications.

There were forty-three messages on our group chat. The first fifteen were from Sukhi and then two from Lisa.

Sukhi: Ali—you home yet?

About an hour later:

Lisa: I'm home—hope you two are okay.

Quickly followed by:

Lisa: Sorry about Darren ☹

Sukhi replied, telling her he was horrible, but she guessed he probably overreacted because of what happened.

And then a tiny alert had popped up:

Lisa has left the group

Soon after that about twenty-five messages came from Sukhi asking where Lisa was and asking me to reply or she'd call the police.

Sukhi! I'm home. I'm sorry I ran off! I typed.

OMG!! ALI!!! WTH!!! She immediately typed back. She must've had her phone in her hand.

I ended up at my uncle's house—the one who lives near town. You okay?

I added:

What's happened to Lisa? Why's she left the group?

The phone started flashing with Sukhi's name. I took a beat and swiped left.

"Aaliyah!" she said in a loud stage-whisper. "Why did you do that? I've been freaking out for hours! Lisa went off with Darren, and me and Harpreet had to wait for ages—it took my mum, like, two hours to get to us! And she was so angry with Harpreet for letting you go off alone!"

"Sukhi ... I'm so, so sorry. I wasn't thinking. I'm really sorry." My voice broke and I couldn't stop myself from crying—again. This was getting majorly embarrassing.

"It's all right. It was awful. You don't understand. People, like, died." She sounded as if she was fighting back tears too.

"I know," I said, crashing on my bed, staring at my lap. "I saw it on the news."

"We were lucky, you know," Sukhi said.

"I guess it was a good thing we ended up with crappy seats and weren't anywhere near the stage like we'd wanted to be," I said. "Did you see anyone else from school?"

"Yeah. I saw Jo Mumford. She was on a stretcher."

"Jo?" I said, my stomach lurching. I'd seen her in the lunch queue just yesterday. "What's happened to her?"

"I dunno, but I asked one of the mates she was

with and she said her leg was seriously injured and she couldn't walk . . ." Sukhi went quiet.

I didn't know what to think, let alone what to say. A wave of nausea rose in my throat. I couldn't imagine it happening to anyone, but Jo was someone we knew. Someone we went to school with. The pit of my stomach hurt just thinking about it.

"Sukhi?" I said after what felt like a long silence.

"Loads of kids lost their parents and couldn't find them, Ali — it was horrible . . ."

"Sukhi?"

"Yeah?"

"I'm *really* sorry for leaving you. I just couldn't handle it after what Darren said. I was so scared, I wasn't thinking."

"Yeah, I get it. He was so nasty . . . I'm sorry I didn't come with you. I couldn't leave Harpreet . . . but he's an idiot. Ignore him."

I stayed quiet. It was easy for her to say. *She* wasn't the Muslim who was going to be blamed for the attack.

The door opened. It was Mum.

"Listen, I'd better go," I said. "Mum's here. I'll call you tomorrow, yeah?"

"Yeah. I'm just glad you're okay. Catch you later," she replied.

I put the phone on my bed and watched Mum cross the room with my Books Are Life mug in her hand.

"Here, have some haldi doodh." She handed me a mug of steaming turmeric milk—the South Asian cure for all illnesses, apparently. Not sure how it was going to help me tonight. "Was that Sukhi?"

"Yeah," I said, taking the mug by the handle to make sure I didn't burn my hand.

"Her mum said sorry Harpreet let you go off like that."

"But Mum, she didn't know I left! I ran away . . ." I blinked hard to get rid of the image of Darren's face.

"Why did you leave your friends? Did something happen?"

I looked at my nails and tears brimmed in my eyes again. I couldn't tell her. "Will you *please* tell her mum it wasn't Harpreet's fault?"

"Okay, I will, don't get upset." I think Mum could tell I couldn't talk about it. "Is Sukhi all right?"

"She's fine." I attempted to take a sip but the milk was too hot.

"And you? Are you all right?" she asked.

"I think you need to stop asking me that," I said, my voice wobbly.

She gave me a reassuring smile. "Just drink that and get to sleep. It's very late." The circles under her eyes were dark.

I pressed the home key on my phone—it was 3:10 A.M.

"Okay," I said, smiling weakly. "Get some sleep, Mum. I'm fine."

She looked at me as if I was totally not fine, but she walked out, gently closing the door behind her.

For the first time in forever, no one tried to wake me the next morning. When I finally got up, I checked my phone. It was 12:30 P.M.

Normally Mum would have been shouting at me hours ago, telling me to get showered and start my homework.

I couldn't face getting out of bed. I felt groggy every time I lifted my head off my pillow. I'd hardly slept all night. I kept dreaming I'd fallen and been trampled by hordes of people trying to get out of the concert hall. In one nightmare I was right near the bomb and blacked out. Why was I having nightmares of being attacked? I hadn't even seen anything. I gave up on sleep, and after I'd sent messages to Sukhi to forward to her sister and her mum saying it was my fault I ran off and that I was really sorry, I ended up rereading *Furthermore* on my Kindle to distract me.

I heard Mum mumbling to Yusuf in his room next door. I was in the small room at the front and he—of course—had the bigger one next to mine. I had plans to take it over once he left for uni, but now I didn't want it—I didn't want him to leave. I wanted him around to protect me like he'd done before he'd left Ratcliffe Academy for sixth form. Maybe I could enlist him as my personal bodyguard if I ever needed to go anywhere near—

Darren.

I shrank into a tighter ball in my bed just thinking about him.

My stomach grumbled. Given I'd puked up my dinner last night, I hadn't eaten anything since yesterday lunchtime. Untucking my knees from my chest, I scrambled out of bed, throwing the stripy pink duvet on the floor. I got a glance of myself in the hallway mirror—it was not a good look. My eyes had dark circles underneath. My hair was a massive brown wavy bush, as if someone had drawn it on a stick person with a fine brown pen. It must've been from all the tossing and turning I'd done.

"Ah, Aaliyah." Mum came out of her bedroom. Her hair was tied back tight and her eyes were puffy—it looked as if she had been crying all night. "You sleep okay?" She stroked my hair.

"Yeah." I focused on the carpet. Guilt panged through me, imagining her crying because of me. "I'm just gonna have a quick shower."

"I'll make you some breakfast." She rubbed my arm before heading downstairs. "What do you want to eat?"

"Fresh waffles and maple syrup?" I smiled cheekily. I had to make things feel normal again. I didn't want her to be upset. If I hadn't gone to the concert, none of us would have had such a scare.

"O-kay . . ." Mum rolled her eyes, clearly trying to make me laugh. "I can do the maple syrup part, not sure about the fresh waffles!" she said from the foot of the stairs.

In the kitchen, Yusuf sat at the table, his head in his laptop. Mum was loading the dishwasher while steam burst out of the kettle, making it wobble on its stand. Through the window, I could see Dad with a hosepipe sprinkling the lawn.

"Have you lot eaten lunch already?" I asked as I pulled out the chair opposite Yusuf. As draining as it felt, I had to try and be normal Aaliyah on a normal Sunday. Even if nothing was the same.

"Yeah, we're not all lazy like you," he said, without lifting his head. It was obvious he was teasing from his voice.

I tutted and sat down.

"Aaliyah," Mum said, closing the dishwasher and opening the fridge. "You want some eggs? We don't have any waffles."

"It's okay, I'll just have whatever you all had for lunch," I said, sweeping crumbs into my hands and leaving smears all over the glass tabletop.

"We had last night's leftover pizza," said Mum. "It's finished now. How about fried eggs on toast?"

"Thanks." I went to the bin and pushed the lever with my foot, dropping the crumbs in before dusting my hands. "Whose is this?" I asked, leafing through a copy of the latest *Glamour* magazine on the counter. It had a hijabi with two other women on the front cover.

"Oh, your abu bought it when he went to get the paper this morning," said Mum, putting some bread in the toaster. "Amazing to see a hijabi on the front!"

Dad always bought Mum magazines when she was ill or sad. My stomach flipped, knowing how much last night must've upset her.

"Do you want to come with me to Sainsbury's? I need to go in a bit," asked Mum.

My insides went cold. How would it feel to go to a busy place full of strangers? I would have to one day, but would it ever feel safe and normal like it used to?

"I don't want to," I said, sitting back on my chair. "Everyone will stare at us."

"What you on about?" Yusuf closed his laptop. "No one's gonna stare at you."

"I just don't wanna go," I said, folding my arms.

After I'd eaten, I put my plate by the sink and headed sluggishly into the hallway to go up to my bedroom. My body felt as if it had run a marathon. As I passed the front room, I heard Dad saying something in a hushed tone, so I stopped.

"I mean, I understand how she feels." Mum was speaking now. "Just do an online shop and pick it up for me, please. I don't think I can face people today either. God knows what abuse I'll get."

"Yeah, you're right. It's probably best to stay in. Everyone is too upset right now . . . His sister was on the news and said he left a note saying he did it for all the kids who have been killed in bombings by the UK. The bloody idiot. Like this was going to bring anyone back."

My ears pricked up. Dad was talking about the bomber.

I wanted to know more. I pushed the door open and went in.

"Oh, hello," said Dad, giving me a tight smile.

The leather sofa squeaked as Mum shifted in her

place and rubbed her cheek. I needed scissors to cut the tension in the room. I sat next to Dad and rested my head on his shoulder.

Dad's school grading was strewn over the coffee table. The TV was on but the volume silenced. The headlines at the bottom of the screen stated the terrorist's name, the rising number of people who'd died and those who were injured. Images of the scene outside the concert hall were being shown.

I froze.

"Aaliyah?"

"Huh?" I think someone was talking to me.

"Aaliyah!" Dad's hand waved across my face.

I blinked and turned.

"I said, what do you want to watch?" Dad handed me the remote. "*Fresh Prince* reruns?"

"Umm . . . not right now. I just want to sit with you and watch the news," I said. Normally I'd be delighted he was giving me the remote, but nothing felt normal anymore.

"I don't think that's a good idea." Dad put his arm around me and pulled me back to rest on a scatter cushion.

"Why not?"

"There's nothing new to learn. No point in upsetting yourself."

"I tell you what," said Mum. "Aaliyah—go and

pray two nafl shukar and thank Allah for keeping you from harm."

She was right, I hadn't thanked God for saving me and my friends. I shuddered as I thought of Jo and her leg and what would have happened if we'd had seats elsewhere in the hall. We shouldn't have gone. If those last-minute tickets hadn't come up, none of us would've been there. Not even Jo.

My phone buzzed in my jeans pocket. I pulled it out—it was Sukhi.

So Lisa's come off the group. And she left after I said he was horrible.

My body tensed.

You think it was Darren? I thumbed into the keypad, wondering if he'd gotten hold of Lisa's phone. My head started getting cloudy thinking about him.

I bet Darren did it. Her message pinged back the same time as I sent mine.

Hope she's okay. I replied and pressed Send.

The thought of Darren made every muscle in my body tighten into a big ball and thrash in my chest. I had to stop thinking about him. But how was that possible when his sister was my best friend?

CHAPTER 8

THE BATHROOM FAN switched on as someone closed the door. Monday morning. I groaned and covered my face with my duvet. I'd hardly slept again last night. I didn't want to face the likes of Jayden and his gang at school. They were definitely going to blame me for the bombing. Last time there was an attack by someone claiming to be a Muslim, I got a note about my dad helping terrorists in London. What would they say to me about the concert right here in Lambert? I wondered if Mum would let me have the day off. She and Dad were being extra-nice; they said they were lucky to have been able to bring me home. And they were right—I was lucky. Unlike Jo and the other fifty-three people who were injured, or the fifteen who had died. I didn't want to go out, but I needed to see Sukhi and Lise. I needed to hug them and remind myself that we were all okay. I grabbed my phone from my bedside table and messaged our group chat even though only Sukhi was in it now. Lisa would rejoin today once she got away from Darren.

U going into school? I typed.

There was no answer. Maybe she was still sleeping or in the shower.

I messaged Lisa separately on her phone number but my message didn't deliver again. None of my messages had been delivered since yesterday. Was her phone still off? Maybe she'd lost it down the back of the sofa or something.

As I went downstairs, still in my pyjamas, I smelled fried onions. Why was Mum cooking on a Monday morning before work? Odd.

"Mum?" I called, hesitating to open the door because I didn't want to smell of onions for the rest of the day. I loved to eat them, not wear them.

"As-salaamu alaikum," said Dad as he came through the kitchen door, holding a huge silver cooking pot, the kind they use to cook wedding food in.

"What's that?" I asked. "I mean, I know what it is, obviously, but what's it for?"

"We're making food at the mosque for the police and forensic crews still working on the scene. And this is our contribution." He smiled proudly.

My heart sank, imagining all the people working at the hall. I blocked myself from picturing the exact work they'd be doing, probably the kind I'd seen on the medical stories on my Snappo feed. "Oh. Right. What did you make?"

"I just finished chopping a salad. Your mum's making some rice. Go help her, ja." He put the huge pot on the hallway mat and opened the porch door. "Actually, Aaliyah, go and get all the drinks from the kitchen and pass them to me."

I sighed, slouching my shoulders. *Onions, here I come.*

The kitchen reeked as if it was time for dinner, just as I'd expected. Mum stood at the hob, humming and stirring sizzling oil and onions with a wooden spoon.

"Mum," I said.

"Oh, Aaliyah, you're down early," She glanced at me over her shoulder. "Why aren't you in your uniform?"

"I don't want to go," I said, lifting the small cardboard box full of fizzy drinks from the table.

"Aaliyah. You can't miss school." Mum went back to stirring the onions.

Right. So she wasn't treating me like a delicate flower anymore.

"I'll come and help you serve the food," I said, without thinking.

"Dad's dropping it off to the mosque. They will be distributing it. I don't think it's a good idea we go near . . . there," she said.

I balanced the heavy box on my knee to open the

kitchen door and walked out. What would it be like to go back to the concert hall? Part of me wanted to see everything in person, but another part of me shriveled just thinking about it. I knew one thing—I'd never ever go to a big concert again.

"Are you not going to work?" I asked Dad, handing him the box through the front door.

"I'm not teaching first period because there's a whole school assembly. I'll go in after I'm done at the mosque," he said. "Right, I'll just go drop off this batch. You go and get ready for school."

"Dad?" I put on my most innocent-looking face. "I don't want to go today," I said.

"Aaliyah, I know. I understand. But it's best to get it over and done with. Trust me." Before he pulled the door shut he looked me in the eyes and said, "Anyway, my jaan, you'll need to see your friends and catch up with them. Go on—get ready." And with that he closed the door.

I loved it when he called me his jaan—his life. I didn't get why he was making his "life" go to school, though. I trudged upstairs to chuck my pyjamas on my bed before having a shower. I had twenty-five minutes before I had to leave. My phone flashed on my desk—it was Sukhi.

I don't wanna go in tbh. She had replied to my earlier message.

Neither do I! Let's skip today—yeah? We could FaceTime instead.

I'm like literally leaving my house and coming to pick you up!

Oh, flip. I'd better get ready then.

Ugh. Okay—just going in the shower. I messaged her back.

I wished Mum and Dad would just let me have *one* day off. They had no idea what it felt like to be blamed for something I didn't do, and asked about "your people and your religion."

When we approached Lisa's street my legs went weak, as if they wouldn't let me go any further. Nowhere near number 49. I was almost grateful to them. I didn't want to stand outside that red front door. I couldn't risk facing Darren.

"Listen, Sukhi," I said, taking my arm out of hers. "You go and get Lise. I'll wait for you here. You guys walk back up and we'll go down Harrington Road instead."

"Darren can't do anything to us, Ali," she said. "I don't exactly wanna see him either."

"Sukhi, I literally can't." The thought of going any further made my stomach dive.

Sukhi stared at my face for a moment. It must've told her everything I was feeling, because she said, "Okay, I'll get her. But don't ever say I don't do anything for you!" She ran off down the street.

Rain started spitting on me. I gathered my blazer around my waist as if it would somehow protect me from the drops falling on my hair.

It wasn't long before I saw Sukhi's long skinny legs running back toward me. "She's not in," she said, out of breath, bending over and holding her knees.

"Huh?" I said, baffled. "Did you even wait long enough for her to get to the door?"

"Yeah!" Sukhi replied. "I rang the doorbell a few times and even knocked. Then her nasty neighbor gave me an evil stare from his garden, so I left."

"Ugh," I said, taking my phone out to dial Lisa's number. "Her number isn't connecting."

"Yeah, I know," said Sukhi. "I tried her house phone yesterday but it went to answerphone. I didn't leave a message."

"Weird," I said, linking my arm in Sukhi's and turning the corner, away from Lisa's street.

We walked in silence down the road. My mind raced with reasons for Lisa going off-grid. Maybe Darren had insisted he drop her to school. Or maybe her arm was worse than we'd thought, and she was in hospital getting it checked out. Poor Lisa. All I could do was hope that when we got to school, she'd be there to tell us what was going on.

Lisa wasn't in the playground, so we knew she wasn't coming into school. Every day Sukhi would go to her form room and Lisa and I would walk to ours, and Lise was never late.

"Erm, Mrs. Alcock," I said, approaching our form tutor's desk.

"Hello, Aaliyah," she said, putting her red pen down on the book she was marking.

"I was wondering if you'd heard from Lisa . . . uhh . . . or her parents?"

Her face was blank.

"Uhh . . . I just wanted to know if she was okay," I added.

"I'm afraid I don't know where she is." She smiled. "Did you not come in together today?"

"She's . . . She's just not answering her phone since . . . That's all," I said, heading to my seat. "Thanks, miss."

Now I was getting worried. If school didn't know and we didn't know, then where was she? It hadn't looked like she'd broken anything on Saturday night, but what if she had? Maybe she had a concussion and felt really sick and couldn't talk or read messages, like the time Yusuf hit his head when he fell off his bike. I needed to talk to Sukhi ASAP after form time. We had to find out if Lisa was okay.

We had a whole school assembly straight after the register was taken. Everyone filed into the familiar large, musty, gloomy hall like robots. Mrs. Owen, our head teacher, stood in front of the stage, dressed in a charcoal gray skirt suit. My year, Year Eight, walked in, shoes thundering over the dusty dark wood floor, and sat in the gray plastic chairs between the Year Sevens and Nines, who had got there before us.

As the last of the Year Elevens took their seats, Mrs. Owen stepped forward. "Good morning, everyone," she said.

"Good morning, Mrs. Owen," we chimed back.

"We've gathered together this morning because we need to talk about what happened on Saturday night at Montfort Hall," she said.

A ripple of murmurs echoed through the school hall and someone cried out loud and stopped as if they were holding back a sob.

Panic heaved through me from my stomach to my chest.

"It was an unbelievably horrific act of terror. It's absolutely normal to feel angry about what's happened and also sad. We are all feeling that way. But we are strong at Ratcliffe Academy. We are going to get through this together." She stopped pacing the front of the hall and smiled at us before continuing, but her brown eyes weren't sparkling as they usually did.

"As ever, your form tutors are there for you. You can also go to the new pastoral head or your head of house—they are all here to ensure your physical and emotional wellbeing. The school counselor has extended her hours, and we are also setting up a support group for you. Speak to each other. Cry. Talk about it with others who were there. And even if you weren't there and feel anxious or affected, the services are also open to you." She started pacing again.

I raised my head above my row of chairs to find Sukhi, but I couldn't see her among the mass of heads. Leon Abbott had his head in his hands. Feifei Wen was wiping tears from her eyes. I felt as if someone was staring at me and glanced right to find Jayden glaring as if I was a piece of muck on his shoe. *How is this my fault?* I thought, and quickly turned back to Mrs. Owen, who had stopped to face us again.

"If you don't want to speak to the school counselor or at the support group, then please make sure you're talking to someone you trust, be it a parent or a friend.

Don't keep your emotions locked in. Please. It will help, and you'll see that you're not alone in what you're feeling." Mrs. Owen had her palms pressed together as if pleading with us.

"Now, I do need to share some very sad news with those of you who may not have heard . . ." She stopped again to face us. "Kerry Edge in Year Seven is in intensive care. Jo Mumford in Year Eight is in hospital; she's had to undergo a life-changing operation, and Natasha Burton in Year Seven is currently in surgery." She stared at the floor for a moment. "Shannon Urry in Year Ten was at the concert on Saturday with her younger brother, Shane, from Year Nine. Unfortunately . . . they both lost their lives." She hung her head low and gulped, then continued. "Sheetal Palmer in Year Seven also lost her life." She wiped a tear from her eye and more people around me started crying. I felt like someone had put an ice pack inside me. I hadn't even considered that the people who died would be from OUR school. I thought all the tickets were sold out and only us and Jo's friends from Year Eight went.

"There will be a vigil for them and the other victims . . ." Mrs. Owen continued, but her voice became distant. It was as if a cloud of fog had overcome me. I couldn't hear or see anything anymore.

CHAPTER
9

"**S**HALL WE GO TO THE VIGIL TONIGHT?" asked Sukhi as we walked home from school down a quiet street lined with townhouses.

"Umm . . . I don't know. I feel anxious just *thinking* about going to crowded places full of strangers," I said, watching my school shoes hit the cracked pavement slabs one after the other.

"Yeah, me too. Wow." She sounded surprised. "I thought it was only me."

"I guess that's why Mrs. Owen told us to talk about it. Maybe everyone's feeling like that?" I said.

"And there's no way to get away from it. It's always on the news. It's all anyone's talking about online. It feels as if it's been a week when it's only Monday."

"I know. I've been avoiding all my apps and ignoring notifications. I reread a whole *Mortal Engines* book in ONE day so I wouldn't have to think about it," I said, my brows raised.

"Well, at least you were doing something useful, you nerd," said Sukhi. "I've just been playing on the PlayStation." She laughed as if she was nervous. "Mum's not even hassled me to do any homework."

"Did you hear any more about Jo?" I asked. Mrs. Alcock had told us that she was in intensive care after having her leg amputated. My stomach dipped thinking about her lying in a hospital bed.

Sukhi stopped walking. I froze mid-step.

"We should go and see her at the hospital, you know. My mum was saying we should take some 'food.'" She did speech marks with her fingers to show me she meant the multiple tubs of food our families usually sent to sick people.

"But what if she doesn't want to see us? She might not want visitors yet—I wouldn't." I could imagine how I'd feel if I'd lost a part of my leg and my school friends gathered around my bed to gawk at me. I'd hate it. I wasn't even sure if I could go into a hospital anymore, let alone think about becoming a doctor. Since the bombing, I couldn't bear the thought of seeing anyone suffer. I didn't think I could handle it.

"True," Sukhi said, linking arms again to get us moving.

"I want to do something to help her, though." I said. "I feel so bad she ended up with tickets closer to the bomb."

"How's that our fault?" Sukhi said. "We paid less, so got rubbish seats—THANK GOD. Can you imagine if we'd actually been given the chance to buy the fansign ones like Jo's?"

"Don't," I interrupted and blinked hard to get rid of the image forming in my head.

As we got nearer to Lisa's street, I started glancing over my shoulder.

"Darren won't be around right now." Sukhi squeezed my arm. She could read my mind.

"I know," I replied quickly. Even if he was, he couldn't do anything to me in broad daylight. *He couldn't*, I reassured myself.

"Shall we try calling Lisa again?" I asked.

"I did." Sukhi raised an eyebrow at me. "Her phone connected, and guess what? She didn't answer!"

"No way! So she hasn't lost it!" I said as we both continued to walk. "What's going on?"

"I don't know. I seriously don't."

We were quiet the rest of the way home.

"Here you are," I said, handing Uncle Aziz a mug of steaming chai, the scent of cardamom drifting from it.

"Thanks," he said, barely looking at me. Even though he and Aunty Rashida had apparently popped in to see how *I* was, all they'd done so far was talk to Dad. I don't think Mum and Dad had told anyone else what had happened because they probably regretted letting me talk them into going to the concert in the first place.

I sat next to Dad, flicking through the magazine he'd bought Mum while they talked. I stopped at a feature about social media influencers because one of them was wearing a hijab. The hijabi social media influencer was a model and said she put it on when she was fifteen. Just two years older than *me*. I was surprised she was so confident wearing a hijab so young. According to the article she put it on to empower herself, because she didn't want to be judged on what she looked like or wore. She wanted to be free of society's expectations of what women should look like. *I should follow her on Snappo*, I thought.

"This country's a mess," Dad told Uncle Aziz. "They claim to be Muslims, but these so-called Islamist extremists are making things a lot harder for us."

I closed the magazine to listen.

"It was better than this when we were growing up," added Uncle Aziz, sipping his tea.

"How?" I asked. "I thought you had to deal with more racism?"

"Well, yeah, in some respects it was harder," said Uncle Aziz. "But we were all in it together. And religion was never an issue. We had one community center, and we all mixed there regardless of our beliefs. Indians and Pakistanis, the Hindus, Muslims, Sikhs and people from the Caribbean and Africa. We struggled together. That's all changed now everyone has their own halls and places of worship."

Aunty Rashida sat up in her armchair and said, "We used to send Eid food to Savita Behen and she'd send us Diwali food. That's stopped now . . . You remember your neighbors from before you moved out here?" she asked.

"Err . . ." I looked at Mum.

She helped me out. "Your daadi's neighbor Savita used to own that corner shop you loved when you were little."

"Ohhh, yeah!" I smiled, remembering the story Daadi loved telling about me running off in my nappy, barefoot, to get sweets.

"Daadi looked after Maureen every day too," Dad added, talking about his mum's other elderly neighbor whose family didn't visit much. "Maureen loved us. They knew we were good people. Now these damn extremists have ruined everything. They've given racists a voice — just the excuse they needed to openly hate us. Everyone blames Islam and Muslims for everything. You're judged as soon as they hear your name." He tutted and shook his head.

"You're a problem even if you don't ever mention Islam and just live peacefully practicing it," added Uncle Aziz, taking another sip of his tea.

"Exactly," said Dad, his face sullen.

"Would you ever move back to Tanzania? Would that be better?" I asked, looking at Dad on my left and then Uncle Aziz across the room on my right.

"No," said Uncle Aziz. "Your dad was only ten months old when he came here, so he was raised here, and I was twelve. We've never been back to Africa. We may have family roots in Iraq, India, Pakistan, and Tanzania, but this is our home. We couldn't live anywhere else."

Twelve. Wow. That was only a year younger than me. I couldn't imagine starting life over in a new country. "Why *did* you leave?" I asked.

"Our family had a lot of money and your dada's businesses were doing very well. You know your daadi had six nannies, one for each of us?" He smiled at me. "But the political climate became too dangerous. People were *forced* to leave their homes and businesses and resettle in villages to look after farmland. There was also a drought and the economy was struggling.

Your granddad thought it would be safer to get out before things got even worse."

"How come you chose England?" I wanted to know as much as possible while Uncle Aziz was being so chatty about our family's past.

"Well, one of your granddad's friends recommended it. So we all came over here, thinking it would be better." He sipped more tea. "But it wasn't."

"What do you mean?"

"We had to start from scratch. We owned nothing. No house. It was cold, we had no heating, no maids, no help, no car. We bought a brand new Mercedes van with our savings—we bought it to trade out of, no one had one back then—but no one would give us insurance because we were brown."

"Wow." My jaw dropped and I couldn't close it. I was sure you could sue if a business did that now.

"The van sat on the cobbled road for two months, untouched, before we found someone in London who would insure us. Your granddad was miserable because it was so hard to establish himself again. He was a respectable businessman back home with lots of staff and a driver." He put his mug on the TV stand.

"We don't have anything in Tanzania now, Aaliyah," Dad chimed in. "No family, no connections. And I certainly don't have the energy to start over. And—" he said, pointing at Mum and telling me for the fiftieth time—"your mum was born here, at the same hospital you were born in! So the people who say, 'Go back home,' can shut up—this *is* home."

"Exactly." Mum nodded in agreement.

I didn't know my granddad had to establish himself again. I thought they'd come here to have a better life. Not because they were forced to leave a good life behind. *Their* story could be in a magazine.

I rested my head on Dad's shoulder and he put his arm around me and squeezed hard. I was proud of my family and what they'd achieved, given the challenges they'd faced.

After Uncle Aziz and Aunty Rashida left, Mum and Dad insisted we go to the vigil. I said I didn't want to, but they told me it was important we pay our respects to the injured and to the people who had died, especially as we were Muslim. We had to show we didn't agree with the terrorist.

I held the bouquet of carnations tightly, my hands sweaty from the moisture on the plastic wrapper. It was in the town hall square at five-thirty P.M., in broad daylight and not near the concert venue, so it would be okay, apparently. I didn't quite believe them. If a bomber wanted to kill people at another big gathering, this would be perfect. We'd be toast in minutes. In seconds.

We followed hordes of people toward the main town square. The road was closed, and two police cars and a fire truck blocked any cars from entering, but the air was still smoggy from the car exhausts on the busy roads nearby. As we approached, I heard someone talking on a loudspeaker, their voice muffled. Then I saw the huge crowds crammed into the square, like pens in a pencil case.

I stopped in my tracks, struggling to breathe as people brushed past.

I could see the packed crowd at the concert right in front of me.

"Aaliyah?" Mum walked toward me while Dad went on ahead, unaware of what was happening. She put her hand on my chest. "Hey, hey. Calm down. It's okay. Everything's okay." She steered me to an empty bench, not far from the armed police stationed at the corner. Somehow they made me feel worse, not better.

Mum pushed me onto the wooden bench and sat next to me. "Aaliyah, you're safe," she said gently as she texted Dad.

"I'm scared, Mum," I cried.

"Shhh," said Mum, wiping my cheeks. "Nothing's going to happen, in shaa Allah. You are so brave,

Aaliyah. I'm so proud of you." She wrapped her arms around me.

"Why don't you stop bombing people?" someone shouted.

I lifted my head off Mum's shoulder. A bunch of guys walked past us, sneering. One of them must've said it.

"And eat bacon!" another one added, their nasty laughter trailing behind them.

"Come on," said Mum, her eyes wide. "Let's go." She tugged my arm.

I dropped the bunch of flowers and froze. My gaze darted everywhere, but I couldn't move.

"They've gone. Look, they've gone," she whispered in my ear. "Come on, let's get back to the car. We'll wait for Dad there." She kneeled down to pick up the flowers and placed them gently on the bench, then put her hand in my sweaty palm to pull me away.

After holding me tight in the car the whole way home, Mum went straight to the kitchen when we got back around seven to "make my favorite meal." Dad told me we would talk about how I was doing later and drove off somewhere as soon as he'd dropped us at the door.

I stepped into the front room to hip-hop blaring

from the TV. Yusuf lay across the sofa with his legs on the armrest, his cap covering his face. He'd got out of coming to the vigil because he had to revise for his exams, but he obviously wasn't revising.

I sat on the carpet with my back to him and checked my messages to see if Lisa had replied. There was nothing. Maybe she'd dropped her phone in water and it wasn't working. Maybe she was embarrassed by how Darren had behaved. She'd never go this quiet for so long otherwise.

Sukhi sent me photos of the speakers at the vigil and the hundreds, possibly thousands, of bunches of flowers laid across the front of the town hall. I scrolled through them, a deep sadness creeping over me.

Something dark fell to the floor near me, and I jumped. It was Yusuf's cap. I put my hand to my chest. I'd thought it was an intruder!

"You dodo, what you doing?" I said, glancing up at him. He'd fallen asleep. There was something strange about his face, so I got on my knees to get a better look.

A massive purple bruise covered his left eye.

CHAPTER 10

"**O**H MY GOD!" I gasped.

Yusuf woke up startled, looking around. "Huh? Wha—"

"What happened to your face?" I stood and bent over him to get a closer look.

"Nuffin'!" he shouted, covering his eye with one hand and grabbing his cap off the floor with the other. "Get out!" He grimaced and clenched his fists as if he wanted to give *me* a black eye.

Mum came rushing through the door with her yellow washing-up gloves on. "What is it?" She took one look at Yusuf and practically leaped onto the sofa next to him. "Yusuf, what happened, beta?" she said, stroking his face.

Yusuf pushed her hand away and scowled. "I'm fine!"

"You're clearly not fine. Now you tell me what happened before I call the police, Yusuf Hamid!" Oof, Mum only said our full names when she was seriously angry. She pulled off her gloves and muted the volume on the TV remote.

Yusuf picked at the print on his T-shirt and muttered, "This guy from my sixth form called me a terrorist as I passed him in the park. I punched him and he punched me back. It's no big deal."

"You stupid boy!" Mum scowled. "As if we don't have enough worries, without you getting yourself into trouble!"

She turned to me, frowning, as if I was involved somehow. Why was *I* in trouble?

Mum pointed first at Yusuf and then at me. "I'm only going to say this once. These are difficult times, but they will pass. People will say upsetting things, but you *have* to ignore them. Do NOT—" she stared at Yusuf—"rise to the bait! This is exactly the time to be a good example and show that Muslims are good people." She picked up the remote again and switched off the TV, slapping it back down on the sofa. "Did the Prophet Muhammad fight back when that woman threw rubbish on him? Hmmm? Well, did he?" She glared at Yusuf.

"No," Yusuf muttered, his head tilted on his hand, looking seriously fed up.

"No," I said when she turned to me for an answer.

"Okay. Yusuf, I'll make you an appointment at the doctor's. We need to make sure there's not been any damage."

"I don't need no doctor." Yusuf stared at the ceiling, not bothering to hide his irritation.

Mum frowned. "Aaliyah, go upstairs and pray your asr salat. Dinner will be ready in half an hour. I need to talk to Yusuf alone."

I dragged myself toward the door, feeling too lazy to wash and pray. Yusuf hung his head low. He didn't seem himself, and not just because of the eye. It was as if the spark had been punched out of him.

As I traipsed up the stairs, it dawned on me that Yusuf had been called a terrorist and attacked by someone in his sixth form college, but he didn't even "look" like a Muslim. He hardly had a beard. He was always in T-shirts and jeans. If *he* wasn't safe, what would they do to Mum?

In the car back from the vigil, the reporter on the news had said loads of women in the UK had reported their hijabs being ripped off, and Islamophobia was on the rise since the concert bombing. Dad told Mum that a man had been attacked with bottles by some drunk men who had tricked him into stopping his car. He warned her not to stop for anyone, even if they made it look like an emergency.

What if the idiot who punched Yusuf figured out where he lived? What if he decided to bomb our house?

Panic swirled through my body. I started to sweat. It felt as if there was no air around me.

I needed to get out.

I ran to the back door, shoved my feet into the black garden slippers on the mat, and escaped into the garden.

The cooler air instantly felt better on my skin. I focused on my breaths to steady them. What was happening to me? Would I always be like this now? Should I tell Mum that I was the one, not Yusuf, who needed to see a doctor?

I sat cross-legged on the freshly mowed lawn and closed my eyes. The sounds of the birds twittering around me seemed louder; I could hear the bees buzzing in the wild flowers near the shed in the warm evening sun.

Wait. What was that noise?

It sounded like an animal yowling. I scanned the greenery, but couldn't see anything. A blackbird splashed in the stone birdbath under the big apple tree.

The yowl came again from near the fence that divided our garden from our neighbor's. I got up to investigate behind the shrubs.

There was a gap where a panel had chipped away

due to age and weather. White daisies crept through it. I crouched down and heard the small cry again, followed by another.

Hidden behind a leafy green bush was a mass of black fur. Our neighbor Mr. Baldwin's cat! He'd been in hospital since an ambulance took him away last week—where had his cat been all this time? It stood with its back arched, its ears were flat against its head, its whiskers too, and its tail was low between its short, cute legs.

It looked at me and yowled once more—a loud drawn-out meow.

"What's wrong? Are you missing Mr. Baldwin?" I asked it in a baby voice.

It swiveled its black and white face. I put my hand out to stroke it and it came toward me with another big meow, searching my face.

"Where's Mr. Baldwin?" I asked, wondering what he called it. "Who's been looking after you?"

The cat rubbed its face and body against my leg. Then it lay on the ground on its back, inviting me to pet it.

SQUEEE! This was amazing!

It had never done this before. But then I'd never really tried to approach it.

I peeked through the gap in the fence to check

if anyone was anywhere to be seen. "Hello?" We'd never seen anybody come round to his house. Did Mr. Baldwin's family even know he was in hospital?

The black cat meowed again loudly.

I reached down to pick it up. It fitted perfectly on my arm, but it tried to wriggle off as I lifted it. "Hello," I said, gently stroking its arched back with my other hand.

It was adorable. My insides warmed and I felt as if there was no worry in the world. Cradling the small cat against my chest, I stood and stopped it from jumping off my hand. "Don't worry," I reassured it. "You're safe with me." Its tail swished.

I gave the cat's soft warm fur one last pat before putting it down. "Be right back," I told it.

In the kitchen, the aroma of chicken curry bubbling in a pot on the hob made my tummy grumble. I washed my hands and searched the cupboard where Mum kept her clean, empty Tupperware. I grabbed two rectangular plastic tubs and put a chicken thigh in one, making sure to wash the spices off like Mum used to do for me when I was little, and filled the other with water, and carried both outside for the cat.

I remembered when I'd first seen Mr. Baldwin carrying his cat and I'd told him his kitten was really cute. But now I couldn't remember if he'd said its name, or told me whether it was a boy or girl. I did remember he'd said it was a dwarf cat and that even though it looked small, it was fully grown, and I'd been surprised. Mr. Baldwin had said because the cat had short legs it didn't like going out, and preferred to be carried around and cuddled. It was a house cat and barely ever came out unless it was with its owner. It must be missing Mr. Baldwin so much. I wondered how the cat had got outside.

After that chat with Mr. Baldwin, I'd pleaded with Mum and Dad for a cat and even made a PowerPoint presentation of all the pros of having one. One of my slides said they were cheap to look after because cats only drink milk, and Dad had laughed and explained that they can't drink cow's milk because it upsets their tummies, and he said they actually cost a lot to keep properly if you include vets' fees. I'd still begged them for days after but finally gave up after Mum told me she was allergic. Why hadn't she said so in the first place? Maybe she just didn't want one. . . .

I could sneak it into the house as a test. If Mum didn't sneeze, she'd have no reason to say I couldn't look after it till Mr. Baldwin got home. But if she did? I was chicken keema, the finest mince meat. I sighed. It was better not to take the risk. Still, there had to be something I could do for the little cutie. It had already been alone for a few days and that wasn't fair.

The evening sun had moved to the front of the

house, and the garden felt a lot cooler than before. I went to the shed at the back of the garden and pushed the creaky wooden door open. Dust floated in the air. The smell of mulched grass from the lawn mower blades tickled my nostrils. I searched Dad's shelves and found a rectangular tangerine box that had no lid—perfect. I emptied out the car cleaning stuff Dad had been storing in it and lined the bottom with one of the large old rags he used for cleaning. It was big enough to cover the cat if it got cold too.

Outside the shed, I could see Mum's profile in the kitchen—she was on the phone. She hadn't seen me. She probably thought I was upstairs praying.

Keeping an eye on the cat, and imitating the kissing sounds I'd heard Mr. Baldwin make to it, I gently placed the box beside it. It sniffed the box.

"I'm going to put you in there where it's nice and cozy," I said, pointing to the shed. "I'll leave the door open for you to come and go, don't worry. Come here."

I walked the box with the cat inside down the stone path to the shed, the cat chittering the whole way. As I placed the box inside the door of the shed, the cat leaped into our garden and followed me. I backed away. "You can't follow me. Stay in there where you'll be safe. I'll just get your food."

As soon as I'd moved a few meters away from it, the cat strolled to the tub in the shed and ate the chicken.

That had been a welcome surprise! I'd tell Mr. Baldwin where it was as soon as he got home, and beg Mum to let me keep it until then. She was probably in a bad mood after seeing Yusuf's bruised face, so I'd leave it tonight.

The sun was beginning to set as I stepped into the kitchen, trying hard to keep the smile off my face. But then I heard shouting coming from the front of the house.

Dad's voice. He was yelling.

A stern voice I didn't recognize answered him.

CHAPTER
11

FROM THE KITCHEN DOOR, I could see Dad holding the front door open with one arm, blocking the entrance. Mum stood behind him in the hallway and flicked through one of her clothbound law handbooks. Yusuf peeked out from the front room, watching what was happening.

"I told you, there is nothing to talk about or see," said Dad. "I know my rights. We've done nothing wrong. Believe me, there is nothing for you to search, even if a neighbor suggests there is!"

"Sir, given the serious nature of the allegations, it would be helpful if you cooperated. If you do not and continue to speak to us aggressively, we will have to arrest you."

A police officer! I put my hand to my mouth to hold back a gasp.

"I am not being aggressive. I am well within my

rights not to let you in my house without a warrant. With respect, you're a Community Support Officer. I don't even think you have the authority to conduct searches, do you?"

The police officer didn't answer. The radio on his shoulder screeched.

"I'm going to discuss this with my wife, who is a lawyer. You're welcome to wait in my front garden," said Dad.

"Very well," said the police officer.

Dad shut the door and turned around. His face revealed the storm brewing inside him. His forehead furrowed and his jaw clenched. When he clocked me and Yusuf watching him, he shouted, "Both of you, get upstairs!" He pointed to the stairs and added, "NOW!"

I ran up the stairs as if I was being chased. I knew he was upset, but why was he taking it out on us? Yusuf stomped behind me and slammed his bedroom door.

Why did the police want to search our house? What did they want to arrest Dad for when all he'd done was make food for them this morning? From my bed, I tried to spot the police officer through my bedroom window, but I could only see the side of his pale face under his cap and his black jacket. I turned my gaze to the neat, pretty front gardens across the road. The man at number 75 was watering his potted plants. He didn't seem aware of what was happening, so he couldn't be the one who'd called the police, right? A few doors further down, an old lady dug into the soil in her flowerbeds. She kept glancing at our house—maybe it had been her? There were no cars in the driveway opposite ours, so they weren't even in. My stomach rolled. Someone we knew—probably waved and smiled at everyday—had sent the police to our house.

Dad opened the door, said something, and the policeman answered.

Then the front door slammed shut and Mum and Dad were talking in the hallway. I couldn't make out what they were saying, so I jumped off my bed, almost tripping over the clothes heap on the floor. *I'd better put them in the laundry basket before Mum sees and lectures me.* I pressed my ear against the door. I still couldn't hear.

By the time I'd opened the door as quietly as possible, Mum and Dad had gone into the kitchen. I gave up and shut the door again. My stomach rumbled, but there was no way I was going to ask for dinner and have them yell at me some more.

I grabbed my phone from my back pocket and checked my messages. Sukhi had sent me a screenshot of 3W's tweet from the night of the attack:

> Sorry. We are so, so sorry.

This was the longest I'd ever gone without thinking about them, I realized. I'd been so wrapped up in my head worrying about Lisa, Jo, and being attacked, I hadn't even thought about how they were. They had nothing to be sorry for. It wasn't their fault.

I opened my laptop on my desk and searched: *3W Lambert concert*. Thousands of links came up. My heart started racing just reading the headlines. One of them said there had been a five hundred percent spike in Islamophobia. *No, really?* I thought.

That article showed up related links underneath it. One of them was an article on *Teen Vogue*: "What It's Like to be Harassed for Wearing a Hijab." It was about a teenager who was shopping in a mall with her mum when an elderly lady came up to her and asked why she didn't wear a scarf like her mum. The girl told her that Islam doesn't force women to cover, but gives them the choice—and this girl *chose* not to wear it. The old woman said she was glad the girl didn't wear it. This annoyed the girl. She told the old lady that even though she was a Muslim who didn't wear a scarf, she wasn't half the woman her mum was and didn't have HALF the courage.

My insides felt weird. I stopped reading and thought about my own strong mum. About how I hadn't defended her at the supermarket when that horrid man screamed at her. My cheeks burned with shame. This girl was right—*I* wasn't half the person *my* mum was. She was so smart and brave, even when people around us were insulting Muslims. Even when they were sending the police to the door.

Maybe it was time that I put on a hijab too. For solidarity. What was the point in waiting till I was older and out of school? Why was I so worried about it changing my personality and my life, when she wasn't? Maybe wearing a hijab would somehow give me strength and inspire me to be better.

My door opened. It was Dad. I quickly closed my laptop.

"Aaliyah," he said, a weary smile on his face. "Come on, let's have dinner."

I think this was his way of saying "sorry for shouting at you."

I smiled back and stood up. He opened his arms, and I walked into them, inhaling the familiar smell of his fresh citrusy aftershave and put my head on his chest.

"I'm sorry, baitay, I was just upset. One of our neighbors filed a false complaint about us," he said.

"About what?" I asked.

"Apparently we're making bombs in here because we're Muslim."

I pulled my head away and looked up at his face, my mouth open. "NO WAY!"

He sighed. "Yes, unfortunately."

"How can anyone even do that?"

"They'd apparently seen the Community Support Officer on the main road and made him come down to speak to us. He seemed inexperienced—he thought he had cause to enter our house, and that's why I was so annoyed with him."

I didn't know what to say. My mind buzzed with thought overload.

"Anyway, it's a good thing your mum's a lawyer. We set him straight."

"What if he comes back with a search warrant?" I asked, putting my head on his chest again and listening to his strong heartbeat.

"He can't. They have no proof. And if they do come back without any, they'll be in trouble. Don't worry, okay?" He leaned down to give me a kiss on my head. "Come on, let's get down to dinner before Yusuf eats all the chicken!"

We both laughed and I followed him out. Good old Dad. He always knew how to make me smile.

I had broken sleep all night. Again. In between thinking about Jo lying in hospital, scrolling through happy photos of me, Sukhi, and Lisa goofing around with silly dog-ear selfies, and dreaming that I'd been blasted off my feet at the concert and police were storming into my bedroom, I probably didn't get more than an hour's sleep in total.

I zipped my backpack and slung it over my shoulder before heading downstairs. I felt queasy. I wasn't sure if it was due to lack of sleep or because I was genuinely sick.

Mum and Dad had already left for work, after firmly telling me and Yusuf not to open the door to anyone, as if we were seven years old. I dumped my cereal bowl and spoon in the dishwasher, wondering if Lisa would be in school today. As I closed it, I saw a squirrel through the kitchen window, jumping over our fence into next door's garden. The cat! How could I have forgotten about it?

I peered through the open wooden shed door and discovered that the cat had clambered out of the box and was sprawled across the concrete shed floor, licking itself. My heart melted, just like it had when I first saw it yesterday. I recalled a news clip I'd seen about pets helping sick people recover quicker. Holding the small black cat the day before had made me so happy. Nobody could possibly feel scared or sad with this cutie around.

Meow. The cat followed me out.

I set the box and the plastic tub of water and some

cold leftover plain chicken in the furthest corner of our garden, where Mum hopefully wouldn't spot it. I lifted the cat, who was now rubbing against my leg, and placed it back in the box. "You stay there. I'll be back soon."

The cat jumped out and started eating the chicken. I watched it for a few minutes and then turned to leave. It looked at me and then trailed after me. I felt a sudden urge to pick up the squished-faced cat and cuddle it. I held it against my chest. It closed its eyes and purred. How gorgeous.

I decided it would be safest with me. It needed me. And before I could stop myself, I tucked the cat in the nook of my arm and went to school.

CHAPTER
12

MY TIN PENCIL CASE clattered to the classroom floor, making me jump in my chair. I looked up from my exercise book and saw Jayden walking past. He must've swiped my pencil case off on purpose. Ugh.

Glancing back at me, he mouthed, *Terrorist*.

His friends jeered from the back of the class.

"Neanderthal," I muttered as I picked up the tin and the spilled pens and pencils and put them on my table one by one.

"Enough!" yelled Mrs. Pickering, our English teacher. "Jayden, sit down quickly, please, otherwise you'll be staying after school."

"It was an accident, miss!" he said.

Feifei Wen turned from in front of me and sucked her teeth at Jayden.

Jonah David stretched over from his table and

gently placed my blue felt-tip on my book. I smiled to thank him and put it next to all the others.

As the class settled down and went back to their stories, my backpack wailed. Oh, flip. The cat must've woken up when the pencil case crashed to the floor. I swiveled around to see if anyone had noticed. The bustle of chairs and everyone chatting probably masked the noise. Phew.

It hadn't been a good idea to bring the cat to school—instead of making me happy, it was stressing me out. Before I left home, I'd emptied my bag and put it in there, stupidly thinking I'd be able to cuddle it in between lessons. But then as I got to school I worried it was going to dehydrate before I could hide in a bathroom stall and give it a drink of water. And what if it got hungry? Would the leftover bits of chicken I'd given it this morning be enough? I had no way of feeding it.

I had to keep the zip of my backpack open so the cat could get air and I could check on it and stroke it regularly, but that increased the chance someone might hear it, or worse, it would scramble out.

I shouldn't have brought it with me. I really needed to think before I did things. This wasn't like me. I had never done anything this impulsive before.

At morning break, I rushed to the Year Nine toilets because they were away from school for a day trip.

The pipes gurgled as I entered, and the automatic lights took a few seconds too long to come on. My phone buzzed in my blazer pocket. It was probably Sukhi, back from her dentist appointment and wondering where I was.

I went into a stall at the far end, which smelled of bleach, and hung my bag on the hook on the door. When my bag was fully unzipped, two pointed ears and bright yellow eyes peeked up at me.

"I'm sorry," I whispered. "I'll get you back home soon."

The cat opened its jaw wide and hissed, showing me its teeth.

I was a real idiot.

I messaged Sukhi, asking her to grab me a small bottle of water from the snack shop and bring it to the Year Nine girls' bathroom because I had to tell her something in secret.

While we waited, I stroked the cat's soft, warm fur and told it I was sorry for bringing it to this strange place. It calmed and snuggled against me. It—because I still didn't know if it was a boy or girl—was getting used to me now.

The door pushed open and slammed closed. I prayed the cat wouldn't meow.

"Ali?"

Phew. It was Sukhi.

I came out of the stall with the cat resting on my arm.

"Errr, what the hell is that?" Sukhi pushed her glasses up her nose and stepped back.

"It's a cutie wootie cat," I said grinning, suddenly proud of myself for presenting her with the little furball. That's what I'd call it—Furball. The perfect name.

"Errr, get it away from me now," she said, inching back.

"It can't do anything to you!" I laughed. "It's a small cat! Don't tell me you're scared of cats?"

"O-KAY . . . a) it's a live animal, b) it's a cat, and c) it's in school." She waved around a small bottle of water as she spoke.

"Thanks," I said, reaching for the bottle, and she quickly handed it to me before I got any closer. "Actually, can you open it?" I said. "I don't want to drop Furball." The cat's ears twitched back and forth.

"You do know you'll be in major trouble if you get caught?" she said, twisting the blue plastic cap and then passing me the water.

I put the bottle to the cat's mouth and gently tried to pour some in. Water went down its chin and over my sleeve. "Aargh!" I handed Sukhi back the bottle and lifted the cat off my blazer sleeve. "You feed it and I'll hold it over the sink."

"Aaliyah! I can't believe you're asking me to do this!"

"Okay, you hold it and I'll feed it," I said, trying to hold back a laugh.

"Ugh, you moo-moo." She took a step forward and then stopped.

"What?"

She poured some water into the blue plastic cap and placed it on the edge of the sink. "Let it drink from there. I'm not going near it. Where did you even get it from?" she asked. "You said your mum was, like, allergic."

"Yeah, she is," I said, taking the cat to the sink and holding it as it wriggled and refused the water. I picked it up again and held him close. "I found it in my garden last night. My neighbor—its owner—is in hospital and it looked really sad. I think I was having a panic attack. I couldn't breathe and I ran outside and heard it. But as soon as I held this little one, it calmed me. I forgot about the concert, bombs, and racists. Everything." I stroked Furball's back. My heart felt as if it might burst with love. "I had nightmares again all night, and this morning when it followed me, I just couldn't leave this baby at home."

"Yeah, I had nightmares too," said Sukhi. "But *that* thing would give me even more!" Her forced smile told me she understood how I was feeling.

After I'd put the cat back into my bag, we headed out of the toilets. I wore my backpack around my front and wrapped my arms underneath it so the cat knew I was there and wouldn't jump out. It seemed to calm and settle in that position. The corridor was quiet apart from a classroom door slamming somewhere. Everyone was outside enjoying the early June sun.

"So is it going to be your pet now?" asked Sukhi, moving away from me, practically scraping along the far wall.

"Nah." I laughed. "It's stressing me out."

"That's probably because you're carrying it around in a backpack at school!" Sukhi raised one eyebrow and gawped at me to make her point.

"I know! But only for one more lesson. I'll take it home at lunch." I frowned. "Anyway, have you heard from Lisa? She's going to go wild over Furball," I said. "I can't wait to show her. I didn't try to call her today because I got late sorting the cat out."

"No, but she posted that pic last night. Did you see it? She's at her uncle's house in Wales."

"Huh? Why?"

"Something about her family getting away after the scare on Saturday. She wrote it's really helped her."

"Did you say anything?" I asked.

"I liked the pic. I didn't want to comment in case Darren saw and gave her grief."

I shook off the bad feeling his name gave me and pulled out my phone to go on Snappo to see the photo. But when I went to her profile, there was nothing there.

"Can you still see the pic?" I asked Sukhi. "I can't."

Sukhi pursed her lips, her brow furrowed. "Yeah, look." She showed me her screen.

Lisa stood with her mum, smiling in front of a traditional stone cottage. I blinked and turned away, my mind cloudy.

"Why can't I see her photos?"

"Looks like you're . . . blocked," said Sukhi.

I rubbed the back of my neck.

"Could be Darren?" Sukhi said, clearly trying to make me feel better.

"Yeah," I said. "Probably was."

A seed of doubt niggled at me, and I shut it down. It had to be him. Lisa wouldn't block me.

CHAPTER
13

AFTER MY LAST LESSON before lunch, I headed to my locker to put my books away, so Furball would have more room to move. It had slept through the lesson and was wriggling against my stomach in my bag. I was going to run home during lunch and put it back in the shed. I felt bad for carrying it in a bag all morning—I wondered how people carried their dogs in handbags. It seemed cruel.

When I got to my locker, I saw a white label stuck to the door. On the label, someone had scrawled in red felt-tip marker:

> I LOVE BOMBING PEOPLE
> Bcus im evil

Heat rose in my cheeks. I clenched my fists but stopped myself from throwing them against the locker. I wanted to scream. Instead, I scanned the corridor to see who was watching and then ripped off the label. Of course only half came off, leaving behind: *I LOVE BOMB*.

If I was in a graphic novel, there'd have been steam coming from my ears.

I quickly scraped off the rest with my fingernail, leaving the sticky residue behind.

Shoving the torn, scrunched-up label in my blazer pocket, I stormed through the corridor and downstairs to the lunch hall.

I wasn't going to let this go. How dare he?

The lunch hall was heaving with kids chatting, eating, clanging cutlery. The smell of pizza and grease wafted from the kitchen. I put my backpack on my shoulders and pushed through a clump of Year Sevens who were leaving and scanned the large hall full of tables. Where was Jayden?

And then I spotted him, with Mark and Rikesh, at the far back. He was hunched over his plate, shoveling food into his mouth like it was about to be taken away. I weaved through the maze of tables, scraping empty chairs out of my way to get to him before he looked up and saw me.

When I saw the glass of orange squash in front of him, I didn't hesitate. I just picked it up and poured the whole glass over his head.

He sputtered, his mouth open, orangey water dripping down his face and chin onto his black blazer.

"I love pouring drinks over evil vomit-heads like you—THAT'S what I love doing," I said and marched away without looking back.

Halfway through the hall, I realized the whole room was quiet, apart from the odd clang. It seemed all eyes were on me. That's when cold liquid poured over my hair and down my uniform.

I spun around. Jayden stood behind me, grinning. His hair was stuck to his face, and his skin had an orange glow. He clutched an empty plastic water bottle.

"What? You thought you'd get away with it?" He leaned over me and sneered.

"JAYDEN WILLIAMS! Get over here NOW!"

Our deputy head, Mr. Atkinson, strode across the hall toward us, pink-faced.

Oh, no. What if he'd seen me pour orange over Jayden? My wet skin prickled.

"Aaliyah, get your PE kit and get changed, and then go straight to my office. NOW!" He pointed toward the changing rooms behind the lunch hall.

"Yes . . . er . . . s-s-sir."

I burned up inside as I shuffled, head down, toward the door.

"That was awesome! Well done," Feifei Wen

whispered in my ear as I walked past her out of the hall.

It was not awesome. I'd never felt so humiliated. Everyone had seen what he'd done. I hoped no one had recorded it. Though it might actually be good if they *had*. More evidence of what a bully Jayden was.

After changing into my white running club shirt and black tracksuit bottoms, and cuddling and apologizing to Furball once more, I headed toward Mr. Atkinson's office, the squeak of my shoes echoing in the empty space. I hoped no one would see me and the walls might swallow me if someone went past.

I had become too impulsive. What was wrong with me? I wanted to kick myself. Dad was going to kill me for getting into trouble at school.

I knocked on the dark wooden door twice and waited. Maybe he wasn't there?

"Come in!" Mr. Atkinson said.

Ugh.

His office stank of coffee. I wanted to put my hand over my nose, but this wasn't the moment to do that. I was already in enough trouble.

Mr. Atkinson sat behind his wooden desk facing the door. "Sit down, Aaliyah," he said sternly in his totally-inappropriate-for-summer brown tweed suit.

I lowered myself into one of the two green fabric-covered chairs in front of him, my elbows tucked in between the silver metal armrests. My hands were under Furball on my lap, my chin over the backpack opening, hoping the little cat felt reassured I was there and wouldn't meow.

He leaned forward, resting his arms on the desk. "Please explain what happened. Jayden tells me you started it by pouring squash all over him. He claims he was eating his lunch and minding his business."

Of course he said that. The thug.

My insides boiled with anger. I opened my mouth to start ranting, then closed it. I had to stay calm otherwise he'd never believe me.

I took a deep breath, pulled out the two scrunched-up label bits from my blazer pocket and placed them gently in front of Mr. Atkinson.

He raised an eyebrow at the white balls of rubbish. "What's this?"

I cleared my throat, focusing on the coffee stains on the wooden desk. "Sir, that is a label I found stuck on my locker at lunchtime," I began. Then from my bag came a tiny yowl.

Oh, flip.

I needed to get Furball home before I got in even MORE trouble.

I shifted in my seat and stroked Furball with my thumb through the backpack fabric, hoping Mr. Atkinson would think the sound came from outside, and blurted out everything that Jayden had said and done to me in the past few weeks. How it made me feel. How the last straw for me was the label. How I hated that he'd publicly humiliated me yet again. I spoke so fast, it was a miracle Mr. Atkinson even understood what I'd said.

"Aaliyah . . ." Mr. Atkinson had both hands up. "Slow down. Do you have any proof it was Jayden who put the label on your locker?"

"Umm . . . no," I said, sitting up in my chair and straightening my back. "But it was definitely him." He'd obviously chosen to target me via my locker because it was tucked away at the end of the maths corridor, which was always quiet and had no cameras.

"We take this sort of bullying very seriously. I appreciate that you've felt harassed and we will look into it, believe me. But—" he stopped and took a sip of coffee before continuing—"you pouring orange squash over Jayden is a separate matter, and we have to deal with it. I am giving you a lunchtime detention."

"But, sir!" I interrupted. I'd never been given detention. I didn't even know what happened while you were in one, but I knew teachers looked at you differently. As if you were a disappointment.

"Aaliyah—listen, please. I know this behavior is out of character. Let's schedule a meeting with your head of house so they can find out why you're behaving the way you are and support you. I'm sure things have been difficult since the concert." His chair creaked as he leaned back to study me.

My mouth dropped open. "How did you know I was there?"

"Your mum called to let us know."

Oh my god, why did she even do that?

"So make sure you're at every lesson on time, and that your homework is in on time, otherwise you'll get yourself into more trouble. Now I have to call your parents."

I dipped my head into my chest and covered my face so Mr. Atkinson couldn't see the tears oozing out of my eyes. Ugh, this was majorly embarrassing.

"Off you go. Get yourself some lunch before the bell rings and remember that you'll be staying in tomorrow lunchtime," he said.

I uncovered my face. "Actually, sir, can I go home? I don't feel well." I didn't—I wasn't even lying.

Mr. Atkinson sighed before picking up the gray handset on his desk. "Fine, go and sit outside and have a drink of water while I call your parents."

"Okay," I said, wiping my wet face. Mum and Dad were going to kill me, especially after what Yusuf did just yesterday.

On top of that I had to get Furball out of my bag before it died.

CHAPTER
14

DAD PICKED ME UP during his free period. He didn't say a word the whole way home. I avoided eye contact and texted Sukhi about the entire incident, responding to her messages asking if I was okay—which I definitely wasn't.

"I'll speak to you later," Dad said sharply, staring ahead, as I climbed out of the car and onto the charcoal block paving on our driveway.

"Allah Hafiz," I whispered before slamming the heavy car door shut. I was tired. I'd been defeated. Thanks to Jayden, the teachers and even my parents thought I was a troublemaker. I was basically as bad as him now. What was happening to me? I needed to sort myself out.

As I took off my shoes and stepped into the hallway, I noticed through the open kitchen window that Mum was on the lawn talking to someone on the phone. The box lay at her feet.

She'd found it.

Oh, flip.

How would I get Furball back into the shed? I slung my backpack off my shoulder and ripped open the zip to its full width. Furball was curled up. My heart pounded harder, convinced I'd killed it. My hand shook as I reached into the bottom of my bag to pull it out.

Furball's back rose and fell, and I breathed a sigh of relief. Furball was asleep—thank you, God.

Through the window, I heard Mum say, "Yes, but I'm allergic and my neighbor is in hospital, and will be for a while because he has severe concussion and has broken his hip. He has no family that can help and it can't live in my garden or my shed. You're the RSPCA, you have to rehome it, just till my neighbor gets home."

She must've seen Furball in the garden this morning and come home during her lunch break to check on it! I shouldn't have left the shed door half open. Somehow I had to set Furball down near the shed without Mum noticing. Then I could claim I'd just found it hidden in the bushes. Mum would think it had come back to sleep in the box.

Oh, fudge—the box. She was going to ask who had prepared the box.

I'd tell her the truth; that I'd stumbled upon it, and

wanted to keep it safe overnight. That I was about to tell her and Dad, but the police were here and I got distracted.

"I'm so sorry I took you to school, Furball," I said pulling the cat out of my bag and giving it a peck on its back. "I'm going to take you outside now and you'll be going to a really nice place where they'll look after you better." I sighed.

Furball meowed as if in response.

An image of a row of cages at an RSPCA shelter popped into my head, with sad cats and dogs scratching at the mesh wiring to get a potential owner's attention.

A knot formed in my belly. How could I leave Furball in a shelter? It was already sad because it had lost Mr. Baldwin so suddenly.

I'd let Sukhi and Harpreet down by running away. I couldn't help anyone at the concert. I couldn't help Jo get better. Not even Lisa, who had had to get away from it all without telling us. But if I kept Furball and gave it the love and attention it needed, that could be my way of helping someone at last. Someone who needed it.

I blew out a breath, cradled Furball against my chest, and headed upstairs to my bedroom.

FRANCE BANS HIJAB

was splashed across the front page of Dad's newspaper in big bold letters and underneath it:

SHOULD THE UK FOLLOW ITS LEAD?

I swallowed as I sat at the kitchen table that Tuesday evening, the comforting smell of Mum's cooking all around us. A strong wave of FOMO rushed through me. Maybe I should start wearing a hijab now, while I still could? What if I waited till I was older and then I couldn't because it was banned?

"You've been in your room all afternoon, according to your mum. What took you so long?" asked Dad.

"Umm . . . sorry, I was just finishing my homework. I didn't want to forget what I had in my mind." I couldn't tell him that I'd been googling how to make a happy environment for new cats and then spent HOURS shredding old newspaper and soaking it in soap to make it clump to use it as cat litter.

"We need to talk," said Dad as Yusuf scoffed his last forkful of food and got up to leave. "You too, Yusuf."

Yusuf groaned and sat back down as I recited bismillah under my breath before scooping some chicken pasta from my plate.

Dad cleared his throat. "Your mum and I have had a chat, and we think you both need to speak to your school and sixth form counselors."

I gulped.

Yusuf laughed in disbelief. "Are you being serious?"

"Yes, Yusuf," said Mum. "Sometimes we can be more affected by an incident than we realize. What happened on Saturday gave us all a shock, and it won't leave us anytime soon, so we need to find strategies to deal with it."

"Yeah, but nothing happened to her," Yusuf said, his hands slamming on the table. "All she saw was a few people crying!"

"Actually, I think Aaliyah is reacting to a hugely stressful event. Which it was for all of us, regardless of what we saw," said Mum.

"She's all right!" He pointed at me.

Well, that was a matter of opinion.

"Aaliyah, you're very quiet," said Dad.

"Yusuf's right. I'm okay. I've been talking about everything with Sukhi, and it helps. I don't need to see anyone," I said, putting another forkful of chicken pasta in my mouth and trying to look totally relaxed about the whole thing, even though inside dread swirled around me. I didn't want to see a counselor. If Jayden found out, he'd think that I'd had to go because of the way I'd reacted to him. He'd love that.

"I'm glad you've got Sukhi, but you're obviously not coping. If you're being bullied, Aaliyah, and you're throwing drinks over people in the lunch hall, we'd appreciate if you would speak to someone more professional," said Dad, his elbows on the table and his hands laced under his chin.

"Wha—" Yusuf pushed his hands off the dining table and laughed. "She threw a drink over someone? Go on, Aaliyah!"

"Shush!" said Mum.

My cheeks flushed. I'd even surprised Yusuf by my stupidity. I'd gone from being good old Aaliyah, to raging—not thinking first—Aaliyah.

"You're not going out this Saturday with your friends," said Dad, glaring at me.

"But, Dad! I've got to return books to the library, they'll be overdue!"

"Aaliyah, we're going to nip this in the bud. You can't act out like this. You've got your future to think of. You'll spend this Saturday in your room, thinking about it," Dad said firmly.

I clanked my fork onto my plate and folded my arms. Yusuf sat grinning at me, clearly ecstatic that I was being grounded and not him.

After dinner, Mum told me to stay at the table and asked Dad to go watch some TV. Yusuf had already gone to his room, and I was sitting twiddling my thumbs, unsure what she was going to say and worried about Furball upstairs.

She sat on the chair next to me with a steaming mug of tea. "After your dad picked you up from school, he spoke to one of his friends who is a psychologist," she said.

"A psychologist? Why?"

"Aaliyah, what you experienced was life changing for some people. And so of course it will have had some form of impact on you, because you were there."

"But I'm okay!" I protested.

"Aaliyah, let's be honest, shall we? You're not sleeping, I've seen how anxious you can get when we're near crowds, you're acting impulsively, getting angry at school, and just not behaving like you usually would."

I hung my head. That was true. But I wasn't over-reacting because of the concert. "So what does this mean? I have to take medicine?"

"No, it means we have to help you process this. Dad's friend said everyone reacts to trauma differently." She swiped her phone and went to her emails and read something for a moment. "It's just like grief—everyone has an individual response. Some people can pick themselves up and adjust but it can take longer for others to find any sense of normality." She took a small sip from her mug and put it on the table. "It's different for everyone — I remember when my friend couldn't cope because of something traumatic that happened to her and then she snapped out of it because something else happened that made her see life from another angle." Mum looked straight at me. "You've got to stop seeing yourself as a victim and become a warrior, Aaliyah. You can do this. Nothing bad will happen to you, in shaa Allah. And talking things through with someone will help . . . I've been reading up about it, I can see you're easily angered or irritable — "

"But Mum, Jayden said I loved bombing people! Anyone would be angry!" I folded my arms and felt my brows fold. She just wasn't listening.

"Okay, look, it could be that you're tired and that's why you're irritable and reacting like this, but I'd still like you to see the school counselor."

"I don't want to talk to someone I don't know, about anything!"

"Aaliyah, today's behavior was so unlike you. Will you just consider it?" Mum pushed her chair back and went to the sink.

"Okay," I muttered.

I wondered if this was the right time to mention that animals help people get better. Maybe Furball could help me process this—whatever *this* was. But I couldn't get the words out. Instead I took two tins of wild salmon out of the tin cupboard and snuck them up my T-shirt.

I went upstairs feeling as if my heart was in my stomach. Nothing was right. It didn't matter how hard I tried. And it was worse watching my life unravel in front of me. I had to do something useful, something that would help make things better.

While Furball ate her dinner from a plastic tub, I stared at myself on my phone in video mode. I had to message Jo on Snappo. It didn't matter that we didn't know each other well. I had to tell her I was sorry about what had happened. I had to tell her I hated the terrorist for what he'd done to her, and to everyone else. I had to tell her I hoped she'd get better soon and that I'd see her again at school, and maybe we could do something together sometime.

The first take was awful, tears streamed down my face so I stopped mid-recording and deleted it.

The second take wasn't much better. My lip started wobbling when I told Jo I was sorry.

By the fifth take, you could tell I'd been crying and I decided that I couldn't send Jo a video. It might upset her more. And I really didn't want to do that.

CHAPTER
15

"**F**URBALL, why aren't you sleeping?" I groaned, covering my ears with my duvet in an attempt to block out the soft scratching sounds coming from somewhere in my room. She—I now knew Furball was a she because I'd googled how to check after dinner and managed to keep her still for long enough to have a look—continued to scratch and rustle something. I peeked out from under my duvet and saw that she had somehow managed to tip my wastepaper basket over and was batting around balls of paper.

Ugh, Furball!

I leaped out of bed to stop her before she spread pencil shavings across the light beige carpet. She continued to paw at the paper balls while I picked up scraps of paper and dumped them back into the bin.

"You are very naughty." I lifted Furball to my face, and she tried to squirm out of my grasp.

I put Furball back into the makeshift bed I'd put together out of a large old plastic tub with a faux fur blanket I'd found in the airing cupboard. I'd placed the bed under my desk, opposite my bed, behind my chair out of direct sight, just in case anyone walked in without knocking.

"Remember, this is your litter tray." I pointed to the filing tray I'd covered with the paper I'd shredded. "If you're gonna pee or poop, do it in there, okay?" Thankfully, she had used it so far, and I'd only had to pick up one dry ball of poop she'd left in the corner of my room.

From googling cat behavior for hours and finding Jackson Galaxy's awesome YouTube channel, I'd learned that Furball might get stressed being in a new place and sleep more because she felt depressed. I had to make her feel comfortable in her new home — I had to make a basecamp. I'd put on one of my old T-shirts and let her headbutt and nuzzle it so she could use it like a comfort blanket for when I was at school to make her feel less anxious.

I needed to buy some dry cat food that I could leave out for her. The tins of salmon I'd snuck out of the kitchen for her last night stank up my bedroom, and I had to open my window wide to air it out. I wasn't going to give her that again in a hurry.

Furball watched as I moved the soft old cushion

I'd given her from my bed, hoping it would help her sleep and feel comforted through the day. As I pulled my head from under the desk, my arm knocked against the table leg and got caught on a splinter of wood.

"Oh, Furball! Did you scratch this?"

She was busy nuzzling into the cushion.

I sighed and turned my attention to the pencil shavings all over the carpet. Being a cat mum was hard work. But it was worth it. Who could stay mad at that cute little face?

I scooped up most of the shavings with my hand, wondering what Mum would say if she heard me vacuuming first thing on a Wednesday morning. My alarm went just as I finished dusting my charcoal-covered hands over the paper basket.

7:05 A.M. Ugh.

Much as I wanted to stay here all day with Furball, I had to go to school.

I had to face detention for the first time in my life.

I managed to get through morning lessons without any drama, even though Jayden scowled at me as he passed. Sukhi said that Mr. Atkinson had told my form tutor yesterday afternoon that Jayden would probably be suspended for a few days after they'd finished their investigations. They wanted to speak to people who had witnessed what I'd told Mr. Atkinson first. Sukhi said Feifei Wen, who hated Jayden for making jokes about her eyes, had put her hand up and offered to give a statement in the middle of French. To say I squealed with delight at the thought is an understatement.

Lisa was still in Wales, it seemed, so we'd decided to catch up with her properly once she was back. Sukhi was keeping an eye on her Snappo account, but she hadn't posted anything more. I told myself she was probably having a really good time and thinking about us made her think about the concert.

"I'll meet you at the gates after chem, yeah?" I said to Sukhi as we left the school lunch hall and I made my way to detention. The saddest thing was that I had to miss library duty because of it, so it was a double punishment.

"All right." Leon Abbott nodded at us as he passed us on the steps.

"All right," I said.

"See you in a bit, bad girl!" Sukhi said, leaning in to give me a hug.

I pushed her shoulder and tutted.

The corridors were quiet and quicker to navigate when everyone was outside or getting their lunch. I was hurrying along, trying my best not to stop to admire the new biology display on the walls, when I saw someone familiar stride past.

The walls disappeared—all I could see was her walking in the sunlight filtering in from the windows above. It was like a scene from a movie—without the *aaaaaaah* background music. I blinked to make sure I wasn't dreaming. Nope. I wasn't. She was still there.

"Lise! Lisa, wait up!" I yelled, as she rushed ahead, her silky blonde hair swinging from side to side. Instead of stopping, she quickened her pace. *She probably has ear pods in.*

Stepping into a light jog, I caught up with Lisa and tapped her on the shoulder. "Oh my god! It's SO good to see you!" I said. "How was Wales?"

She hung her head and walked faster.

"Lise? Wait for me!"

She glanced at me but kept moving.

"Hey, Lise! You okay?" I said, worried that maybe she was upset and couldn't talk.

She stopped dead in her steps and spun around. Her brows crumpled.

"Don't talk to me. And I'm not walking to school with you anymore either."

"Huh?" *Did I hear her right?* "What have I done?"

"I bet you knew him. You all stick together—you make me sick." Lisa eyed me from head to toe in disgust.

"Knew who? What are you on about?" This couldn't be happening. It hadn't been that long since we were hugging and dancing together at the concert. And now she hated me? How was that even possible?

"Darren's right," she shouted as she marched away down the corridor, her voice angrier than I'd ever heard it. "It's better if I don't hang around with people like you."

People like me?

"What the hell do you mean by that?" I yelled after her.

"Well, you never know when one of you Muslims might blow us up," she hollered, right before she disappeared around the corner.

CHAPTER
16

I GASPED. It felt like Lisa had punched me in the chest.

I don't know how long I stood there in the corridor, but it was long enough for Mr. Atkinson to spot me and ask why I wasn't in detention.

I sat in a daze for the next half an hour in the empty classroom. One of the physics teachers was at the desk at the front of the lab marking work. The rhythmic ticking of the clock rang in my ears as I tried to gather my thoughts and make sense of what had happened.

Lisa didn't want to hang out with me because I was Muslim. Because she thought I was *dangerous*. THAT'S why she'd come off the group chat, ignored our calls and blocked what I could see on her Snappo account. It all made sense now.

And there I was, worrying about her. Wondering if she was okay all that time. Dense.

My *best friend* thought I was a terrorist. And I

was letting myself feel bad for something that had nothing to do with me. That I hated too. I closed my eyes and prayed. I recited the opening verses of the Quran, repeating the one asking for help, and immediately calmed, then asked God to help me stop being scared and letting others treat me like this. Help me stop being a victim, like Mum had said. Help me find a way of showing everyone they were *wrong* about us. I imagined Him high above looking down at me, and felt a sense of strength and relief, as if God was seeing my pain and He was listening.

Hot tears spilled onto my arms on the desk and I let them roll until something released from deep inside me.

In that moment, I decided I'd had enough.

Everything felt clearer, as if I'd snapped out of a dream-like state. As if someone had slapped me and woken me up. I couldn't allow MY life to fall apart because of some idiot who bombed the concert I happened to attend. There was no point in me sitting here feeling sorry for myself. I had to do something. And it had to be big.

Later that night, I sat on my bed and wondered how other Muslims coped with this sort of hate. How did they carry on? My eyes fell on the magazine, which Mum had let me bring up. I jumped off my bed and grabbed it from my desk to reread the article about how wearing a hijab had empowered the social media influencer. I then googled the word *hijab* on my laptop and another *Glamour* magazine article popped up about why Muslim women wear a hijab. The answers made my fingers tingle. Some of them wore it because it was part of their identity and it helped them be mindful of their speech and behavior. One girl wore it because it helped her to spiritually connect with her religion; one because it meant no one could judge her for her beauty but instead her mind and who she was; one wore it to smash stereotypes and show people Muslim women were more than cooking and cleaning and to show people that we're not terrorists. . . .

I closed my laptop and looked out the window. I realized I'd been thinking about this all wrong. I'd been scared that I'd get attacked if people knew I was Muslim, but actually, what I needed to do was *show* I was one. It was the only way I could fight this hate.

Instead of shying away from my religion because some evil criminal terrorists thought it was okay to kill people, I had to show that we weren't all bad—there were more of us wanting to live in peace than the few murderous losers who didn't.

I was going to wear a hijab.

THAT was the answer.

To remind people that being a Muslim didn't mean you were dangerous and that *nothing* had changed.

And, like the women in the article, it could help me be more mindful of my behavior. No more orange squash dumping. No more letting friends down and running away. It would be my constant reminder to check myself and help me stop and reflect before I acted. I needed it more than I realized.

Wearing a hijab would empower me to be true to myself and be an ambassador, like Mum was at work. I'd show everyone a proper Muslim wasn't anything like the few bad ones plastered all over the news.

It was time I came out and was confident about who *I* was.

It was time to fight back.

"**A**ALIYAH, you don't have to do this." Mum watched from her bed as I rummaged through her scarf drawer that evening. "It's more important that you have a good character that inspires others than wear a hijab just to look like a Muslim. You can wear it when you go to college—when you're sure you're going to keep it on."

"But Naani always says, 'If you look like a Muslim, you'll act like one because it's a constant reminder.'" I looked at Mum through the mirror. She was frowning. She looked torn, as if she couldn't disagree with her mum, but she also didn't want to agree because it would mean she was telling me I could wear it.

"It's not a great time to be putting one on, baitay," she said. "You're still young, you can wait."

"Mum—this is the perfect time." I pulled a plain

navy one out of the drawer and folded the square into a triangle.

She sighed and got off the bed to help me tie it. She set the scarf on my head and showed me where I should position the fabric before wrapping it around my head. She grabbed a hatpin from her dresser and put the sharp bit in between her lips.

"Don't stab my scalp," I said, flinching as she put her hands on my head to glide the pin in place.

"It looks risky, but I've managed to get through twenty years of wearing one without hurting myself." She smiled before placing both hands on my shoulders. "You're so beautiful, ma shaa Allah, Aaliyah," she said. "Inside and out."

I smiled at her and glanced at the mirror. I'd worn a scarf before whenever I'd prayed, but never the way it was done now, purposefully wrapped around my face to cover every strand of hair, and pinned in place to avoid it slipping.

I looked different.

A pang of doubt sprung from my stomach. What if everyone thought I'd changed?

But I hadn't. I was still me. Aaliyah, the good girl, hopefully saved from her raging impulsiveness.

The next morning, I took a deep breath before stepping into the kitchen to present myself for the first time in a hijab in my school uniform.

"Aaliyah!" Mum was at the table, her finger hovering over Sukhi's mum's contact page in her phone. Crumbs of toast with tiny specks of strawberry jam were on the plate in front of her. "You can't wear my silk scarf to school!"

"But it's the best one!" I pulled the milk from the fridge and yawned. I didn't know how I was going to get through the day having only slept for three hours after trying out various hijab styles from YouTube. "It's the smallest one and I can tuck it neatly into my shirt collars."

"Go and change it." Mum twisted to look at me, and I could tell she wasn't happy. "One: it's expensive and my favorite, and I can't believe you even thought you could wear it, you cheeky madam." She got up from the table and went to the sink. "Two: you can't go to school in a bright scarf, they will want you to wear a sober color, like black, to match your blazer. Three: you'd better go upstairs now, fold it neatly, and put it away before you get it dirty."

I plunked the plastic milk carton on the table and tutted as I turned to go upstairs. "I don't want to wear a black hijab," I muttered.

Mum sighed. "I'll take you to buy some tonight, in shaa Allah. You can try beige or white." She dropped the washing-up sponge. "While you're up there, can you switch off that game you're leaving on in your room? It's really weird. Sounds like you've got a mouse scurrying around up there."

What game? Then it hit me—she meant Furball! Oh, no! I thought that podcast she listened to might mask any noise. Thank god Mum usually left for work before me and got back after I did, so she wouldn't go in my room. Dad always had the TV on loud, so he'd never hear Furball, and Yusuf always had headphones in his ears. But I had to be more careful. I could leave some music on low for now, and then as soon as I got back from school I'd google how to make Furball a scratching post and a ball made of wool or something to keep her happy in her cat quarters under my desk—her own little space.

The doorbell rang as I stepped off the stairs after changing my scarf into a standard cotton one. The milk and cornflakes from breakfast sloshed around in my tummy. This was the first time Sukhi was going to see me with a hijab. I'd written ten different messages last night when Sukhi had messaged about Lisa being back in school and being weird with her, but I'd deleted them all. I couldn't find the courage to tell her I was going to do this. It felt too hard to explain over messages. I slipped on my school shoes and shoved the magazine with the hijabi influencer in my bag. I filled my cheeks with air, like a puffer fish, and slowly exhaled before opening the door.

Sukhi stared at me, her eyes wide. After a second too long, she looked away, and when she looked back she was smiling, obviously trying to act normal. "Here." She passed me the next two books in the *Noughts & Crosses* series I'd asked her to get from the school library while I was in detention.

"Thanks." I leaned through the porch into the hallway and put the books on the glass console table, then went outside, squinting as the bright morning sun hit my eyes. If she could act like nothing was different, so could I.

We continued in an awkward silence for about a minute. A bus hissed and stopped to let some kids off on the main road. My skin prickled as I braced for them to yell something nasty at me. Thank god they didn't. They were all too distracted trying to get to school.

"So, erm . . . what's with the scarf?" asked Sukhi.

Well, that didn't take as long as I'd thought.

"You wouldn't understand," I said, focusing on the

green weeds springing out between the cracks in the pavement slabs.

"Try me," she said, linking her arm in mine.

"I'm a Muslim and proud of it," I said, holding my head up, pushing my shoulders back, and trying to look confident.

"You were a Muslim and proud of it before too, though," Sukhi said.

"Yeah, well, now I wanna represent," I said.

Sukhi stopped walking, so I did too. "What do you mean?" she asked.

"Well, whether I wear a hijab or not, I'm the same person, and when people can tell I'm a Muslim just by looking at me, they'll know we can be good people."

"Oh, Ali," she said, stopping to wrap her arms around me and my backpack. "You're not just good people. You're the *best* people."

I stiffened at first, but then relaxed and put my arms around her too. To be honest, I needed the bear hug.

CHAPTER 18

WHEN I WALKED INTO SCHOOL, I got some looks so I kept my head down—I didn't want any confrontation. I'm not sure if Sukhi noticed, and I didn't say anything because I didn't want to make a big deal of it. I put on my biggest, most confident smile when I left her to go to morning form time, but inside I fretted about Jayden dissing me the moment I walked into class. Lisa wouldn't notice me now that she sat right at the front—obviously to avoid me—so I had no idea what her reaction to my new look would be. She'd probably hate me more.

I quickly scuffed into my chair, my eyes rooted to my table, but soon after the register was called, I learned Jayden wasn't around when Mark told Rikesh that Jayden had been suspended! Maybe things would get better from today, especially if he wasn't here. What. A. Relief. I breathed out.

Girls giggled, poking each other in the hallway as I passed, while they stood around moaning about lessons. *It might not be about you*, I told myself. My stomach tightened when a caretaker muttered to another, "Bet she was forced to wear that . . ." It was as if someone had pressed the mute button on a TV remote and all the sounds around me were more pronounced. I wanted to scream and tell them it was actually *my* decision, but what was the point? They probably wouldn't believe me anyway.

At break, it was hard to ignore the curious observers, whispering and staring while I sat on the field sharing a cookie with Sukhi. Even though I'd thought people might stare, it didn't make it any easier. I wanted to mention them to her, but then we'd both be looking their way, and they'd know they were bothering me. There was *no way* I was going to eat in the lunch hall today.

In geography, I put my hand up to answer Mrs. Carter's question, and by the way she observed me, I could tell she was wondering why I was wearing a hijab, but thankfully she didn't say anything. Jonah David, who sat with me in geography, had smiled as I pulled out my chair. He didn't comment on it either, but I decided to see his smile as support.

As I headed out of library duty after lunch, my scarf felt loose around my ears, so I stopped to adjust it in the corridor while reading a poster advertising the end-of-year summer fete, the school event of the year, where the whole school and their parents *and* their neighbors came to enjoy the outdoor entertainment and competitions and stalls. It was going to be the weekend before the summer holidays on 9th July. The list of attractions was longer than last year's, and it looked much better. Last year Mr. Atkinson had put on a playlist of dodgy nineties dance music. They had loads of stalls selling new and used things, different types of food, inflatable sumo wrestling suit fighting, archery and football penalties. Almost all of Year Seven had turned up, and me and Sukhi and Lisa had waited in the long lines to try out all of the activities. This year they were bringing in actual rides and a proper radio DJ so it would be even more of an attraction for the school kids and people from the local area.

The thought of a big crowd made me shiver. But this was outdoors and in school, not a famous pop concert full of strangers. It would be different, I reassured myself, and blocked the panicky thought trying to take over my excitement.

"Hey!" someone thundered behind me.

Before I could turn to see who it was, two hard fists shoved my back with full force. The air went out of me as I went hurtling toward the stairs, landing on my chest with my hands splayed. My heavy backpack toppled onto my head. I'd just missed the top step.

I lay, staring at the stone floor, my heart pumping a trillion times a second. Two black Doc Martens stopped about a millimeter before my nose.

"You silly head-covering Muslim cow!"

I raised my head. Sasha, Jayden's sister in Year Nine, glared down at me, gritting her teeth. Her best friend Natascha smirked over her shoulder.

"First your lot try and kill us at a concert. You made Jo lose her leg and then YOU get my brother suspended!" she shrieked.

My head pounded. As I pressed my hands on the cold floor to push myself up, a spray of stringy, gloopy spit landed on my cheek.

"That's what I think of you," Sasha hissed.

UGH. That was it. I wasn't going to take this. "You—"

But the sound of shoes thumping away and cruel laughter echoed in the corridor. They'd gone before I even got to say anything. Cowards.

I sat up on my knees and looked around, trying to get my breathing under control. The glob of phlegm was slowly rolling down my hot face. No one else was around. How convenient for Sasha. They must've planned it, knowing it'd be quiet outside the library on such a warm day.

I dug in my backpack for a tissue to wipe that racist ignoramus's germs off me. How was what happened to Jo my fault? I felt bad enough as it was, but I didn't bomb the concert. Why would I bomb a place I was at? That my friends were at? Why would I bomb a place at all? If this was in our religion, like people said, why weren't all two billion Muslims around the world blowing everyone up? Stupid. Stupid. Stupid.

UGH. My raging brain was about to explode out of my ears.

The bell rang. Soon everyone would start pooling in from outside. I had to get to the toilets to sort myself out and redo my scarf.

Mrs. Owen was walking past the toilets just as I pulled the door open. When I called her name, she turned and raised her brows.

"Umm, miss . . . I, err . . . need to talk to you about something," I said.

"Can it wait? I have an important meeting."

"Erm, well . . . it's about Sasha Williams, in Year Nine."

"What about her?" she said, letting out a heavy sigh.

"She—she . . . err . . . attacked me a few minutes ago . . . because I'm wearing a headscarf . . . I think," I said. My words weren't coming out quick enough.

"What do you mean, attacked you?" she asked, glancing at her watch.

"She pushed me—"

"Are you hurt?" she said, before I could finish.

"Uhh, no, miss," I said.

"Well, let's leave it at that for now, and let me know if she does anything else." She began to walk away and then stopped, spun on her toes and added, "By the way, it's not the most appropriate place to wear one of those at the moment, is it, Aaliyah? Perhaps you should consider wearing it to the mosque and not at school."

She strode away, and my mouth properly dropped.

Was EVERYONE at this school narrow-minded? I didn't even go to the mosque unless it was Eid! Everyone else seemed to be able to wear what they wanted. Why couldn't I?

CHAPTER 19

AFTER SCHOOL, I went to the Co-op to buy Furball some dry cat food. Co-op seemed to be the cheapest place to buy pet food on Google because they had an offer on, and I remembered they had half an aisle for pets so I'd definitely find something. It was on the main road, so no one from school would dare hurt me there — I hoped. Still I walked fast, my shoulders tense, worrying that something bad might happen.

As I got near the store, an older woman in a hijab stepped out and smiled at me. "As-salaamu alaikum," she said and my heart felt as if it might burst. If she'd seen me a week ago she wouldn't have known I was Muslim, and probably would've ignored me, but this was like being part of a cool not-so-secret society.

Mum had once said that what she loved most about visiting London's Regent's Park Mosque was how everyone, no matter their race or background, said As-salaamu alaikum, wishing peace on you as soon as they spotted you. This was the first time I had been recognized as a Muslim without Mum with me. I felt accepted, and my insides warmed. "Walaikum as-salaam," I replied as I smiled back and stepped into the store.

The cool air-con hit me and I lowered my head, remembering that not everyone was going to be as accepting as the old woman, and I prayed the staff would treat me the same way they always had. A nice shop assistant offered to help me choose the right food when she saw me googling each tin on the shelf. And she didn't look at me like I was a total weirdo because of my headscarf, which made me feel more relaxed. She also gave me some used folded cardboard boxes and explained how to make a DIY cat scratcher using the rough, grooved sides. She showed me some catnip toys and said I could buy a calming plug-in diffuser to help keep Furball calm, and stop her from wanting to run around scratching everything in sight.

I breathed out as I left the store. No one had given me any dodgy looks, and I felt proud of myself for sorting out Furball's life, like a good cat mum. I held my head high. I could totally get used to wearing a hijab.

As I got nearer to our house, I passed Mr. Kumar's convenience store. I jangled the change in my blazer pocket to check if I had enough, ignoring the traffic that had slowed for the pedestrian traffic lights. After the day I'd had, I deserved a treat.

Someone yelled across the road, where a few people had gathered. I stepped closer to the curb to see what was happening, then ducked behind a telephone box, peeking my head out.

Darren was shouting at an old woman wearing a hijab, who winced and rubbed her arm. It was the same woman who had smiled at me outside Co-op! I closed my eyes for a second, unsure what to do. A heaviness settled in the pit of my stomach and I became aware of my breathing. There was no way I'd be able to help her. I *couldn't* face Darren.

The old lady's torn carrier bag flapped against her in the breeze. Lisa crouched beside them, looking panicked as she tried to stop fruit from rolling on to the road. Darren's face was pink with fury, and he was shouting at Lisa now. He kicked a bunch of bananas from her hand and stomped off, fists clenched. Lisa stood slowly and put her hand on the old woman's arm. I couldn't hear, but it looked as if she was apologizing for Darren's behavior. She kept glancing back at Darren and then she ran off after him.

I took a big gulp of air. Darren was the worst human I'd ever met. How could he attack an old woman? Lisa was just as bad for going after him.

The man from the kebab shop across the road was now helping the woman. Who'd have thought Lisa and Darren would turn out to be such horrible people? I tried to pull in deep breaths to calm myself. I really needed some comfort food.

Inside the shop, I went straight to the chocolates and stared at all the shiny wrappers. I tapped the side of my head to push Darren's face out of my brain. Hopefully forever.

It was hard to choose what I should spend my eighty pence on; it was all I had left after buying Furball's food and toy. I had no idea how I'd get more cash for the next batch, now that I'd spent my Eid money, but I'd worry about that later because I probably had enough for a couple of weeks.

As I stood in line to pay for my double Twix, Mr. Kumar was talking animatedly to the elderly man at the counter. Mr. Kumar's brown bald head gleamed under the spotlight above him.

"Yeah, it's terrible." Mr. Kumar shook his head. "They need to sort out these people. These Muslims are ruining lives everywhere right now."

The man paid for his newspaper and nodded in agreement.

My nostrils flared. I couldn't believe Mr. Kumar had said that. He had always been kind and friendly, but now I wasn't sure he'd even serve me. I turned to put the chocolate back on the shelf, but then I stopped. I wasn't going to shrink away. *I have to face him in my hijab—that's the whole point of it. He won't hurt you,* I told myself, rubbing my thumb over the shiny gold chocolate wrapper repeatedly. I had to represent.

As the elderly man hobbled away, giving me a dirty look, I stepped up to the counter, set down my Twix on a stack of newspapers, and smiled politely.

Mr. Kumar glanced at me and punched some numbers into the till.

Maybe he hadn't recognized me in my hijab. I cleared my throat. "How are you, Mr. Kumar?"

"I'm fine, thank you." He scanned my face, and his mind must have made the connection because he raised his eyebrows and said, "Mr. Hamid's daughter?"

"Yeah," I said, managing to hold on to my smile.

He smiled back. "Ohhh . . . you're so grown up, I didn't . . . recognize you! How is your father?"

"He's fine."

"Is he still at Judgefield School?"

"Yeah, he's Head of Science now," I said, holding my shoulders back, surprised he was being so nice, after saying something so awful about Muslims just moments ago.

"Oh, brilliant! Tell him Anand still talks about him—he's studying medicine, you know?" he said, the pride obvious in his voice.

"That's great!" I said, recalling how Dad used to give extra lessons to Mr. Kumar's son after school in the front room when he was doing his exams.

"Hmm, yah. That's eighty pence, please."

I handed him my coins and took the chocolate off the stack of newspapers. "Bye, Mr. Kumar," I said, trying to sound as cheery as possible.

I left the shop, hoping I might have reminded him that Muslims weren't all evil. We were the same people he'd always known, not anything like the random vile terrorists he saw on the news. We were his customers. His neighbors. Just regular humans, like everyone else.

What. A. Day.

I flumped on my bed with my English homework after making Furball's cat scratcher and sighed. Everything felt like it was spiraling. A few weeks ago, I had my two best mates and the worst that happened in a typical day was Jayden saying something nasty. But now things had ramped up to what felt like the highest level in an online game.

I couldn't focus on my homework. I wanted to call Lisa, but that was impossible. I picked up the facedown framed photo from my bedside table, a selfie Lisa had taken on my birthday of all three of us grinning outside

Pizza Hut, our faces stuck to one another. My chest felt heavy and I put the frame back facedown. Sukhi was at a mehndi party, so I couldn't even speak to her. I still hadn't been able to tell her what Lisa said yesterday. It was too painful. And embarrassing. I blocked the image of Lisa looking at me in disgust. I'd rather pretend it never happened than have Sukhi telling me Lisa didn't mean it, or worse, Sukhi fighting with her because of me . . . or even worse, understanding Lisa's reasons for saying it.

I aimlessly swiped across my phone, back and forth, trying to find something to distract me, when my thumb landed on my music app. And then it hit me. I hadn't listened to 3W since THAT night. I blinked hard to get the traumatic concert memory out of my head. I could do it. I could totally listen to them again. They weren't connected to the bombing. I didn't need to think of it when I heard them sing. They'd seen me through all my days until the concert. And then I went and abandoned them at their hardest time. Maybe listening to them again would make me feel better.

I selected the first song in 3W's playlist, "All Alone."

Big mistake.

The instrumental at the beginning made me shrivel inside. The words dug deep into my soul. Tears spilled on my English book and I didn't care that the drops crinkled the pages.

We used to be so happy. Lisa and Sukhi and me. Jumping, laughing, singing together. And now I was all alone.

Sukhi was amazing, but she didn't really understand what it felt like to be judged and hated for being a Muslim. Everyone loved Sikh people—they never made the news for bad things. She didn't even really understand what it was like to be judged for being too brown. She was much paler than me, and most people wouldn't even know she was Sikh unless she told them. And Lisa, well, she didn't care about me at all. 3W was right. We were all alone, really.

"What the hell is that?" Yusuf stood in my doorway, face scrunched, pointing down at Furball as she lay sprawled on my rug.

I jolted. Oh, flip.

"Errr . . . it's a cat. What's it look like? A horse?" I wiped the snot off my face with my T-shirt sleeve and tried to hide the panic tickling my spine.

"What did you bring it up here for? Get rid of it!" He tutted, barging into my room. Furball sprang under my desk in one leap.

"What are you even doing in here? What d'you want?" I asked him, pressing Pause on the music. My heart beat double-time, hoping he wouldn't spot Furball's bed, food, cat scratcher and litter tray.

"I need your Sharpie set," he said, rummaging around my desk, lifting my folders and books.

I jumped off my bed and elbowed him away. Quickly grabbing the pens from my drawer, I flung them into his chest. "There. Now go."

He gave me a side-eye. "You'd better take that stinky thing back to its home before Mum finds out," he said, and walked out.

I let out a huge breath, glad he hadn't figured out that this actually *was* Furball's home.

CHAPTER
20

SUKHI LINKED ARMS with me as we slowly walked home after school on Monday under an almost-white sky. It was sticky and warm and really needed to rain. If it did, I'd welcome it. And my hair might not even get wet because it was covered. Bonus.

It was my third school day wearing a hijab, and I was already getting used to wearing it with my uniform, as if it had always been a part of it. School had been uneventful and I was glad of it. I had library duty at lunch, which kept me out of sight of Sasha Williams and her mates, and I'd made sure I left the library behind other people so I wouldn't get caught alone again.

"You're so lucky you were grounded on Saturday, Ali," Sukhi said, her eyes ahead as we walked. "Oh my god, town was *so* busy. They had some festival on and it took me *forever* to get to Central Library. And I hated having to walk through the crowds."

I shuddered—I was glad I hadn't been there if it was that crowded, but was still upset about how my weekend had gone. "I didn't feel lucky. It was so boring, Sukhi. Mum and Dad were in a bad mood because Mr. Grimshaw, our neighbor opposite, had a go at them while they were tidying the front garden about the latest terrorist attack in Australia. They wouldn't even let us watch any TV! They said it was all too negative."

"Oh, right." After a few seconds, she looked at me. "How come they didn't come to my mum and dad's anniversary party on Saturday? It was weird not to see them this year, even though I knew you probably couldn't."

"Mum said she had a headache. I think they're stressed by all this stuff that's going on. They've been acting really weird." I tried not to breathe through my nose and dodged some dog poo someone hadn't bothered picking up. "Anyway, I'm glad they didn't go because then they would've left me at home 'cause I was grounded, and I'd have felt even worse."

"Yeah, true! They're dealing with a lot, I suppose." Sukhi adjusted her backpack.

"Yeah . . . I tried to read and then forced myself to listen to my whole 3W playlist. It took me a few goes to be able to get through a full song without blubbering, but I'm getting there. I still can't look at their pics on Snappo, though, can you?"

"I'm okay with it. I just don't think about the concert . . . So how's your new pet?" Sukhi quickly changed the subject.

"Ha! Furball is *amazing.*" I felt my face relax. "Because I had nothing better to do all weekend, I made loads of balls made of wool and googled videos of what cats like and basically spent every day playing with her in between trying out different scarf styles. She sleeps curled on my bed and when she hears Yusuf she hides under my desk. It's definitely her safe place." I smiled thinking about her, looking forward to snuggling when I got home.

"Well, I'm happy for you, but don't be inviting me to your room—sorry, *cat palace*—any time soon." Sukhi grinned. She was so cheeky. Shame she was scared of cats. Furball would love to snuggle with her.

The front door slammed shut so hard that I felt the vibrations all the way in the kitchen and jumped in my chair.

Yusuf must be in a bad mood. Again.

I pulled my earphones out and paused the 3W track I was listening to, putting my pen down on my maths worksheet. I wondered if Mr. Grimshaw had harassed him again. Mum and Dad thought he'd been the one who had called the police on us last Monday after the vigil. He was being more difficult than ever—telling Yusuf to take his cap off and not walk around like a "hooligan." Ringing the doorbell to complain that the front of Dad's car was a few centimeters over the edge of our driveway and threatening to call the council to report him.

Mum had told Yusuf and me firmly not to talk back and give him more "ammunition." But it was hard not to worry when Yusuf was always throwing a temper tantrum, and Mum and Dad were arguing and having a go at us about the tiniest of things.

"Look at this!" Yusuf stormed in and slammed what looked like a poster on the kitchen counter. His hair was gelled off his face and his button-down shirt was open over his Nike T-shirt. "They're rallying now."

Dad looked up from the biology papers he was marking, dropped his pen, and gestured to the dining table. "Bring it here."

Yusuf put the white A3 poster in front of Dad. It had a sketch of a man with pale hair and a mask over his mouth doing a Hitler salute. Underneath the sketch it said:

WHITE ZONE

in big white letters against a black background, followed by, in smaller font:

TAKE ACTION — JOIN US AND PROTECT THE BRITISH WAY OF LIFE

Dad turned it over so we could no longer see it and leaned back in his chair, stroking his beard for a long minute, his brow seriously furrowed.

"Does that mean only white people are allowed in this country or something?" I asked. "Because that's ridiculous."

"Yeah, like we're in Hitler's Germany or something." Yusuf stood behind Dad, his jaw clenched.

"Where did you find it?" asked Dad.

"It was stuck on a lamppost near Victory Park." Yusuf leaned over Dad to take the poster back.

"Leave it," said Dad. "I'm going to hand it in to the police."

"They ain't gonna do nothing!" said Yusuf.

"Yusuf, if you're going to speak, use better language," said Dad, lifting his pen again to continue marking.

Yusuf rolled his eyes, tutted and went to leave the kitchen, but stopped at the door. "There's loads of posters out there, Dad. Photos of them are already going viral online."

I searched my Snappo to check if anything about the posters was on there, but couldn't see anything, just my usual cat, hijab and running videos. Maybe he meant it was going viral between him and his mates?

"We ain't gonna take this lying down." Yusuf pulled the door shut and stormed upstairs.

CHAPTER 21

A FEW DAYS HAD PASSED since Yusuf had found the poster and stormed off to his room, and the house had been kind of peaceful and normal since, which was a relief. I'd successfully managed to avoid any more drama in the lunch hall with Jayden after his suspension ended because I'd brought sandwiches from home.

This week at school I'd offered to help Janae, who sat next to me in physics, Sheena in chemistry, and even Daniel in English, by passing them my notes, hoping they'd remember that I was still Aaliyah and not a dangerous terrorist.

It was Sports Day and I was feeling good about it. This was my chance to be the usual Aaliyah—the always-willing-to-help-her-house-win Aaliyah—and be as equal as everyone else on the athletics track. And it would be so cool if I won my race. I'd love to run around celebrating and stick my face in Lisa's to show her I didn't care what she thought of me, even if it had taken me a whole week to pluck up the courage to even think of facing her after what she'd said.

I switched off the 3W song about loving yourself, said bye to Furball—who was hovering near her litter tray, clearly needing privacy—and headed down. I tied my hair in a messy bun before grabbing my scarf. The best thing about wearing a hijab was that I saved at least ten minutes every morning because I no longer had to try and get my hair to look right. I smoothed my hijab around my face and took a breath before I looked in the mirror in our hallway. *There,* I told myself. *All your worries are covered. No one can see them. This gives you power, it doesn't take it.*

I thought about the post I'd come across on Snappo when looking at running videos, about a women's beach handball team who had been fined for not wearing bikini bottoms because they wanted to cover their butts. When I'd searched for more details, so many newspapers were outraged and the team had support from around the world, criticizing the board who had fined them for not letting the women cover up and dress how they wanted. Some pop star I'd barely heard of had even offered to pay the fines. It gave me hope that people who actually used their brains would also support Muslim women who didn't do sport, for the choices *they* wanted to make. There had to be more of the nicer people in the world than racists like Sasha and Jayden. I guess I just had to find them.

After having lunch, I walked quickly toward my locker. I smiled at Feifei and her friends when she passed, and anyone else who looked my way. I was focused on proving I was the friendly—not a terrorist—Muslim at school.

YOU BETTA TAKE THAT THING OFF YOUR HEAD, OTHERWISE YOUR DEAD!!!

The walls echoed with the *WHAM* of lockers slamming, kids shouting over each other, their shoes scuffling away as I froze.

Another note, this one written on a greasy folded-up piece of lined paper, had been wedged into my locker door. So now I'm dead if I wear one? My stomach flipped. I wasn't going to let this person—I bet it was Jayden because of the dodgy spelling, or maybe even Sasha disguising her writing—tell me what I could wear or do. Especially not them. But there was something else as well. When I unfolded the note with the tips of my fingers, trying not to touch any of the greasy bits, a small rasher of pink, crispy meat fell out of it and onto the floor. It looked and smelled like bacon.

I flung the note away, closed my eyes and sighed heavily. Barbaric. Barbaric. Barbaric.

No actually, correction. Evil. Evil. Evil. I wanted to storm into Mrs. Owen's office and bring her here. She was our head teacher—it was her responsibility. She could pick up the note and see for herself what kind of horrible people she had in this school. I wasn't going to touch it.

Then again, what was the point? There was no point in telling any teachers, or anyone in this stupid school. Look what happened when I told Mrs. Owen that Sasha had attacked me. Absolutely nothing. She would probably just agree with the note writer. No one wanted me to wear a hijab. Not even Mum.

I had thought that by coming out visibly as a Muslim, I'd be able to make people see we weren't bad. Instead I was just getting abused and attacked, and now I was getting actual death threats.

I pulled out my PE kit, throwing the books I didn't need back onto the metal shelf, and banged my locker shut. As I turned into the main corridor, heading toward the changing rooms, I bumped straight into Lisa.

She gave me a closed-lip smile. A tiny one. As if she wanted to stop and talk. I gave her a side-eye and walked off.

I keeled over on the grass at the edge of the makeshift athletics racetrack, out of breath from the hundred-meter sprint. I ignored Jayden and his mates jeering at me from a distance and hoped Mum and her parent friends had somehow missed it.

"Here." Sukhi passed me my water bottle.

"Thanks." I sat up, squinting in the hot sun, and took a big sip, then poured water over my scarf to cool myself down. Before the race, I'd redone my hijab and worn it like a headwrap with a bow on top and left my neck clear, so it wouldn't flap up on my face as I ran. Mum had said I looked like the writer Zadie Smith when I'd practiced it last night, and that didn't bother me one bit, even though I was aiming for more of author Tahereh Mafi chic.

"It's not your fault you fell over Leanne," said Sukhi. "No one would've seen that coming."

"I know, right? Just my luck I was going too fast and didn't have time to stop when she buckled—our house lost because of me. Ah, well . . . there's always next year." I sat with my knees to my chest, watching the two-hundred-meter race, which was about to begin. I'd really wanted to beat my bronze and get a gold medal this year, even silver. It would've been amazing to have helped my house win so they'd know

I hadn't changed just because I looked different, but I guess it wasn't meant to be. It was my fault for dropping out of running club to do library duty.

Kids who had already run, or were waiting to, chattered all over the field. The Year Eight two-hundred-meter runners were focused, arms ready, in position to run for their lives. A lump formed in my throat when I realized Jo would've been running in this race if she hadn't lost her leg. She was still in hospital. I hung my head and stared at the dry patchy grass beneath me, swallowing. Her whole life had been ruined by that one evening.

The whistle blew and off they went, everyone giving it their best shot.

Once they'd passed and everyone had cheered them on, I searched across the field to see if I could spot Mum. I wondered if she'd seen me fly over Leanne and land flat on my front. Ouch. She probably hadn't, otherwise she'd have run onto the track and embarrassed me even more. I brushed the small graze on my palm, I'd been lucky I'd got away with only grass stains.

I spotted a group of parents, Sukhi's mum among them. A bit further away, Mum stood alone under a tree in her work suit, handbag over her shoulder, staring at her phone. She was probably taking a call.

The race finished and the next group positioned themselves. Mum was still standing at the edge of the field, but her eyes were focused on the racetrack, her face stern. Her arms were folded, so her call must be over. Why didn't she go join the other parents? Usually she'd be right at the center, chatting and laughing away.

And then I realized.

I should have known something was off at the weekend. For the first time in years, Mum and Dad hadn't gone to Sukhi's parents' party. Mum never missed it, but this time she said she had a headache, and Dad stayed home too. My mum and Sukhi's mum must have had a fight. I'd never seen them standing apart like this. I realized I hadn't heard them speak on the phone for ages, and Mum had Sukhi's mum's contact page up on her phone last week—she might've been deleting it.

I bet they had fought about the terrorist being a Muslim.

A wave of nausea washed over me. Everything was changing because of these terrorists, and not just for me. It looked like Mum had lost a best friend too.

I needed to do something. But I had no idea what I should do.

CHAPTER
22

As I slung my backpack off my arm to unzip it in front of my locker, I found a post-it note stuck on the small compartment at the front. My stomach dived.

It had been a week since the last note on Sports Day, and I'd prayed that one would be the last. I'd had evil looks all week whenever Sasha and her gang and Jayden and his mates clocked me, but I'd been able to get away from them, ducking into the library or getting as close to a teacher as possible.

What did Jayden want to say now? That he was going to kill me for just being myself today? For breathing?

And why was he leaving me notes?

He probably didn't want to leave any evidence on his phone or computer, I realized. *That's* why he left notes. Clever. For a Neanderthal.

I peeled the post-it off my backpack and held my breath.

You look beautiful.
Your new scarf suits you. ☺

Well, I certainly wasn't expecting THAT.

A slow smile spread across my face as I folded the note and put it in my blazer pocket. Clearly it wasn't from Jayden. Who could it be from? My mind was blank. But at that moment, it was enough just knowing that someone out there was on my side.

A locker jolted open behind me. It was Lisa. She looked over her shoulder and smiled. I looked to see if she was smiling at someone else, but no one was there.

Could the note be from her?

No, it wasn't her writing. And the ink was from a fountain pen—the letters wider and inkier than from a regular pen—which Lisa didn't use, even though her dad was always telling her to.

I wanted to shove the note in her face, maybe stick it on her forehead, but I stopped myself. She left the locker area before I'd finished reloading my bag for afternoon lessons.

Sukhi turned up just as I clanged the door shut.

"Did you see her?" I said. "Why isn't Lisa talking

to *you*? You're not Muslim." It just came out. Blurted without thinking.

Sukhi adjusted her backpack strap, then pushed her glasses up her nose. "Yeah, I saw her . . ." she said. "Look, she says hi to me now and again but she won't talk to me for real. I think she might be sorry for shutting us out? She probably doesn't want to get between us."

"Well, ain't that generous of her?" I scoffed as we left the locker area and stepped into the corridor. Every time I started to feel bad for Lisa and blame her behavior on her brother, she reminded me that she was part of this decision. She could easily speak to me at school where Darren couldn't stop her. She could've put a password on her phone, but she obviously didn't want to.

Without Lisa, I felt as if I had a gaping hole inside of me. But she didn't seem to care about me at all. Not the way I cared about her.

"Anyway, here," said Sukhi, passing me a white A4 envelope.

"What's that?" I asked.

"I dunno, Feifei Wen passed it to me as I came out of the toilets. She said it was for you."

"Feifei?" I pulled out two sheets of paper stapled together. The top page had a table on it and lots of signatures down one column.

"What is it?" Sukhi nudged my shoulder as she got closer to read it with me.

A wave of fire rushed up from my stomach. "A . . . petition . . . to ban me from wearing my hijab."

"OH MY GOD. Are you serious?" said Sukhi, her hands on her face. "As if spitting on you and leaving death threats on your locker wasn't enough, now they're petitioning to get your scarf banned at school?"

My heart pumped through my ears. "You know what, Sukhi, they can do what they like!" I lifted the petition in front of my face and tore it to pieces, dropping it to the floor like confetti. "They're not going to tell *me* what to do or wear. I'm gonna carry right on. This is MY choice, not theirs."

"Yesss!" Sukhi punched her fist and pulled it to her hip as if she'd won something. "Do you think Feifei wanted you to have it, so you'd find out they were organizing this? To help you?"

"Yeah, maybe," I said, desperately hoping that was the reason. Feifei hated Jayden. He'd given her a really hard time in Year Seven. There was no way she'd support that racist idiot. Right?

When I got home from school in the spitting rain, I saw a police car parked outside our drive. I spun on my heels to walk back to the main road as dread slapped over me. Why were they here?

I walked around the block and came up my street from the other side and lurked at the corner, messaging Sukhi, waiting till they left, having to constantly wipe my phone on my blazer to clear the screen of rain. Luckily the car was facing the main road and they weren't long at the door.

A police officer stepped out of our drive, and I ducked behind a car. He crossed the road and went to Mr. Grimshaw's house. He looked like the one that had come to our house last time but I couldn't be sure. Their laughter echoed down the still street, and it seemed like they were friends.

Mr. Grimshaw said something that made the police officer laugh even louder and then he turned and waved goodbye. I crouched, pretending to do my laces and waited till I'd heard the car drive off.

When I finally got home, Mum was livid. "Can you believe this nonsense?" she shouted. "Grimshaw said we're forcing you to cover up. That it's illegal. And I had to explain wearing a hijab is a personal decision. And you're not being forced!"

I closed my eyes in disbelief. Had Mr. Grimshaw actually sent another police officer to our house because of *me*?

Like, OH MY GOD, what did it have to do with

him anyway? We didn't go calling the police about *his* wardrobe choices.

After I'd vacuumed my room, hoping it would drown out my frustration, and taken the cat litter out, I unraveled my hijab and dropped onto my bed. Why was I doing this to myself when I didn't have to? But I couldn't see myself not wearing a hijab anymore—every day, it felt more a part of who I was.

These people wanted to strip me of my identity. Of who I was, and who I wanted to be. *They* were the ones who wanted to take away my choice, not my parents.

I stroked Furball's head as I gazed out my bedroom window at the gray street. It was no longer safe to be out in my own neighborhood in case someone called the police on me.

"Life's hard, Furball," I said, lifting her up and kissing her little nose. "But we have to be strong, right?"

Furball closed her eyes and purred. She loved being held. And I loved holding her. Maybe that's why I'd found her. Maybe I was meant to be there for Furball so she wouldn't be left alone, and she was God's way of giving me comfort and making up for all these vomit-brains around me.

"You're the only one that doesn't judge me and loves me for who *I* am. Thank you, my little fluffball. You're the best," I said, lying back on my pillow and pulling her to my chest. The warmth from her little body trickled into mine.

My phone pinged once, then again. I grabbed it and saw that Sukhi had messaged me. She'd sent a screenshot of a photo on some random account on Snappo. It was a photo of ME in my hijab walking in the playground with a red cross across my head and red font below, saying:

BAN THE HIJAB. IT DOESN'T BELONG HERE AND IT'S RUINING OUR COUNTRY.

Sukhi's next message said:

WTH, Can you believe it? I've reported it. What now? Can you talk?

I closed my eyes. I didn't feel like talking. I felt like crying. Why were they picking on me like this? What had I ever done to them?

The next day, I slid straight into my chair at form time, feeling as if all sixty eyes were on me. My eyes were sore from crying, so I kept my head down. I'd spent a long time on my prayer mat last night, asking Allah to make this easier for me. All I wanted was to be my best self, but it was hard when everyone was being so nasty. And after I'd sobbed and begged Him to help, a sense of peace settled deep inside. This was a test, and I'd get through it. Somehow. I just had to make sure I kept wearing my scarf so it could continue to motivate me and help me stop myself from retaliating when I was pushed, like last night when I'd wanted to tell the haters on Snappo what I thought of them, and then remembered that wasn't good representation. It was like when Mrs. Owen picked only the best students to represent the school when we had visitors. I wanted to be the best rep for Muslims at school.

When the bell rang for first class and everyone started piling out, Mrs. Alcock asked me to stay back. *Why does she want to speak to me? I haven't done anything wrong.*

"Erm . . ." She cleared her throat. "Aaliyah, we've had complaints about you wearing your headscarf in school." She fiddled with her pen lid.

I swallowed.

"Not just from the children, but, umm, parents too."

"But why? I'm not doing anything wrong," I asked. My cheeks burned. I glanced at the door behind me and saw Lisa standing in the doorway, listening, as if she wanted to come and help. I gave her a none-of-your-business look.

"Well, people find it—" Mrs. Alcock hesitated—"offensive. Especially after—"

"It's just a piece of cloth!" I butted in. "It's not hurting anyone."

"I'm sorry, Aaliyah, it's got nothing to do with me; it's a management decision and I've been told to tell you . . . we don't need the bad publicity. Parents are threatening to go to the media—"

"The BAD PUBLICITY!" My nostrils flared. "You have no idea what bad publicity is!" I stormed out of the classroom door, pushing past Lisa's shoulder.

So for some reason, me wearing a hijab was making the school look bad. But forcing their opinion down my throat and not allowing me to express myself was fine.

Oh, I'd make the school look bad all right, I thought. And they'd totally regret it.

CHAPTER 23

IT WAS WEIRD, the more I was told not to wear a hijab, the more I wanted to. The school couldn't tell me how to dress if they didn't have a good reason, and "bad publicity" was probably the WORST. If the cloth wrapped around my head didn't harm anyone, what was their problem? I wasn't going to give in. Nope.

I stayed in the library after school to avoid bumping into Jayden and Sasha Williams, who were hanging around the front gates for some reason, and to finish my biology project in peace, away from Yusuf and his blaring gaming chats with his mates online.

After I'd finished, I stared at the doodles on my table and thought about Jo in hospital. Was she ever going to come to school again? How was she feeling? Sukhi said her mum had seen a post on Facebook raising money to convert Jo's house for wheelchair use. Would she be using it forever? I grabbed my phone and forced myself to send the message I'd been writing and deleting to Jo for weeks. I thought it might be better if I wrote down what I'd tried to say in the videos I'd recorded, but I kept chickening out. Today, I went straight to my app and pressed send without rereading it. If I didn't, I'd end up looking at it every day for the rest of my life. Once it had swooshed off, I slumped in my chair. There. I had done it. I had *finally* told her I was sorry about what had happened and hoped she was doing okay. I wasn't sure if she'd reply, but in a way I didn't need her to as long as she knew I was thinking about her.

When I finally left the library, the streets were quieter. The sky was covered in thick fluffy clouds and the traffic had calmed down, leaving just a few cars backed up at the pedestrian crossing. There was no one outside the front gates—everyone was probably home having their tea. Even so, I kept my head down and scurried through the streets.

As the pavement narrowed near the parade of shops on the main road, I stopped to let an old woman lugging a polka dot shopping trolley pass, making sure I gave her my biggest I'm-not-a-terrorist smile. Something caught my eye: three huge posters stuck to the green metal security shutter of a shop that had closed down months ago. They showed the same sketch as the WHITE ZONE poster Yusuf had brought home. The same boy with pale spiky hair and a mask over his face. But these posters had more text. I got closer and read:

> **STOP THE INVASION.**
> **STOP ISLAM.**
> **STOP REFUGEES.**
> **BRING BACK OUR SAFE WHITE NEIGHBORHOODS.**
> Join us in taking back our country.
> Saturday 9th July 12–4 p.m.
> Lambert
> Call Darren for more info: 07203 768349

This was on the same day as the summer fete in two weeks! Fury rose within me as I'd never felt it. I pulled out my phone to check my contacts list. I still had Darren's number stored from the time I'd had to call him to pick us up from the cinema in Year Seven. I didn't think to delete it, and now I was glad I hadn't. I checked the number on the poster against the Darren in my phonebook—it was the same. Now he was *spreading* his lies and publicly calling for others to join him.

I wanted to release the swear words at the tip of my tongue and scream. If I could breathe fire I'd have scorched the posters right off the shutters. I would've burned the shutters down.

Instead, I looked around and imagined what anyone would think if they saw a hijabi shouting and swearing, and I stopped myself. I took a photo of the posters on my phone and stamped back up the main road. Toward Lisa's house.

I'd taken the longer, busier route home from school, so I was only a few blocks from Lisa's. Now I took the shortcut through the village green—basically a big field with some play equipment on it. My heavy brow wrinkled as squeals of laughter came from the little kids being pushed on the swings and going down the slide. What were they so cheerful for? Wait till they got to high school, I thought. Even the cooing pigeons in the trees annoyed me. A boy on a bike came from around the corner and sped toward me. I slowed to avoid his wheels as I passed the sweet-smelling trees and bushes lining the edge of the green. A squirrel scrabbled up a tree trunk on my right, sending a flock of birds cawing into the sky.

My hand cooled instantly as I pulled the yellow metal gate open on the other side of the green. I ran through it toward Lisa's house. I'd had enough of Darren and his racist ways. I had to confront him. Maybe I'd change his mind. Maybe he'd remember how we all used to play badminton in his hallway and realize he had nothing to worry about.

I turned into Lisa's street and immediately spun

on my heels and ran back around the corner, hiding behind a hedge bordering the house at the intersection. A group of guys stood on the pavement a few meters away—a few doors from Lisa's house, leaning on a white van, smoking. My heart felt as if it'd stopped. I hadn't been this close to Darren since that night at the concert. I'd gone out of my *way* to avoid him, even when I'd seen him shouting at the old lady. And today, like a numpty, I was heading right for him. I hadn't thought things through. What was I going to say to him? I was wearing a hijab that he'd want to rip off the second he laid eyes on it. I wouldn't be able to say a word. Just thinking about him made me want to shrink into a hole, how did I think I could actually STAND UP to him? If he was that scary when he was alone, what would he be like in front of his friends?

I slunk back into the tall prickly hedge to catch my breath. *Slow down*, I told myself, gripping my elbows. I could hear them talking, but my heartbeat was louder in my ears. Focus. Breathe. I took in a big gulp of air and crouched next to the hedge.

They laughed wildly. A small insect buzzed around me, I swatted it away and leaned into the hedge, edging closer around it into Lisa's street. Two other guys were with Darren. I knew it was him when Darren spoke.

"Yeah, it's gonna be mad!" he said. "I'm bringing a

couple of baseball and cricket bats as well. They won't know what's hit 'em."

"Once the crowd is powered up at the rally, we'll sneak off and get as many people as possible," said his mate. "The police will be distracted, and we'll show these brownies that we're serious about stopping the invasion!"

"Nine July!" screamed the other.

"Yeah!!" they all hollered together.

I put my sweaty fingers to my lips to hold back a yelp as I fell into the dry spiky hedge. Were they talking about the rally on Darren's poster? Were they actually planning to beat up anyone who was brown or Muslim in the streets? I had to do something. Should I go the police? Ask Mum or Dad for advice? But what if Darren found out I'd told on him?

I had to think of something—and it had to be fast.

CHAPTER
24

I WENT STRAIGHT UP to my room when I got home, flung my school headscarf on my bed for Furball to nuzzle, and decided I'd focus on my maths homework after I'd finished zuhr, the afternoon prayer. It might settle the choking feeling in my chest and settle my breathing, and get Darren out of my head.

I plunked my textbooks on my desk, knocking over my deodorant and perfume bottles. I put them back in place, but took the lid off the perfume Lisa had given me for Christmas even though she knew we didn't celebrate it. I moved it under my nose and inhaled the sweet, warm smell. It took me straight to the moment when Lisa had given it to me in my bedroom. I'd ripped the snowman wrapping paper off and squealed—it made me feel so grown up. We'd hugged and sprayed it over our wrists just like those Snappo influencers.

I put the perfume back and told myself to stop thinking about how nice she used to be—I had maths homework to do. Rummaging around my school bag again, I couldn't find my calculator. I must've left it in my locker. I'd have to borrow Yusuf's.

I pulled my door shut to make sure Furball didn't follow me. Yusuf's bedroom door was ajar and he was chatting with someone. I raised my knuckles to knock but something he said made me stop.

"Yeah, we're gonna sort their 'white zone' faces! Don't worry, bro! They *think* they can do us damage? Let them try, just let them try!"

Some animated sounds came from his call.

"Yeah, man . . . Brothers unite!" Yusuf said.

Oh god. Oh, no, I was having déjà vu—this was the same stuff I'd heard earlier that afternoon but from different people in a different place. Both of them wanted to hurt each other. To wipe each other out. Like threatened lions killing invading lions to claim their territory in a wildlife documentary. And one of them was my own brother.

Yusuf was an idiot. He couldn't get involved in this sort of stuff. He wasn't thinking. This wasn't going to be like when he was at Ratcliffe Academy and the boys fought with Darren's year at St. John's in the school fields because they hated each other's schools. This would be a million times worse.

I pushed the door in and barged into his room. He was sitting on his bed in shorts and a white T-shirt, the smell of freshly sprayed deodorant lingering in the air. He lowered his laptop lid and scowled at me. "Get out."

"I need your calculator," I said, going to his cluttered desk.

"Get out of my room, Aaliyah!" His eyes narrowed and he pushed his laptop open again. "Sorry," he said to the person on his call. "It's just my sister. Hang on."

"I'm going nowhere till you give me your calculator. I have to hand in my maths tomorrow. I need it."

He bounced off his bed, threw open his desk drawer and shoved his Casio in my stomach.

"Ow!" I rubbed the short sharp sting on my tummy with my elbow.

I wanted to talk to him, but it didn't look like he was going to get off his call. I gave him eyes before leaving his room. It was probably better if I thought about what I should do first anyway. Surprise myself and think things through. No more impulsive Aaliyah blurting out the first thing that popped into her head.

In my room, Furball rubbed against my leg as I sat at my desk and typed "stopping terrorists" into Google. But that just threw up boring government documents and links. So I typed: "stopping racists from fighting—what can you do."

That brought up lots of articles about racism in America. But halfway down the list, one headline jumped out at me:

Ways to Fight Hate Crime — Community Responses

I clicked on the link and a blog post with a list of suggestions came up. The post said you should join forces with others, speak up, pressure leaders and teach acceptance. I leaned back in my chair and stared out onto our road. That all sounded great, but how could I do any of it? I was only thirteen.

I grabbed my phone and put out a post on Snappo:

Fed up with all the hate and fighting. Why can't we all love each other and be kind? Signed a sad 13 year old 😣 #3WConcertBombing

Within a minute someone random told me not to be sad, there were kind people in the world and I should focus on the good things and stay away from the news.

Ha. I had done everything to stay away from the news these past few weeks. If only they knew it made me hyperventilate.

Didn't they know that some of us had no choice but to live with the consequences of the concert? Focusing on the good things hadn't stopped Jayden and Sasha from tormenting me. It hadn't stopped Darren and his mates from organizing a racist rally as a cover for beating up anyone that wasn't like them.

I could understand why Yusuf wanted to stand up for us, but he was choosing the wrong way to do it. I was scared he'd end up in prison or worse, dead, if he tried to fight those racist thugs.

After twenty minutes of gearing up my courage, I barged back into Yusuf's bedroom. "I heard you, you know," I said, staring as he sat hunched over his desk. "I know you're planning a fight."

He cocked his head and glared at me. "Shut up and stay out of it. And get out my room, I'm revising. In fact"—he pushed his chair back and strode over to grip my shoulders—"if I catch you coming in here and listening to my conversations again, you're dead." He pushed me toward the door. I put my hands out to stop myself from falling. By the time I whirled around to yell at him, he'd put his ear pods in and turned up his music.

I trudged back to my room to reread the blog. And I was so glad I did. In a way, it agreed with Yusuf. It said there was no point in staying silent. If a hate group was coming to your town, you had to act. But it also said you should never attend the hate rally. Instead you should bring people in your community together. It gave examples of stuff you could do, like hosting meetings, sharing meals together and trying each other's food, praying together, or organizing parades and other entertainment.

Oh. My. God. Why hadn't I thought of that before? I could do something positive that would bring us all together. Like it used to be years ago.

I could get Sukhi to help me organize an event! I grabbed my phone to message her about my genius plan.

We could get everyone together at the summer fete to raise money for the school kids that were hurt at the concert. That way Jo's parents could afford to convert their house for wheelchair access for when she left hospital. Money could never make up for what happened, but it might help Jo adjust more easily. And we'd have *shown* her that we were sorry and cared about her.

Everyone from school and people from the local area would be there too. They'd want to support it because it was for the Ratcliffe Academy concert victims. AND it was on the same day as Darren's hate rally—if we worked together then no one would go to it. And then Yusuf would be safe.

I might even face the thought of big crowds full of people I didn't know. And finally confront my fear of Darren. Maybe I would stop hyperventilating every time I saw him.

CHAPTER 25

THAT NIGHT, I fell asleep snuggling next to Furball with visions of everyone in Lambert smiling and happy together at the summer fete. And maybe because I actually slept properly after so long, the chirping birds didn't bother me the next morning. The people chatting at the bus stop, the sharp morning breeze and music blaring from cars made me feel alive.

Sukhi had another dentist appointment, this time for her braces to be fitted, so I left for school on my own. I almost skipped my way there in my head, even though I kept my feet firmly planted on the actual pavement. If I could get Yusuf to come to the fete and away from Darren, *and* raise money for Jo and the other Ratcliffe Academy students who were injured at the concert, everything would get better. I just knew it. I tucked the flaps of my scarf further down my shirt collars as I walked. Maybe people in Lambert would finally realize that all Muslims weren't bad and would never want to hurt them like that vile terrorist.

As I turned the corner onto the quiet side street that led to the school, my head jerked back violently. I lurched forward and my knees locked. Someone had yanked my scarf from behind. I spun around, panic rising through me, but whoever it was had disappeared. My stomach went rock hard and my ears throbbed. I scanned the parked cars and terraced houses and re-adjusted my hijab. No sign of anyone.

A minute earlier I'd wanted to skip, but now I wanted to run to school. To somewhere safe. A minute earlier I was happy. Now my every limb shook.

It wasn't easy running when my whole core had turned to ice. I finally made it to the end of the road, where more kids traipsed along the pavement toward school. My heart was beating so hard, I was sure if I touched my chest, I'd feel it trying to thud out.

Who pulled my scarf? It could've been Jayden, or Sasha, or Darren—or anyone. I had no idea. What I did know was that I didn't want to walk alone again.

After I'd finished covering for Mrs. Patel in the library at lunch, I met Sukhi on the field. I sat, trying to seek out the handful of Black, South Asian, and

Chinese kids, smattered about like a little ground pepper that had accidentally fallen in a saltshaker. I wondered if any of them had ever been attacked for who they were. There were a few Muslims in Year Ten and Eleven, but I didn't know them, and as much as I wanted to, I couldn't just go up to them and ask them how they felt. They probably wouldn't talk to me anyway.

"You're quiet today," said Sukhi, her words muffled through her new braces. I could barely hear her above the kids screaming and chatting across the school field. "Ali?" She leaned her face into mine.

Without warning, my eyes prickled with tears.

"Ali, talk to me. What's happened?" Sukhi asked, her blurry body now turned toward me, her knees knocking into mine.

"It was something, but then it wasn't," I managed to say between sobs. I was glad we were sitting at the edge of the field where no one could hear or see me.

"What do you mean?"

"Someone pulled my scarf in the street—but they didn't get it off 'cause it was wrapped around my head tight. So nothing really happened."

"Oh my god! Who?"

"I don't actually know. I didn't see anyone."

"I bet it was Jayden! Who else would do that?" Sukhi shook her head.

"Sukhi, it could literally be anyone ... I mean, everyone seems to hate Muslims right now."

"Yeah, but look at what he did yesterday. Blatantly pulled your water bottle out of your backpack and chucked it down the corridor." Sukhi pulled out a daisy from the grass. "And I can't believe when I complained, Mrs. Owen said he'd been 'triggered' and the concert had affected people in different ways and then stared at *your* scarf, as if it was your fault he did that!"

I shrugged and sighed. I had no way of proving it, even if it was Jayden. And what difference would it make anyway? He got away with everything—even chucking water bottles down corridors when Mrs. Owen was around.

Sukhi studied me as if I was interesting to look at. It made me wonder if I'd imagined it. I mean, nothing happened and no one was there. Maybe I had.

"Forget it." I wiped my face with my hands. "People go through a lot worse. Just ignore me."

Sukhi pursed her lips. After a long second she said, "Why does everyone say that Muslim women are forced to cover up? You aren't."

I shrugged. "They're not; you hardly see proper hijabis in Pakistan or even India—none of my family there wear it. If it was forced, every Muslim woman would wear a hijab and they obviously don't—my mum's friends don't. There's not one way to be a Muslim, it's up to you how you express it." I looked at the school buildings in the distance. "I guess people say that because some women *are* forced in some cultures. My mum gets so upset when she deals with cases in court where some Muslim families treat their women badly. She says they've twisted the religion and want to control women because of what their culture and tradition back home has taught them."

Sukhi threw the now petal-less daisy into the grass. "Yeah, like my uncle's always telling me to wear a salwar kameez at home, and he always makes me feel like I'm doing something bad if I don't."

"Yeah, Mum says it's always men telling women what to do and how to dress."

Sukhi looked at me for a moment. "Do you feel hot in it?"

I laughed. It was a fair question, one I'd often wondered about before I started wearing a hijab. "It's weird, but I don't. I like the way it keeps my hair off my neck and face, and also"—I swatted away a small fly buzzing near my cheek—"I won't get any nits."

She snorted. "Oh my god, that's so true!" Sukhi pulled another daisy from the grass. "So do you wanna talk about the fete fundraiser idea?"

"Oh, yeah," I said, sitting up straight, feeling more energetic. "I thought we could do a collection for the

Ratcliffe concert bombing victims." I ducked as a bee came buzzing far too close.

"The PTA is already planning a collection at the summer fete," she said in a matter-of-fact way, pulling out another daisy and picking its tiny white petals out one by one.

"Yeah, but ours would be different, it would be organized by actual school kids!" I said proudly.

"The PTA are working with the student council, Aaliyah," said Sukhi, looking at me over her glasses.

"Oh . . . okay," I said, feeling deflated. Maybe there was nothing I could do to bring everyone together. I was just a kid. It was stupid of me to even think I could keep Yusuf away from the rally, and get my ex-best friend to help us do something good. It was even more stupid that I thought I could do something about the hate spreading through Lambert. So dense.

"But," Sukhi said, tapping my arm to get my attention, "*we* could help the PTA, which is obviously bigger and more organized than just us, and that would still count?"

"Oh, yeah!" I sat up. "And we could speak to the student council to find out more about the PTA's plan for the fete and ask if we could help *them* raise money for the concert bombing victims."

"Yeah, that's a good idea. So then we're helping everyone involved."

"I'll speak to Jonah. He's my form student council representative. And you speak to yours . . . who's yours?" I knew how the student council decided on things because I had been a member in Year Seven; we just needed them to bring this idea to their next meeting.

"Leon Abbott, I think," Sukhi said.

I stared at my school shoes. "It's weird how since the concert, I get upset so quickly. As if I'm made of eggshells. I got so worked up about raising money, I hadn't realized that we didn't *have* to do it all by ourselves. We could just help the PTA. Duh!"

"Yeah, you worry too much," she said as if it was just a normal thing to say.

"Can you ask your mum if she'll let us help too?" I asked. Sukhi's mum was on the PTA. "That way we'll have someone to directly speak to at the student council and the PTA? Maybe she could come over this weekend and we could all plan together?"

The fundraising might just be the thing that would get Mum and her talking again. I focused on the grass between my fingers wondering why they had fallen out. I daren't ask Sukhi what had happened because I didn't want it to affect us. I only had one good friend now, and I wasn't going to lose her as well.

I SLID AROUND MY CHAIR in citizenship on Friday. The one lesson I used to look forward to because I sat between my two best mates. But now it was just awkward. Lisa had moved to the end of the table near the door, and a quiet Syrian boy called Sami who'd recently moved to Lambert had taken her spot.

Mr. Wilkinson thankfully hadn't asked Lisa why she'd changed seats. What if she told him in front of everyone that it was because I'm a Muslim? I wondered what he'd say.

As I sat waiting for class to start, Lisa walked in. WITH Sukhi.

Lisa had the skull-and-crossbones scarf she usually wore around her neck — on her head. My body stiffened. Was she having a laugh at my expense? And how could Sukhi betray me like this?

Lisa smiled as she sat down near the door. She

smiled at me just like she used to. What was going on?

I glared at Sukhi as she put down her backpack and pulled out her pencil case. She grabbed my exercise book and wrote: *PEACE OFFERING* on the back page.

Whatever she meant, I was not impressed. I think my face said it all.

Sukhi whispered, "Let's talk after lesson, yeah?"

Mr. Wilkinson stood in front of the whiteboard. "You've worked hard on your end-of-year assessments, so I thought we could have a free lesson. You can decide what we discuss."

Jayden's hand shot right up. Mr. Wilkinson ignored him and nodded at Leon, who said, "I wanna talk about the police brutality protests happening in America."

We need to talk about what's happening at home in the UK first, I thought.

"Okay," said Mr. Wilkinson. "What else?" His blue eyes scanned all of us.

"I want to talk about friendship," said Lisa, her flushed cheeks more visible than usual because her hair was covered and off her face.

Both Sukhi and I glanced at her and then at each other.

"Okay, Lisa. . . . Anyone else?" He wrote the suggestions on the whiteboard. A few more hands went up.

I raised my hand slowly. I had to speak up. That

blog had said that's what made a difference. So it was time.

"Yes, Aaliyah?" Mr. Wilkinson pointed his pen at me.

"I want to talk about identity and freedom of expression . . . maybe even hate crimes?"

A murmur went around the class. I felt all sixty eyes on me as I focused on Mr. Wilkinson.

Leon chimed in, "Yeah, I think that's a good one."

Wait, was someone actually agreeing with me?

"Yeah, me too," added Sukhi.

I glanced over at Lisa, who nodded and said, "Me too."

Then Sami, who sat next to me, and another kid, and another.

Feifei put her hand up. "I hate it when people ask me if I'm from China. Why can't I be both British and Chinese?" She swept her short black hair to one side of her face.

She was right. People asked where my parents were from, and when I told them England, they always seemed surprised and asked where my grandparents were from. As if that was the most important thing about *me*.

Sami put his hand up slowly and then straightened it as if he'd found his confidence. "I hate that people look down on me because I had to leave my country.

They assume I lived in a desert tent with camels. As if I've never used a computer or played with anything other than dirt." His eyes were fixed on Mr. Wilkinson's face. I think he was nervous. "I think focusing on what is different about us divides us, and we need to change that by looking at what we have in common."

He was right. Even though he'd been here a week, I'd never heard him speak. I was really surprised by how well-spoken he was. He sounded American and not like I'd assumed he would. *I* was one of those judgmental people he was talking about. I bit my lip, feeling bad.

Leon Abbott said, "I hate the way some people look at me and my big brother when we walk into a shop. They stiffen up and you can see that they think we're gonna cause trouble." He eyed Jayden and added, "I'm proud to be Black and I love my 'fro—I don't care what people think of it—I don't go around telling people how to wear their natural hair, do I?" He gave the cutest grin, showing off his dimples. "It's not my fault I wear it so good."

There was a ripple of laughter. Leon always knew how to lighten the mood when we were discussing a heavy subject.

Suddenly, I felt supported. As if I wasn't alone. Maybe other people were affected by hate crime at school, but I hadn't thought about them until today because I was so focused on what was happening to me.

"Anyone else want to share how their identity is challenged or how they're not allowed to express themselves?" Mr. Wilkinson scanned the room, and when Lisa raised her hand, he nodded at her.

"Ummm, I'm not challenged—" she began.

Jayden cut in. "You are mentally, with that thing on yer head!"

"Jayden!" Mr. Wilkinson barked. "Last warning. Lisa, please continue. You won't be interrupted." His eyes were firmly planted on Jayden.

Lisa's cheeks were almost fuchsia pink. "Uhhh . . . as I was saying, no one challenges my identity, and I'm free to wear what I want, but my best friend . . . errr . . . Aaliyah . . . she can't, and it's so not fair, which is why I'm wearing this scarf. To support her."

My skin tingled. What was she doing? I wasn't going to fall for her tricks. She probably had a plan with Darren.

I caught Sukhi smiling at me from the side. I stared at my nails.

"Umm . . ." Jonah put his hand up. "I know I don't look it, but I am different. I'm Jewish and some people hate to hear that. People are still antisemitic, and with everything on the news right now, I can't wear my kippah outside of my house. I only put it on once I'm in the car, near the synagogue. I don't feel safe to say I'm Jewish."

I couldn't help staring at him. So *he* was like *me*. He couldn't wear his symbol of religion because he was scared he'd get attacked. Maybe I wasn't the only one struggling to express my identity. I'd have to talk to him at lunch. I'd never spoken to him about anything other than homework before, but maybe I could approach him by first asking him to speak to the student council about raising money for Jo and the other Ratcliffe students affected by the bombing.

Sukhi hooked her arm through mine as we stepped into the corridor after the bell went, Lisa walked next to her. "We're going to the toilets," she said, a twinkle in her eye.

The corridor was flooded with kids and their backpacks. I felt sick. I didn't know what their game was, but I didn't need more problems to worry about right now. I'd dealt with Lisa emotionally—accepted that she hated me. I didn't need to go through it all over again or for her to pretend she was still my best friend.

"I don't need the toilet," I said.

Sukhi rolled her eyes. "Ali, please will you just listen? We need to talk. ALL of us."

I let out a deep sigh and followed Lisa and Sukhi in.

We heard someone flush. Sukhi put her finger on her lips, which meant we should wait till they'd washed their hands and left.

"Umm . . . Ali . . . I . . ." started Lisa, after the girl had left and the door had shut behind her.

I kept my eyes on the non-slip floor and shuffled my feet, waiting for this to be over.

"Ali, I . . . I'm really sorry for what I said . . . and did." Her voice cracked.

Oh, flip, she was going to cry.

"I shouldn't have listened to Darren. I thought he was protecting me, but now I know he's an idiot and won't stop till he's hurt someone . . . He . . . He made me watch all these weird videos about regular people you'd meet anywhere planning attacks and they were totally fake. I only found out because one trended on Twitter and made the news. He made up stuff about Muslims and how they're ruining England."

But Lisa had known *me* and my family since we started high school, so what did any of that matter? I kept my eyes on my frayed laces. They needed replacing.

Lisa's voice got more animated. "But the worst was when he pushed an old Muslim woman so her shopping went all over the pavement. He's evil. It's like he can't see what's real anymore. He doesn't listen to

Mum, or Dad . . . if he's around. All he cares about is what his dumb racist mates down the pub think." She paused. "Ali, I know I've been horrible, but PLEASE forgive me. Please. I've really missed you."

My eyes stayed glued to my laces. I didn't know what to say. *Lisa did look distressed the day Darren attacked that old woman . . .*

"Ali?" Sukhi lightly elbowed me in my ribs.

I looked up to see Lisa's pink face streaming with tears. She seemed genuinely upset.

The words came flooding out before I could stop them. "Honestly? I've missed you too."

I shuffled my feet.

Lisa moved forward awkwardly, her arms out for a hug. I let her hug me. The familiar smell of her perfume comforted me and I slowly lifted my arms and hugged her back. Sukhi watched us, smiling, like a proud parent at their toddler's sports day.

"Lise. Do you really think I'm dangerous?" I asked as a tear rolled down my face on to her blazer.

Lisa pushed my shoulders back away from her, and put her face in mine. "NO! I swear, Aaliyah. I was just so scared after the concert bombing. I was scared of everyone. I let Darren get into my head."

She grasped my face and made me look at her. "Ali, I was so ashamed of myself after what I said to you, I couldn't look at you. Darren had hyped me up before school and I'd come in ready to say it, but I regretted it as soon as I'd said it. I'm really sorry. You're my best mate. My Ali. How could you be dangerous? I'm an idiot."

"Yeah, you are." Sukhi stepped in for a group hug.

I stepped back. "If you're serious, Lise, then show me you mean it. Unblock me on Snappo and put a password on your phone so Darren can never get between us again."

Lisa's eyes widened. "Yeah, I need to do that. I forgot because I don't go online much anymore." She pulled her phone out of her bag and swiped to get into Snappo, then went into settings to unblock me.

"Now the phone password." Sukhi stared at Lisa with her hands on her hips.

"He made me take my password off so he can get in any time, you know," said Lisa, going into her password settings. "And he's added his Face ID onto my phone.

"OMG, Lisa!" said Sukhi, her mouth wide open.

"He can't do this," I said. "That's not normal behavior. Yusuf would never touch my phone, let alone add his Face ID to it."

"Actually, even my parents don't do that," added Sukhi, her brows raised above her glasses.

Lisa had her face in her screen.

"Why didn't you tell your mum or dad?" Sukhi asked.

"Dad's away at some important *Médicins Sans Frontières* conference and anyway, because he works in London, by the time he gets home, I'm in bed. I've barely seen him since he took time off because of . . . the . . . you know."

I swallowed. She meant the concert.

"And Mum's always on long shifts at the hospital, so when she's home, she's either asleep or out of it 'cause of the medication she takes. I actually did tell her the other day when she asked me why I'd been quiet—I told her everything Darren's done and when I finally looked up, she was snoring! So I just left it. I can't be bothered to go through it again." Lisa shrugged. She paused and bit her lip for a second before she deleted Darren's Face ID and changed her password. "There, done. He can never get between us again."

"Now can we have that group hug?" Sukhi stepped in closer putting her arms around me and Lisa.

We all laughed and rested our heads against each other's.

Lisa's scarf slipped.

"Lise?" I said.

"Yeah?"

"You can take the scarf off your head now. You don't have to do this."

"Yeah, I do."

"What about Darren?"

"You're my best mate. I want to. And that's that," she said.

A feeling of warmth rose inside me. Everything had to get better now.

CHAPTER
27

MY BED SHOOK. A bomb? I jolted up from my pillow and looked around my pitch-black room. Then I heard voices and realized it must have been Yusuf slamming the front door.

Furball leaped off my bed and I fumbled around my cluttered side table for my phone and pressed the home button: 2:05 A.M. Saturday 25th June. Obviously Mum and Dad had stayed up waiting for him. Yusuf was going to be in big trouble.

Trust my annoying brother to interrupt the best dream I'd had in weeks! 3W had come to play at the school fete, and Will had taken me aside and leaned in close to tell me how awesome I was for getting everyone together again.

After a few frustrating minutes of trying and failing to listen to the muffled conversation downstairs, I allowed myself to drift back to sleep, hoping to find out what Will was going to say next.

After my shower, I dumped my damp hair towel in the laundry basket on the upstairs landing and headed toward my bedroom. I stopped at Yusuf's door. I wasn't being nosy, I told myself. I just needed to see what state he was in after coming home late. To find out if he was okay.

I turned the doorknob as quietly as I could and stepped into his room. It was pitch dark with the thick blue curtains drawn. The farty boy smell was stronger than usual because the door had been shut all night. Yusuf lay in a heap at the edge of his double bed. His room was a mess, clothes on the floor and stacks of folders and papers all over his desk. I knew he'd be angry if he saw me, but I had to know what those papers were.

It wasn't his work. I knew it wouldn't be. I hadn't seen him do any revision for his last exam these past few days. The writing on the dark posters was in bright yellow font that I could just make out in the gloom. It said:

RISE UP AGAINST THE FAR RIGHT

Next to the posters was a typed-up sheet with smaller print. But I couldn't read it.

I really need to look up exactly what "far right" means, I thought. All I knew was that Hitler was on the far right, so whatever it was, it couldn't be good.

I pulled my phone from my back pocket, put the flash on the camera and aimed the camera at Yusuf's desk. Yusuf was still in the same position with his duvet over his head. The flash lit the room for a moment. But he didn't move. Phew. I slipped my phone in my pocket again to head out.

On my way to the door, I trod on a creaky floorboard and Yusuf stirred. Oh, no. I gulped and took another step so I'd be away from his desk if he woke and caught me. I could pretend I'd come in to check on him—which was actually my initial plan.

Tiptoeing as if I was a burglar, I made it to the door. I glanced back at the bed—Yusuf seemed to be in the same position—took a deep breath, and slipped my hand between the door and the frame, opening the door only wide enough for me to squeeze out. Light streamed in from the landing window. I shut the door softly and listened, but Yusuf didn't make a sound.

I let out a breath.

Oh. My. God. I didn't want to do that again in a hurry.

My mattress dipped as I leaped onto my bed, phone in my hand. Furball was lapping water under my desk, and my insides calmed just looking at her. I went into Photos to read what was on the paper next to the posters on Yusuf's desk. The page was mostly blurry. After all that effort, I could just make out the title:

PLAN OF ACTION AND ROLES:
SATURDAY 9TH JULY

Ugh! Of all the rubbish pics I'd taken in my life, this had to be the biggest fail. There was no way I could risk going back into his room to read the rest. But still, this was *proof* that Yusuf was involved in something dangerous.

CHAPTER
28

M UM AND DAD grounded Yusuf for the weekend for coming in late and not telling them where he'd been. I thought about asking him, but I knew it would be pointless. At least he didn't have any fresh bruises, or none that I could see.

I'd cleaned my room, got rid of Furball's old litter and done my homework, even found out what "far right" meant, and Yusuf had *just* surfaced. I quickly finished my message to Jonah David about our joint geography homework and switched off my playlist before I started brainstorming activities for the fete fundraiser to make sure we raised lots of money.

"Aaliyah!" Mum shouted from downstairs. "Come here!"

"I'm working, Mum!" I'd listed seven fundraising ideas to give to the student council and PTA but I needed more.

Suddenly my door pushed open. It was Mum with a half-full laundry basket in one hand and her iPhone in the other. I quickly spun my desk chair to face her and hide Furball, who was thankfully asleep in her bed.

"We need to talk," she said, lines strewn across her forehead.

Silently, I willed Furball not to wake up or move at the sound of Mum's voice. I tried to look completely calm and normal. I sat up straight, and placed my hands in my lap, as if I'd just had elocution lessons at a posh school. "Why?"

"The school sent an email to parents on Friday . . . last night. I just saw it. They're banning the hijab. Starting Monday."

"Seriously?" My mouth went dry.

"Seriously," she said.

"Oh my god, can they even do that? Single me out like that?"

"Well, they're not singling you out, really. They've banned all religious symbols from school grounds."

"What for? What's the reason?" I asked. If I frowned any harder, I'd get wrinkles.

"Apparently, it's in the best interest of our pupils," she said, doing quote marks with her fingers. "And, to be honest, I actually think it is."

I gawked at her. "How can you *say* that?"

"Listen, my beautiful baby girl, you have your whole life ahead to wear a hijab. I don't want you getting into fights or being bullied because of this. It's not safe for anyone right now, and for a Muslim woman, it's downright dangerous."

"Why are you still wearing one, then?" I asked.

I pulled the charger cable out of my phone to message Sukhi and Lisa. We needed a plan.

"I'm a lot older than you, and I've been wearing it a long time. It's a part of me. It *has* crossed my mind before, but I don't think I could ever take it off," she said, looking around. "It helps me be a better person. Makes me stop myself when I'm about to say or do something that wouldn't be in character with being a good Muslim. And anyway, it's not like the courts often meet hijabi women. They assume we're all locked up in the kitchen."

I was just about to tell her, "EXACTLY! That's why I wear it!" when her face lit up.

"Look at your room!" Mum was clearly trying to change the subject. She scanned the space and smiled so wide, I could see all her teeth. "I can't believe I'm seeing the day where your laundry is in the basket, and you're regularly vacuuming. And you even opened your window to air it out without me asking you to! UNBELIEVABLE! You've really matured recently, Aaliyah. I'm proud of you."

I heard a faint rustle from behind me. Oh god. My face dropped, she was going to spot Furball. I knew it. I rubbed an eyebrow, waiting for her discovery.

I gave her a fake smile — the kind I used to put on for photos when I was being forced to pose as a kid, full of teeth. I needed her to leave before her delight in me evaporated as quickly as it had appeared. "I suppose it was about time, right? You've got plenty to do," I said, trying my best to stop my leg from jerking. Little did she know that the cleaning was because of Furball and me not wanting to give Mum a reason to come into my room.

"Aww, yes. Looks like this is one room I won't have to worry about from now on." Her hand lingered on the door handle. "But your bed could be made better." She stepped toward it and bent to lift the corner of my duvet off the floor.

Oh, no, she was going to see where Furball had scratched the base of my bed before I'd made the cat scratcher! I reached forward from my chair fast to block her and neaten the duvet myself. "Sorry, I'll work on perfecting it."

"How are you doing, Aaliyah? Are you sleeping better?" She stepped back.

"Yeah, kind of," I chirped, hoping she wouldn't want to talk about the concert again. I'd much rather block it out. As long as I didn't see Darren's face, or think about what actually happened to the people at the concert, I was doing a lot better than that first week. And I guessed focusing on wearing my hijab and avoiding bullies at school was a massive distraction.

"Your dad said he wanted you to go to the supermarket with him, but I told him you're still not keen on anywhere big and enclosed that's full of strangers."

"Thanks, Mum."

"Do you think we should try and go soon, though?"

"No! I don't need to!" I closed my eyes and blocked the image of the crowd in the concert hall coming into my head. For some reason I was fine in school and outside, but the thought of a big indoor space like a supermarket made me shudder.

"Okay, okay . . . AAAATHCCHOOOO!" She wiped her eyes with the back of her hand. "Ugh, this weather is really affecting me this year. I'd better go and take my antihistamine."

My stomach rolled as she left my room. I glanced under my desk and saw two bright yellow dilated pupils staring at me. Furball was sitting up, her ears sharp. I bit my lip. "What if it's not the weather affecting Mum this year, my little fluffball?" She stretched toward me, and I picked her up and plopped her in my lap.

As Furball settled in, purring, I looked out of the window and thought about the dumb people who believed a piece of cloth was dangerous. That having a faith was scary. Who'd made this ban happen? We *had* to get it reversed.

This wasn't just about me. This was about all of us at school being able to express who we were. Like we'd discussed in the citizenship lesson; this was about not letting anyone divide us, but instead coming together by *respecting* our differences — not trying to erase them.

For the first time ever, I felt like I had a bigger purpose running through my veins. I wasn't going to let them make me feel like a victim. We were in the twenty-first century, so why was Mrs. Owen dragging us backward? Why was she giving in to pressure from parents and racist people in the neighborhood? I had to try and speak to her. *Make* her see sense.

CHAPTER 29

THE HEAT OF PEOPLE'S EYES burned into me as I walked down the corridor in my hijab on Monday morning. Feifei did a double-take. And it seemed as if the whole class stopped when I walked into form. Even Mrs. Alcock froze in her spot.

After Mum had told me about the ban, I'd asked myself multiple times over the weekend why I was doing this to myself. Maybe I should take it off, get rid of the stress and hassle it was causing me. But then, every time I thought that, I realized if I did take it off, they'd have won. All the bullies—Jayden, Sasha, the parents complaining, and far-right people like Darren—would have got me to do what they wanted, they'd have taken away *my choice*, and I couldn't let that happen. And so I'd walked into school with my head high, smiling like that emoji with the rosy cheeks and cheesy smile.

"Miss?" Jayden strode into the classroom, his hands in his pockets. "Why is she still wearing that towel when it's triggering for me?" He sneered in my face as he passed me to get to his seat at the back of the room.

That's what Mrs. Owen had said when he'd thrown my bottle! She agreed seeing my hijab triggered Jayden's bad behavior? So unfair.

Mrs. Alcock ignored him, but then looked at me. "Aaliyah, please come and see me when the bell goes."

Someone snorted and a whirr of whispers rushed through the room.

Soon after the register was taken, the bell for first lesson went. "I'll see you in the toilets," Lisa whispered as she stood up to leave the classroom. We'd agreed to meet at break so we could talk about getting the ban reversed and make a plan. We were sure that the hate in school would only get worse if it wasn't.

"Aaliyah, why are you wearing a religious symbol when you know it has been banned?" Mrs. Alcock said, fiddling with her black pen, her lips pursed.

"I wasn't sure when the ban came into place, miss," I lied.

"It's with immediate effect. So please take it off right away. As your form tutor, I'll accept it was a mistake today, but I don't want to see it again."

"Okay." I quickly headed to the door before she

told me to take it off in front of her, and ran to my next lesson, hoping I'd get away with keeping it on—because the teacher hadn't been asked to speak to me like Mrs. Alcock had—or just being reminded to take it off again.

It was the last swimming lesson for the term—thank god. I'd got chatting to Sukhi and Lisa in the toilets after form time, so just managed to get on the bus to go swimming before the driver shut the door. Mr. Bull, our PE teacher, gave me a look as I dashed into the empty seat near the front of the bus on the bottom deck.

I pulled out my phone and scrolled through Snappo—past the cute cats, hijabi influencers, and running videos. I'd unsubscribed from the medical story accounts because every time I saw a video of an operation, I couldn't help thinking of Jo and everyone who got hurt at the concert. There was no way I would become a doctor, I knew that much. The "Low Battery" notification popped up. Oh, flip—I'd forgotten to put my phone on charge last night because of Furball distracting me.

That cat caused me more grief than I wanted. But she made me happy, so I had to get on with all the mess and poo that she left my way. I slid my phone back into my trouser pocket, shifting to stop my diving skin suit from sticking to my behind. It was always annoying wearing it under my uniform before I left for school, but at least I didn't have to strip twice in the dirty changing rooms. It was funny they'd banned my hijab but they allowed everyone to cover their hair with a cap in swimming. And they'd never made a fuss about my diving suit covering my whole body. They couldn't ban the suit, could they?

The bus slid to a stop at the traffic lights near the library. I stared out of the window at the street cleaner cart, its front bristles rotating fiercely, and then I froze.

Yusuf was standing outside a café talking to two older men, one bald and clean shaven, the other with a graying beard. He'd left the house at 7:30 A.M.—was he skiving his revision lessons for his final exam? I shuffled in my seat. I'd never seen these men before. They weren't Dad's friends, and they definitely weren't guys from his sixth form. Were these the people he'd been staying out late to meet?

Yusuf glanced up as he spoke and caught me staring. His smile dropped.

The lights changed, and the bus drove forward. I twisted around to see Yusuf's face grow smaller and smaller as he gazed at the back of the bus.

At lunch, Sukhi waved Jonah over to our picnic table as he walked out of the school lunch hall. He was with Leon, who came too.

"So we wanted to talk to you about helping the PTA," Sukhi started, and then looked at me.

"We were wondering if we could support the student council and the PTA to raise money for the concert . . . you know . . . fundraiser." I couldn't finish my sentence, thinking about Jo. I took a sip of orange juice and searched Jonah's face to see if he knew what I meant.

"Oh, okay," said Jonah, raising his eyebrows as if he was thinking. "I'll bring it up at our next meeting this Thursday. How is Jo doing? Do any of you know?" His eyes rested on Lisa, who was busy scooping up some pasta into her mouth, as he slid into the empty seat next to her.

Lisa sat up. "She's been moved to a physio ward so she can learn to move without her leg. I haven't seen her, though."

"Oh, okay," said Jonah, bowing his head, and everyone else did too.

I shuffled, thinking about how Jo might be feeling. She'd replied to my message with three heart emojis, which made me feel even more sad about what she was going through. But I was relieved she'd messaged — it meant she didn't hate me.

After a moment, Jonah asked, "So what did you have in mind for the fundraiser?"

Leon sat down next to Jonah. "The student council are planning on doing a bucket collection and some people are doing sponsored events."

"Oh, like what?" Lisa asked, raising her voice above the thumping of a basketball someone had brought outside.

"Like how much ice cream you can eat in ten minutes." Leon grinned, clearly imagining how much fun it would be.

And I thought about how gross it could be if that person couldn't handle all that ice cream. "Ewww, I'll make sure I don't stand anywhere near the eaters!" I laughed out loud and then scanned around, hoping no one was staring at me in my hijab. I'd gotten away with it so far by telling teachers I didn't know the ban started today. When I'd felt nervous, I'd reminded myself I was an ambassador for good Muslims. And it really helped every time I told myself that.

"Aaliyah, tell them your ideas." Sukhi shoved her bunched-up food wrappers into her empty crisp packet and nudged me.

"Uhhh . . . so I was thinking instead of just going around with a collection bucket we could do activities involving the teachers to make sure we raise a big amount. Like charging one pound to throw a wet sponge or a paper plate full of squirty cream at a teacher."

"I'd pay fifty pounds for that one!" Leon laughed.

Jonah smiled. "Yeah, that's good, and everyone can get involved as well. You don't need to be an expert ice cream eater or anything."

Lisa put a straw through her orange juice carton and faced Jonah and Leon. "We also thought some of the kids who have music lessons could do a performance, which people buy tickets for. All money going to the fund, obviously."

"Yeah, just like twenty minutes or so, nothing too long," I added, clicking my sandwich tub shut. "But we could charge five pounds per ticket and hopefully people might pay that. Do you think we could use the hall for the performance, or does the whole fete have to be outside?"

"I can't see why we couldn't use the hall for a short performance. I reckon Mrs. Owen would love that. Thanks, guys!" Leon beamed.

"Yeah, we'll mention all of this in the meeting and if we need more help on the day, it'd be great if you guys could join us," said Jonah, looking at Lisa.

My shoulders relaxed for the first time that day and I smiled. I was finally doing something about what had happened. Making up for what that vile terrorist had done. And being a little part of organizing something that was important was kind of cool.

Now I just needed to make sure our plan to get the religious symbols ban reversed went smoothly too.

"Miss, I haven't got my book," I said, loading all the books I'd taken out back into my bag. "Can I get it from my locker, please?"

"Yes, okay, be quick Aaliyah." Mrs. Justin, my music teacher, frowned and turned to do the register.

I ran toward my locker so I wouldn't miss too much of the lesson, slowing down at the end of the corridor when I heard someone shout. Was there a fight breaking out in the corridors mid lesson? I crept round the corner and stopped when I saw Mrs. Owen standing outside her office with Mr. Wilkinson. Oh flip. If she caught me with my hijab, I was dead. Luckily I'd worn it loosely so I could quickly drop it around my neck if I needed to. I started to unravel it and paused when I heard Mr. Wilkinson from across the corridor. "This isn't France! You can't do this!" he said.

He was the one shouting? He didn't seem like a teacher who would argue with anyone. I couldn't imagine it. But then, he was always firm with Jayden. More than any other teacher.

"It's triggering for our children and causing trouble. We can't have distractions and fights breaking out that impact learning—we need to keep religious and cultural items out of school," said Mrs. Owen.

I peered around the wall again. Mr. Wilkinson was pink faced and pointing a hand at Mrs. Owen. "But you haven't followed the proper process. You're supposed to get a ban like this approved by the governors first. I've read the school policies."

"I am taking it to the governors. It's on the agenda for our next meeting. And quite frankly, it's none of your concern. You're not senior leadership. We're done here."

They were arguing about the religious symbols ban! Had Mrs. Owen not followed the rules? I pulled out my phone to message Lisa and Sukhi. We had to chat. This was massive.

That evening, I'd just finished editing the final draft of mine and Jonah's joint geography homework, so I thought I'd have a break and play with Furball. I put on my 3W playlist at a low volume—it was getting easier to listen to them just like I always had—and picked Furball up and sat her on my lap. She loved being held and stroked. Recently she'd started bouncing across the carpet to give me a short, sweet meow when I got back from school, giving me a near heart attack if she came too close to my door as I entered or left my room. I needed to somehow get extra pocket money to buy another calming plug.

My phone rang. It was Lisa.

"Oh my god. Guess what Feifei told me?"

"What?"

"She heard Mr. Wilkinson and Mrs. Alcock talking about the ban after her lesson."

"No way!"

"Yeah! Feifei was going back to the classroom after lesson because she forgot her pencil case and she said he was telling Mrs. Alcock that the governors were meant to agree *before* she put the ban in place, not after."

"No way! So I heard right?" I couldn't believe it.

"Yeah! I think so."

"Lise, maybe this means we have more support in school than we think?"

"Yeah, maybe," she said. "Anyway, I'd better go. My mum's calling me to help her with the shopping. Just thought I'd tell you before I forget."

"Thanks! I'm gonna start making a list of ways we might be able to convince Mrs. Owen she should reverse it before she speaks to the governors." I didn't have the guts to go up to her and tell her she'd broken the rules, and she obviously wasn't going to listen to Mr. Wilkinson. Maybe we could just *show* her why she'd got it wrong.

I put the phone down and went back to stroking Furball's soft black fur, when the door flew open. I gulped.

"What the hell?" said Yusuf. He glanced behind him into the hallway as if he'd realized he should be quiet and shut my door.

Furball wriggled in my lap.

"Get out, Yusuf!" My jaw clenched.

He stood near my door and said, "So obviously this is a thing—what is it, your new secret pet or something?"

I looked at Furball in my lap, unable to speak. I didn't know how to explain myself.

"So Mum's got swollen, itchy eyes because of you?" He laughed.

"No!" I said, squirming on my bed. "It's hay fever!"

"Well, if you don't want me to say anything," he said, crossing his arms and putting one foot on my wall, "you'd better not say anything about me being out today—'cause you know you'll be in HUGE trouble with Mum *and* Dad."

"What were you doing, anyway?" I asked. If he was going to blackmail me, he should 'fess up.

"I had some business to sort out." He glared

at me and then at Furball. "How'd you get it inside anyway?" he asked, now holding onto my door handle. Oh, phew, he was going to leave. "You're getting well sneaky."

"Uhhh . . . it was already in the house—I think it's Mr. Baldwin's cat and he's not here, so it must've come in," I lied. Sort of.

"You'd better take it back next door, then, where it belongs." He narrowed his eyes at me. "And I'm telling you, if you say anything about me talking to those men, I'm dropping you in it, yeah?"

I nodded so he'd leave, and he did, making sure I knew he was serious from the side-eye he gave me before he shut my door.

I stroked Furball again, who slept peacefully in my lap. How long would I be able to keep her out of a shelter now that Yusuf had seen her here? I sighed.

CHAPTER 30

"**O**KAY, YOU READY?" I faced the school gates on Friday, checking my scarf was still in place, then clenched my backpack strap and took a deep breath. I'd worn my hijab like a yoyo for days, stressing every time a teacher or Jayden or Sasha looked my way, but I couldn't carry on doing that. I'd had enough. It'd taken us all week to prepare for this, and there was no backing out now.

"Yup." Lisa gently pulled on her cross stud earrings, and then adjusted her long diamante cross necklace so the chain hung equally on each side.

"Fighting ready with my dastaar!" Sukhi held her white-turban-covered head high. She looked like a queen with a crown.

I linked arms with them. "Let's go!"

Nothing and no one was going to break us today. We were going to send Ratcliffe Academy a message.

The whispers and snickers spread through the playground like a ripple effect. But we'd agreed that we'd stare ahead and avoid eye contact. *Focus on the building,* I told myself. *Focus.*

As we walked inside, Mrs. Thornton, the receptionist, stood up at her desk, probably ready to tell us off, but we marched past her office window and pushed through the first set of double doors toward Mrs. Owen's and Mr. Atkinson's offices. Our plan was to protest in the busiest corridor, right outside the head and deputy head's offices. Oh, yeah.

My stomach dipped as soon as I saw the dark mahogany chairs that always sat outside their offices. What would they say when they saw us? My spine tingled. But I couldn't let fear distract me. *Focus, Aaliyah. Focus.*

We'd only just sat on the chairs, Sukhi and Lisa either side of me, when Mrs. Owen's door burst open. "What is the meaning of this?" The corners of her mouth curled down.

Oh, flip. She did NOT look happy. But what was I expecting? A pat on the back?

"You all know the rule. Take those religious symbols off this second and go to your form rooms!" She pointed toward the reception area.

We didn't say a word. We'd agreed we would be silent until it was absolutely necessary.

From the side compartment of my backpack where my water bottle usually went, I yanked out the rolled-up banner I'd made and raised it above my head.

> IT SHOULD BE
> OUR CHOICE
> NOT YOURS

Sukhi followed. Hers read:

> FREEDOM OF EXPRESSION
> IS A RIGHT

And finally Lisa held hers up:

> THIS BAN
> ENCOURAGES HATE
> IS THAT WHAT YOU WANT?

Mrs. Owen looked as if she was going to explode. The phone rang in her office. She turned to answer it, then hesitated, her eyeballs popping. "I don't want to see you when I come back out. You *will* go to your form rooms, NOW!" Her voice boomed in the corridor as she stormed into her office and slammed the door shut.

The school bell went.

Everyone was going to come in any minute. We all looked at each other, trying to stifle our giggles. It was going better than we expected.

The first bunch of kids thundered through the doors. I straightened my back, holding my banner high, and focused on the wall in front of me.

Some kids laughed as they passed. Some stopped to read the banners and take photos. Some must have messaged others because soon a huge crowd had gathered in the corridor. It was getting harder to focus on the wall ahead. My arms ached and I fought to keep them raised.

"TRAITOR!" Sasha pushed through the crowd and stopped in front of Lisa. "To your own brother!" She tutted. I couldn't see her face properly, but I could feel her angry energy. A chill went through me.

Lisa stayed still, holding her banner high.

Sasha clenched her fists and pulled her arm back. Oh my god, she was going to punch Lisa right here in front of Mrs. Owen's office!

"SASHA WILLIAMS!"

She froze, her arm mid-air. Then lowered her fist and tossed her hair and turned.

"Get to form!" It was a teacher.

Sasha sucked her teeth and kicked Sukhi's shin as she left. Sukhi didn't twitch.

Everyone else who had gathered scattered, walking on slowly as Mr. Rudd approached our chairs. "Has Mrs. Owen seen you yet?"

Silence.

"You realize you're asking to get into a lot of trouble, don't you?"

Silence again.

He sighed. His shoes clopped down the corridor. Once he was gone, the only sound I could hear was the faint rumble of cars going by outside.

I dropped my arms and whispered, "Oh my god, did that just happen?"

"Stupid cow!" said Sukhi, scowling and rubbing her leg.

"When do we get to go to the toilet and stuff?" said Lisa. "We didn't discuss that."

Mrs. Owen's door opened. She was a little less pink than before. Maybe she'd calmed down.

"Now. Girls. This is not the time nor the place for a sit-in. I'm giving you a last chance. If you don't remove yourselves this instant, I will have you removed."

My leg jerked. What would they do? I focused on a speck of dirt on the pale sky blue wall in front of me to calm my nerves.

She didn't say anything for what felt like an eternity. Then she said, "Very well. You have made your decision. I am calling your parents and you will be removed for disrupting school life and refusing to comply with instructions."

I exhaled and slouched as she stormed away.

Now what? My stomach lunged. It was a silent, peaceful protest. Surely Mum and Dad would understand.

"Someone's been trying to call me." Lisa pulled her phone out of her bag. "I felt it buzzing when Mrs. Owen was talking."

She tapped her password in, and her face drained of color.

"What's up, Lise?" I said.

"It's Darren," she said. "He . . . He . . ."

"He what?" asked Sukhi.

"Someone posted a pic of us on Snappo and he's fuming."

I felt sick. He was going to hate me even more. If that was even possible. And now he'd be angry with Lisa too. I shouldn't have let her join in.

Lisa sprang up and picked up her backpack. She dropped her banner on her empty chair. "I'm going home. Try and speak to him before Mum leaves for her shift. I'll message you later."

"Lise," I whispered after her. "Stay safe, yeah?"

She nodded, yanking her long necklace over her head and shoving it into her bag as she went.

Mrs. Owen came out of her office, looking twice

where Lisa had sat. "Where's Lisa?" But she didn't wait for an answer. "You are all suspended with immediate effect. Your parents will be notified as soon as I can get hold of them."

My jaw felt as if it'd hit the floor. I glanced at Sukhi—hers was the same.

Mrs. Owen let out a thin smile. She looked almost pleased by the panic creeping over our faces.

Mum and Dad were so not going to be okay about me being SUSPENDED!

SUKHI UNLINKED HER ARM from mine to enter the convenience store first. It was scorching hot, and we'd decided we needed ice lollies before we got home, especially since Mrs. Owen had put us in immediate detention and we'd had to sit in silence all afternoon. As I entered the store, I checked to see who was serving and if the shop assistant looked at me funny because of my hijab. He didn't look up from his phone, and I breathed out. As Sukhi slid the freezer door open and grabbed my favorite cola-flavored lolly, my eyes fell on the newspapers.

AMERICAN SENATOR SAYS "ALL MUSLIMS ARE TERRORISTS" ON VISIT AHEAD OF ANNIVERSARY OF LONDON BOMBINGS

My toes curled. *How could he say that publicly and get away with it?*

"Come on," Sukhi said, handing me my lolly after paying. The ice-cold wrapper stung my hand. "Aaliyah?" she said, when I didn't move. "What's up?"

"Huh?" I said, my shoulders dropping. "Look." I pointed at the newspaper.

"Ugh. But they're, like, idiots. Everyone knows that. Ignore it, come on." She headed toward the door of the shop.

"Sukhi, it's hard to ignore when they're always attacking you."

"Yeah, but they're not attacking *you,* are they?" she said, licking her lolly, completely unaware of the storm rising inside me.

"You don't get it, do you?" My nostrils flared. "Every time anyone says something like that, people start accusing *all* of us. So, yeah, he is attacking *me.* When someone goes out there and attacks a random Muslim guy or rips off a woman's hijab or screams at *my* mum for wearing one, it affects me, okay?"

She stopped, took her orange lolly out of her mouth and said, "Okay, I get it. I'm sorry." She looked me in the eyes and I knew she meant it. "I won't say anything like that again," she added.

After a minute of us walking in silence, she spoke again. "I do know what it's like a little bit, though . . . my mum's uncle was beaten up after the last terrorist attack in Canada. They thought he was Muslim because he has a long beard and wears a turban and kurta."

"Oh no, sorry." I licked my lolly, feeling bad.

"I was a kid. I don't remember it, but everyone was talking about it at Christmas when that Muslim family got shot in Canada. They were worrying about my mum's family's safety."

"Well, that sucks even more if you're Sikh." I swallowed. Now the racists were just going for *anyone* who wore traditional Indian clothes. They were truly the *worst*.

When Sukhi dropped me home, we wished each other luck for the hurricane that was to come and reassured each other that we were only two weeks from the summer holidays, so it didn't matter that we'd be missing lessons. The teachers usually spent the last two weeks clearing classroom displays and letting us watch films anyway.

I gave Sukhi a big bear hug. *I* probably wouldn't have understood why anyone would feel directly attacked before this stuff had happened to *me*. I wanted her to know I was sorry for snapping, and we were still good.

I put my key in the door and stepped into the cool porch. *Ah, shade.* Thankfully, Mum's kitten-heeled court shoes and Dad's and Yusuf's smart leather lace-ups weren't there yet. I'd have some time to decide what I'd say about the protest and being suspended before they got home.

I picked up the post from the doormat and went through it one by one, putting each envelope on the hallway console table. A leaflet telling us to get our lawn treated. A menu from the local pizza place.

But, wait, what was this?

Whoever created it had printed it and folded it at home and not on proper leaflet paper:

LEAVE ENGLAND
GO BACK TO YOUR OWN COUNTRY
YOU DON'T BELONG HERE
WHITES ONLY

My chest tingled. I jumped when someone walked past chatting outside on the street. How did they know we weren't white? Mr. Grimshaw. It must've been him. Unless it was Darren? Or one of his mates? Or some total stranger who'd been watching our house?

I closed my eyes and took a slow breath to calm myself and put the leaflet down on the console table. I took a photo of it and typed a Snappo post.

> Just found this posted through my door telling me I don't belong to my own country ☹

I was born HERE. My mum was born HERE, my dad came when he was just a few months old, my grandma came here when she wasn't even 21 and hasn't been back for FOUR DECADES—where do you want us to go?

But I couldn't bring myself to upload it. It would probably attract more haters. I already had too much noise in my head. I needed to block it out.

Upstairs I dumped my school bag in its place, opened my laptop and put on a playlist of 3W's saddest songs. Sitting on my bed with Furball on my lap, I stared out at the row of semi-detached houses, letting my tears roll.

This was the only country I'd known. And English was the only language I spoke fluently. England was *home*.

And to make it worse, I'd been kicked out of school for standing up for my right to be who I was. To be me.

I showed Mum the poster as soon as she got back from work, trying to delay the "school suspension" conversation for as long as possible. She didn't seem to be angry with me, which was really weird. Her scarf was coming loose and her lips were chapped, probably from talking all day—maybe her phone had been on silent and she hadn't checked her messages yet.

She read the leaflet and scoffed. "What if I posted leaflets through their doors telling them to go back to where *they* came from?" she said, chucking it back on the console table.

I scratched my shoulder blade. "Huh?"

She put her tan leather work bag next to the envelopes, then rifled through the front compartment and pulled out her mobile. "The first people here weren't BORN in England. Most English people are descended from *immigrants*. People had to come here and settle first." She swiped her phone to camera mode.

She was right. *Let's all go back to where WE came from*, I said in my head to the imaginary leaflet writers. *If I don't belong here, neither do you.*

"And Prophet Isa, peace be upon him, came from the Middle East. Are they going to reject him too?"

That's true, I thought. We called him Isa, Christians called him Jesus, but whatever you called him, he *was* Middle Eastern. He definitely wasn't English.

"Who are you sending that to?" I asked her as she snapped a photo of the leaflet and moved it to the side of the console table with a tissue.

"The police. Don't touch it. We can't contaminate it with more fingerprints. They might be able to get one off this."

I traipsed back upstairs, my stomach still rolling, feeling like I was going to be sick on the stairs. There was so much to think about.

My phone was on silent, but the screen flashed every few seconds. I ignored it and lay back on my pillow, thinking about everything I'd been through since the concert. So much had gone wrong.

And Mum and Dad hadn't even found out about the school suspension yet.

CHAPTER 32

"YOU WILL TAKE OFF YOUR HIJAB." Dad ripped a piece off his roti and wrapped it around a kofta. The teacher in him was on fire. "Your mum already told you about the hijab ban at school and said you weren't to wear it, and you *still* staged a protest during school hours and disrupted lessons without any advice from your elders, who quite frankly know better than you." He grunted and ripped some more roti.

"What do *you* advise, then?" I sighed. "I need to do something about the ban."

"I think you've done quite enough," Dad muttered, not raising his head from his dinner plate. "After dinner, go and get your phone and leave it in the kitchen. It's confiscated this week. We don't need you creating more trouble for you and your friends."

"But . . ."

I sank into my chair. What was the point of

protesting when I couldn't even get my own dad on my side? Instead of praising or supporting me for standing up for my rights, he was punishing me, just like Mrs. Owen.

"There are other ways to fight the ban, Aaliyah," said Mum, adding steaming meatballs from the pot into the serving bowl on the table. "Why don't you write a letter to the governors?" She was obviously trying to defuse the tension around the table.

"Why would they listen to me?" I dropped my head lower than it already was. "You don't."

There was silence.

My mind wandered to the leaflet posted through our door earlier. "I'm scared," I said after a few minutes of listening to everyone chew their food.

I only realized I'd said it out loud when Dad's head sprang up. "Scared of what?" he asked around the food in his mouth.

"You saw the leaflet. They want us gone. What if they bomb us?" My whole body shook. "What if they bomb us *here*?"

"Aaliyah, no one is going to bomb anyone. Stop this." Dad's brow furrowed, and he didn't look very reassuring.

"This is not the time to show fear, Aaliyah." Mum patted my shoulder before raising the jug to pour more mango lassi into my glass.

"I'm full." I put my hand over the cup. Even though the smell of sweet mango was tempting, it was too thick and filling for my knotted stomach.

"You have to eat properly," she said, moving my hand and pouring the lassi in.

I pinched my lips. "I'm scared," I said again, fighting back a sob. Great, I was back to being a shivering, crying wreck.

Yusuf spoke up. "Nothing's gonna happen, Aaliyah. I'll make sure of it." I didn't think he'd been listening. He was so quiet, I'd almost forgotten he was there.

"What, like, be a hero and sort their 'white zone' faces at the far-right rally?" I blurted, then covered my mouth when I realized what I'd done.

Yusuf's eyes almost popped out of his sockets. His face reddened as he lifted his chin and glared at me.

Mum looked at him, then me. "What's going on?"

When neither of us answered, her voice went to another level. "TELL ME NOW!"

I swallowed. "Umm . . ."

Yusuf pushed his chair back to leave the table. "Why don't you ask *her* what she's hiding?" And then, to me, "Idiot."

I held my breath, waiting for the attention to turn to me. I could see sweet, innocent Furball peacefully asleep in her bed, not knowing she was about to be tossed outside.

"Sit down," Dad said to Yusuf through his teeth. "You're going nowhere until we have some answers."

Yusuf sat back down, his head low.

"Aaliyah—speak," commanded Mum.

"It was nothing. I got confused."

"Aaliyah Hamid, you had better stop lying, otherwise you won't see the outside world for a long time," said Dad, leaning over his plate. "If you know about something Yusuf's planning, speak now."

"Don't be scared of him," said Mum, pointing at Yusuf. "He can see we're putting you under pressure. He can't blame you for telling us."

I slumped in my chair and closed my eyes. "He's going to fight the far-right people at their rally . . . I think. But I've got no proof!" I added, hoping he wouldn't say anything about Furball.

"No, I'm not!" Yusuf sucked his teeth. "Why don't you tell them about your new cat, eh?"

I closed my eyes. Ugh. *Sorry, Furball.*

"You only saw it once!"

"Twice!" Yusuf shouted and folded his arms.

"It's just Mr. Baldwin's cat! It needed a cuddle and some food, I wasn't doing anything wrong!" My face burned.

"Thank you, Aaliyah," said Dad. "You can go upstairs. We'll speak to *you* later. Right now, we need to speak to Yusuf."

CHAPTER
33

I CLOSED MY EYES and bowed my head as I pulled the kitchen door behind me and prayed to God to help me. I'd only wanted to look after Furball because she was all alone, and she'd ended up kind of looking after me too. I'd never meant to lie to my parents. I just hoped they'd understand.

After sprinting upstairs, I grabbed Furball from the top of my chest of drawers and put her in her bed under my desk so that when Mum or Dad came in shouting, they wouldn't frighten her.

Breathe, I told myself as I got under with her and stroked her head, hoping she'd fall asleep while I tried to listen to what was happening downstairs. Dad was yelling.

"I can't do anything right, Furball."

Furball nuzzled my hand.

"Why did I tell on Yusuf?" I said. "I know I want to do things peacefully, unlike him, but now look what I've done."

I gently pushed her cushion next to her so she wouldn't feel me leave once she was asleep, and tried to figure out how I'd tell Mum and Dad I'd kept her here for three weeks.

The doorbell rang and I crawled out from under the desk. *Who was that?* Uncle Aziz's car was parked outside our driveway. I breathed out. They'd be here ages since it was a Friday night. Maybe I was safe . . . at least until tomorrow.

I switched on my phone and it went crazy with silent notifications. Sukhi had messaged on our chat, so I went straight to the app.

Everyone's talking about our silent protest!
Look!

She'd sent screenshots of comments and posts on Snappo. A flush of adrenaline tingled through my body. I couldn't hear Mum and Dad shouting at Yusuf anymore. Maybe we'd made a difference. Maybe getting suspended was worth it, if it got people thinking.

I sent Sukhi five shocked emojis and started scrolling through the comments. Some kids said what we did was epic. One said we looked like the girl band Little Moxies, all "religioned" up. That made me laugh. I stopped when I saw comments from Sasha and her gang. But then, I couldn't help myself. I shouldn't have read them—they made my blood blaze. They said they'd rip all of our "headdresses" off if they saw us again. One said religion is the root of all problems. Another said we didn't belong here. Racist ignoramuses.

Lisa hadn't commented on anything on our group yet. I was about to reply to Sukhi, when there was a small knock on my door. *Uh-oh. Here we go.* Uncle Aziz hadn't distracted them. I dropped my phone, jumped into my chair, and opened my laptop. Mum entered.

"Right," she said, hands on her hips.

"Is Yusuf in trouble?" I asked quickly before she launched into me.

"Of course he is! But that's not why I'm here."

I inhaled the lingering smell of perfume I'd sprayed to mask the smell of Furball's food and litter and held my breath for a moment.

"Aaliyah, it's great that you helped Mr. Baldwin's cat, but you *have* to tell me when it comes next. We need to get it a proper home! It can't roam the streets from neighbor to neighbor."

Wait, what? Mum thought I'd only had Furball over. She didn't realize the cat was living here. I *couldn't* say anything now.

"She was lonely and I wanted to help her," I said, scrolling through my Word files on my laptop to look like I was working. I made sure I didn't move from in front of Furball.

"Aaliyah, you know there's absolutely no point wearing a hijab if you're going to lie and hide things from us, right? You should have told us about Yusuf and that you've been bringing a cat up here. What has got into you?"

I bit my lip. She was right. I'd been focusing so much on looking like a Muslim, I'd let the important things slip. I wasn't being my best self by hiding Furball from Mum, but I didn't have a choice if I was going to keep her out of a shelter. Surely God would understand? I was helping a vulnerable animal when it needed me—and I wasn't really hurting anyone. Mum was mostly okay. I wiped my moist palms on my jeans.

I could feel Mum scouring my room. "It might explain those strange sounds we've been hearing, which you say are music videos or games."

I always grinned when I lied to her, and she knew it—I couldn't look at her. But I also couldn't bring myself to tell her about Furball. "She's missing her owner, Mum. I just wanted to help. She wasn't here long, I mostly see her outside. But I'll tell you if I see her again." Even as I was saying it, guilt flooded my chest. *I should get rid of Furball before I become a serial liar,*

I thought. But how could I? Where could she go? Mr. Baldwin had *still* not come back home.

"I understand why you wanted to help it. But sneaking it upstairs! Honestly, Aaliyah, I don't know what's going on with you!" She sniffed the air. "You're using too much perfume, by the way. Go easy."

"Okay," I started typing, trying to look busy so she'd leave.

She opened the door and I almost relaxed my shoulders but then she shut it again. "Aaliyah . . . How are you feeling about what happened at the concert? Do you think you've processed it?"

I winced at the memory of Darren screaming at me. "Yeah, I think I have," I said, blinking hard to push his face out of my mind.

I wanted to tell her Furball had helped me too when I couldn't cope and felt alone.

"Hmmm . . . Shall we book you in to see a counselor now you've had some time to think? You have managed to not throw drinks over anyone for a while, but you're directing your energy toward the wrong things, like breaking school rules."

I kept my head down so she wouldn't see my flushed face. "I'm just trying to focus on school, Mum."

She sighed. "Okay, get that done quickly and come down and say salaam to your bareh abu. He's leaving soon. Your dad and I want to talk about this suspension properly and about what you're going to do next week."

Ugh. I didn't want to think about it.

Wearing a hijab and all the drama that came with it might have helped me focus on something other than the concert, but fighting for my right to express myself was a different kind of pressure I didn't know how to handle.

I felt something on my face and sprang awake, gasping.

Oh, phew. It was just Furball pawing me.

I checked the rubbish old-school alarm clock Dad had given me when he came up to take my phone away. The red digital display said it was 12:30 A.M.

I stroked Furball as she padded over my stomach and leaped off my bed.

CREAK.

I sat up straighter. Someone was in the hallway.

Another loose floorboard groaned. I froze. If it was Mum or Dad or Yusuf going into the bathroom, I'd have heard the extractor fan switch on with the light by now. Maybe it was a burglar. Or worse.

Everything was silent for a few long seconds. I pulled open one of the curtains next to my bed to check if there was a car or anything dodgy going on outside. No one. The usual neighbors' cars were on the road. It all looked normal.

The house was completely silent now.

Just as I went to close the curtain, I saw a silhouette move beneath my window.

NO WAY.

Yusuf was slinking out of the driveway!

I flung the curtain wide open, scrambled to my knees to duck my head out of the window underneath the net curtain and followed his outline down the road. He had his hands in his pockets, and his shoulders swayed in his typical way when he walked with purpose.

Where was he going? To meet those men?

He'd snuck out after midnight, after Mum and Dad had told him off—wow, brazen.

I lay back in bed—there was no way I'd fall asleep now. I needed to figure out where he was going. He was clearly involved in something dodgy and I had to stop him.

CHAPTER
34

"**Y**USUF!" I yelled at the bathroom door in frustration the next day, Saturday. He'd been in there ages. He was definitely going out—the stench of his after-shave wafting through the gap underneath the door made that clear. I wasn't sure if the aftershave was for a girl or to make himself smell more manly for his new man-gang.

I'd tossed and turned last night and finally decided how I could find out more. The only way was to follow Yusuf. The rally was a week from today and I was running out of time. He'd kill me if he saw me, but I had to risk it.

My laptop pinged. I went to my desk and pulled the charger cable out to take the laptop to my bed. It had to be either Lisa or Sukhi. I'd managed to message them before I gave up my phone so only they knew I didn't have it and that they'd have to email me. Sukhi said her mum was proud of her for standing up for our rights, so of course *she* still had her phone. Lucky. At least her parents got it.

Meet you at 1?

It was Sukhi. Oh, brill, library day! I had the perfect excuse. Especially if Yusuf was meeting those men at the café on the main road. I'd have the best view from inside the library.

Look at Lisa. She looks soo annoyed, came another message, with a screenshot attached to it.

It was a photo of Lisa and Darren on his Snappo account. Her arm was in a sling and he was squeezing her uninjured shoulder with a rifle in his arm. My spine tingled. He had a gun in his hands. An actual gun. She didn't look happy or comfortable. The caption said:

> Clay pigeon shooting with my sis. Getting ready for combat.

My stomach tightened. How did she get hurt?
What happened??? I asked Sukhi.
You okay, Lise? How'd you hurt your arm? I started typing in a new email before Sukhi told me she'd already asked her how it happened and Lisa hadn't answered.

It was my fault Lisa got suspended, and now Darren

was making her hang out with *him* and not talk to us, all because she supported a protest—for me. For all I knew, he might've hurt her too.

The bathroom door opened and the extractor fan grew louder, snapping me out of my daze. Yusuf was out of the bathroom. I had to hurry. I waited until his bedroom door slammed shut, then dashed in—spluttering at the strong taste of his wood-scented aftershave in the air—used the toilet, checked my scarf, and ran back into my room to grab my wallet, library card, and books.

Furball sat on my windowsill, watching the world outside through the net curtains.

"You going to be good?" I asked her. She squinted at me before turning back to the window.

Downstairs, I popped my head into the kitchen. Dad was at the table with his back to the doorway, reading something on his iPad and shaking his head. "Ratcliffe Academy got an inadequate rating at the latest school inspection for the leadership and management criteria!"

"Did they?" Mum said, sounding worried, as she washed something in the sink.

I stayed at the door so I could hear more before they noticed me.

"I can believe that! Honestly, ever since that Mrs. Owen took over, the management has suffered. They didn't even have a proper pastoral care team until after the concert—just the deputy head. It's a disgrace. And look at all the staff leaving! Peter at work told me her husband is Richard Owen, the guy who's running for election for Britain First."

"No way!" said Mum, closing the tap and picking up a potato peeler.

"Yeah, it's him. We're going to have to get more involved with the school. We can't push back on this ban, in case they make life more difficult for Aaliyah, but we have to make sure they keep seeing our brown faces. It's only going to get worse—some girls from a London school couldn't go on their trip to France last month because they were told to take their hijabs off and they refused to." Dad rubbed his head. "I think this religious symbols ban at Ratcliffe Academy and the way the school is changing its policies is because they're trying to get more votes for Britain First. And this ban is their way of showing voters how much more they can achieve if they win the election."

"What's Britain First?" It just came out.

Mum and Dad turned to look at me.

"People who hate anyone that's different to them," said Dad.

"Nothing for you to worry about!" Mum gave Dad a look, as if making sure he wouldn't say any more. "What else did you hear?"

It was obvious they didn't want me to know that Mrs. Owen was dodgy, so I said, "Not much. I was just going to ask if I could go to the library."

Mum dropped a potato peeling onto the worktop next to the sink. "With Sukhi?"

"Yup."

Dad picked up his iPad again and continued to shake his head as he read.

"Okay—be back in an hour and bring back some milk for me, please?" Mum turned to me, her hair golden-brown in the sunlight. "Take a couple of pounds out of my purse." She nodded at her handbag, which hung on the back of a dining chair.

"Will do," I said. "But I might be a bit longer. Once we get the books, I want to go through the extra homework they gave us for our suspension."

I slipped into my maroon leather Converse, put my canvas tote on my shoulder, and shot an email to Sukhi from my laptop.

Can't make it till 1.30 ish—can you come a bit later? I didn't want to tell her what was going on with Yusuf—not yet. I needed to find out more myself.

Yeah, that works, she emailed back.

I slammed my laptop shut and put it on the console table in the hallway, then headed out of the front door before Yusuf came down.

I decided I'd wait for him at the bottom of our road close to a car. That way, I could follow him if he took a right out of our house toward the main road, or hide behind the car if he headed in my direction.

Ten minutes passed, and I was seriously bored. And hot. I'd already counted my coins to buy Furball's food and litter twice, and Yusuf still hadn't left the house. The sun beat down on the tarmac and burned through my scarf. I wished I'd worn my sunglasses. Every time a car stopped at the intersection, I had to kneel down and redo my laces to look like I'd stopped on the way home. I hoped the same car didn't drive past again and see me in the same spot looking like a loser. Or worse, some racist neighbor, who could accuse me of planning an attack.

Another five minutes passed, and I finally saw Yusuf heading toward the main road.

YES. Result.

I held back until he was almost near the top of the road before running to catch up. This was going to be riskier than I'd thought. Now I had to pass our house and hope Mum didn't see me and ask me why I was back from the library within fifteen minutes.

I stepped into a light jog, the books in my tote

hitting my side as I ran past row after row of neat, sunlit front gardens. As I got to the top of our road, I slowed in case Yusuf was still there.

He wasn't. There was a queue of cars at the traffic lights, and Yusuf was nowhere to be seen. I headed toward the library, hoping I'd see his back come into view. And it did. He was walking, hands in pockets, shoulders swaying, in the direction of the café. Brilliant. I could totally keep track of him there.

Except he walked right past the café and stopped at the traffic lights. Not so brilliant.

I ducked into the pharmacy. An old man in a fabric sun hat frowned at me as I blocked the open door. "Sorry," I said, trying to look as friendly as possible, and moved aside to let him hobble in.

I peeped out in time to see Yusuf getting into a red car. Oh, flip. How was I going to find out what he was doing now? How was I supposed to stop him getting into trouble? Maybe I should just talk to Dad.

CHAPTER 35

JONAH: Hey Aaliyah. Haven't seen you online. You okay?

Jonah had emailed me on my school email account on Sunday.

After I topped up Furball's litter and food and put the extras in the drawer under my bed, I emailed Jonah back, telling him about my phone ban.

JONAH: Oh, that sucks. Sorry. Feifei and Leon were wondering how you're doing too. It was weird without you guys in citizenship on Friday. Mr. Wilkinson lost it with Jayden! Think he's probably going to be suspended again too for starting a fight with Leon in the lesson. He threw a chair and was caught swearing at Leon.

ME: NO WAY! Poor Leon. And good riddance.

I switched off the track I was listening to so I could concentrate on our chat.

JONAH: What you did outside Mrs. Owen's office

was brilliant. You should've seen her face. What are you going to do next?

ME: I have no idea what to do tbh. I don't want to get anyone else in trouble.

JONAH: Well, we've got your back. We'll support you whatever you do. I think you're doing the right thing.

He added a fist bump emoji.

ME: Actually my mum said I should write to the governors. But I can't really see that making a difference.

But I'd love to know if they'd rather support a nasty petition and Mrs. Owen's dumb excuse for the ban instead of our right to express ourselves the way we want.

I added the shrugging emoji.

ME: Also who else has got my back? ☺

JONAH: All of us—me, Leon, Feifei, even the new boy Sami said "nice one" as he walked past your protest! Leon said you should've told us about it and he'd have worn his cross too. I would've worn my kippah.

ME: Oh, wow. That would've been awesome.

But then I realized they'd have got suspended too, so maybe not.

JONAH: Why don't you speak to the governors directly at the summer fete next weekend? They'll definitely be there. The student council's been asked to look after them and you're helping us with the fundraising anyway, so they'll just think you're a part of the council.

ME: Oooh! That's a good idea! I'll start thinking about what we should all say!

JONAH: We? Who?

ME: All of us. If you guys want to.

JONAH: Cool.

There was a long pause. I didn't know what else to say. So I rounded up our chat.

ME: Thanks, Jonah. I'm off school for three days but back on Thursday, so let's meet up at break or lunch with the others and see how we can convince the governors.

JONAH: Yeah, or if you want, we can set up a group chat. Do you have Connectstra?

ME: I can download it! That would be much better actually. Gives me something to do this week! ☺

Furball settled in my lap as I pressed Send, and I smiled. We were going to be making our own kind of student council group. If we managed to reverse the ban, life would be so much easier at school. It would prove to people like Sasha and Jayden that they were wrong and we had as much right as anyone else to dress how we wanted.

I forwarded our email chat to Sukhi and Lisa. Sukhi replied straight away. Lisa didn't. In fact, I realized now that she hadn't replied to anything all weekend. Maybe she wasn't checking her emails—she hardly ever did.

I'd try and call her again as soon as I figured out what we could say to the governors. Should we tell them Mrs. Owen didn't follow the rules? But what if she'd already told them about it and they'd agreed? Then we'd look like troublemakers and they'd never listen to us. I wished I had my phone so I could call her from my bed. I didn't even have her number to call her from our landline, plus no way did I want Mum and Dad overhearing and going off at me again.

"Dad," I said, stepping into the front room.

"Hmmm . . ." He was fixated on the CNN channel blaring out at top volume and did not move a muscle when I flopped down on the cushion next to him.

I folded my arms.

Finally he muted the volume and turned to me. "What is it, Aaliyah?"

I sat silently and focused on the thinning denim on my knees, the thread coming away. If I poked my finger in, I could make a satisfying hole.

"Aaliyah?" he said, his voice firmer.

"You said I should get your advice. So that's why I'm here."

"Go on, then." He put the TV on standby mode and shifted his knees to face me. "And thank you for actually listening to what I said and coming to me first."

"Mum said I should write to the governors—but I'm thinking of speaking to them at the summer fete instead. What do you think? You're a teacher—would it work? Would they listen to me?"

"That's not a bad idea," he said, sitting back into his cushion and folding his arms. "As long as you do it with respect and maturity."

"Obviously," I said, and rolled my eyes, but not enough so he would notice.

"Do you know what you want to say?"

"No, not yet . . ." I hesitated. "I'm still not sure I'll be able to go through with it."

"Why not?"

"Because . . . I don't feel safe. What if someone tries to attack me? It's not just kids at the fete, you know. Everyone from the area will be there. People from other schools too."

"I'll come with you."

"Err, no, thanks!" I looked up at him and laughed. "I can't be seen hanging out with my dad!"

Dad's face dropped. As if he'd been thumped with the reminder I wasn't little anymore.

"What if Yusuf comes with me?" I said, trying to hide the uneasiness in my voice. "It'd be good to have some backup, but he's not a teacher so no one will run away from me either." I grinned cheekily.

The fete was the same day and time as the rally. If Yusuf took me, he wouldn't be able to go and fight there. Now I just needed to get Dad to *make* him come with me without telling Dad what was going on and risk Yusuf hating me for life. It was the only way to keep Yusuf safe. And away from Darren.

"Actually, missy, like it or not, I'm already going to be there. To help the PTA with the collection for the . . . victims of the bombing." He twiddled his thumbs.

I looked down, thinking about Jo.

"I'm helping your mum with the raffle draw."

"Oh, right." I hadn't realized he was doing stuff at school with the other parents. With all the focus on the protest, I'd forgotten to ask Jonah which of our fundraising ideas the student council had agreed to with the PTA. I'd better do that as soon as I got back upstairs, I reminded myself. There was so much to think about, my brain hurt.

"But, you know, I wouldn't want to cramp your *stayal*," he said, flicking his hand out like a fashionista. "You can pretend your old dad isn't even there."

CHAPTER
36

MONDAY. The summer fete was in five days and the ban was still in place, even though we'd protested. It wasn't exactly easy fighting it from my bedroom and not *actually* being at school. I still hadn't decided how I was going to catch the attention of the chair of governors at the fete and convince him that Mrs. Owen had got everything wrong. And time was running out.

First, though, I had to figure out how to stop Yusuf from going to that rally and maybe fighting with my best friend's racist brother.

I almost wished I could reschedule my attempt to talk to the governors until things calmed down with Yusuf. But after the sit-in protest and Jonah's supportive emails and us all starting a group chat, there was no way I could back out. Especially since this was the only chance I'd get to speak to the governors about reversing the ban without Mrs. Owen glued to them.

This was the first time I'd had to fight for anything. I was finally doing something important with my life, but Yusuf was seriously disrupting things. With all my worry about him, I couldn't focus as much as I wanted. But I had to do something. Otherwise us getting suspended and Lisa having to hang out with her racist brother all week would be for nothing.

I picked up a pencil from my desk tidy and pulled a scrap piece of paper from underneath Furball to write down some ideas so I'd be ready for when we all chatted next. I had to get the ban reversed. Somehow. School would be unbearable if it was kept in place; everyone would believe they were right: that because we were different we were a problem.

I sat at the dining table reading *The Hate U Give*. The front door slammed shut and Yusuf appeared in the kitchen doorway, glaring at me.

He hadn't spoken to me since Friday night when I'd accidentally told on him and his plans. And I had avoided him in case he suspected I was following him. I still wasn't sure if he'd seen me before I'd ducked into the pharmacy and he'd got in the car.

I waited for him to launch into me, but he didn't. Probably because Dad trailed in after him. Phew.

"As-salaamu alaikum." Dad pushed past Yusuf and dropped a bag of shopping on the floor. He'd asked me to go with him, but I still didn't want to face a big building full of strange people. It made my spine tingle and the hairs on my neck stood up just thinking about it.

"Walaikum as-salaam," I responded, looking between Dad and Yusuf, who was still hanging around for some weird reason.

"Tell her, then," said Dad, nodding toward Yusuf.

Yusuf hung his head low and mumbled something.

"Did you hear that, Aaliyah?" asked Dad.

"Umm . . ." I said, worried that this—whatever this was—was going to make things worse between me and Yusuf.

"You might want to repeat that," said Dad, opening the fridge door and starting to put the groceries away.

"I said—I'll come with you to your school fete. You're my little sister and I should be looking out for you," said Yusuf, his arms crossed, his foot tapping on the tiled floor. "It's not safe out right now."

"Oh," I said, surprised Dad had already asked him. "Right . . . thanks."

Yusuf opened his mouth to say something else and then didn't. He looked at Dad and said, "All right, I'm going up to pack the books I don't need anymore."

His empty eyes glanced at me before he turned

to head out of the door. I remembered how on my first day at secondary school, he'd walked me into the grounds to make sure I knew the route. How did he go from *that* to this?

"Okay," said Dad, his head in the fridge.

As soon as the kitchen door shut, I got out of my chair and went to the fridge. "How did you get Yusuf to say yes?" I asked, picking up a milk carton from the shopping bag on the floor and handing it to Dad to put away.

Dad glanced at me and took the milk. "He's got no choice. I've spoken to his friends' parents as well, and we're all making sure they keep away from that rally."

I smiled at Dad. I had literally had the best idea ever.

Dad bent to pick up a tub of Greek yoghurt from the shopping bag and added, "I told him you've been bullied, and he has to look after you. I've also messaged those rally organizers on that poster, Peter and Darren, about the fete fundraiser for the bombing victims. You should've told us about Yusuf before, Aaliyah. I'm not happy . . ."

Dad's words became muffled as I stepped back in shock. He didn't just say he'd invited the *hate group* to the summer fete?

"Why would you even do that?" I screamed, running out of the kitchen, a thick lump forming in my throat.

Of all the people you could invite to a school fete to bring people together, my dad had decided it would be a good idea to invite a bunch of racist, Muslim-hating thugs. I couldn't believe it.

"Aaliyah!" Dad shouted after me.

I ignored him and slammed the front room door. I couldn't believe he had invited not just the guy who had threatened me and taken my best friend away from me, but his whole group too.

I slumped onto the carpet and stared at the silver flowers on the wallpaper.

A knock on the door—I crossed my arms and turned away from it.

"Aaliyah." It was Dad. He crouched in front of me and put his fingers on my chin to lift my face to his. "I'm sorry," he said. "I should've told you properly—I wasn't thinking."

Tears of frustration rolled down my face. I couldn't look at him.

"I did this for you," he said.

"How is inviting a gang of thugs to MY school fete, while Yusuf's there, going to help me? You've ruined EVERYTHING!" I cried and threw his hand off my chin.

"Listen," he said, sitting cross-legged on the floor opposite me. "I consulted some community leaders at the mosque and we felt it was the best way to deal with the situation." He paused to look me in the eyes, but I turned my face away.

"If they come and support the collection, they won't be at the rally, or not for long," he continued. "We'll have achieved the impossible. Everyone will be together, working for the same cause. Kids like Yusuf and his friends will be safe, and hopefully these people will see that we're not bad. That we can work together."

I glanced at Dad, who was pulling at his shirt collar, loosening his tie.

"Aaliyah, listen, we have to extend our hand of friendship. If we don't, things will just get worse."

"They probably won't come anyway. They want to chant at their racist rally," I said. "They hate us."

"Well, then, it's their loss, isn't it? If they can't forget their stupid opinions and get behind a fundraising event when they've been especially invited, that says a lot about them."

I supposed he was making some sense. "How did you invite them? How do you even know them?" I asked, facing Dad. I wondered if he'd clicked that Darren was Lisa's brother.

"I don't," he said. "I just sent a text to the number on that poster Yusuf brought home and told them to come."

My brows arched so high, my eyelids hurt.

"Give it a chance. I'll have the police on standby—

don't worry. We have to extend our hand and show compassion. You never know, it might just change their minds . . . It might not," he said, pushing himself off the floor. "But we won't know unless we try."

He pecked me on my head before walking to the door. I forced myself to smile at him. Maybe he was right. Maybe it would change their minds. But it didn't mean I wasn't scared.

CHAPTER
37

I WENT UPSTAIRS, my head pounding. I had to get Darren's face out of my brain. I had to focus on what I *could* do and not on what I couldn't. I had to make the most of my days off school and come up with a plan.

I sat at my desk and opened up my laptop, occasionally throwing Furball a woolen ball to bat around. Then I messaged the group on Connectstra—they'd all be home from school now. Leon had named the group "The Gamechangers."

Hey! Shall we make a plan for the summer fete?

Jonah pinged back right away.

Yeah. When do you want to?

Feifei was online too.

I'm free now if everyone else is?

Sukhi? Leon? I pressed Send.
About a minute later Sukhi was online.

Yep, let's gooo!!

Followed by Leon.

Give me ten minutes. I'm finishing up a game.

After ten minutes we all joined an audio call, and
I opened up a Word document to make notes, like a
proper nerd. Just like I used to when I was a student
council member in Year Seven.

"I know this all kicked off because of my hijab,"
I started. "But this is bigger than me. We've got an
opportunity for all of us to be listened to. To finally
speak to adults who can change things in the school
without having to go through Mrs. Owen. And I think
we all should do something."

"Like what?" asked Leon.

"I don't know, let's brainstorm together—but
I'm thinking we could *all* do speeches about bullying
and talk about our cultural and religious experiences
like we did that day in the citizenship lesson? Tell the
governors we're not going to put up with racism and

hate in school anymore. That they've got to do more about people like Jayden and Sasha and their mates. They can't decide how their classmates dress or look. Why should they be allowed to roam our corridors like they own them, making us want to hide?"

"Yesss!" said Feifei. "I want to see the governors' faces when I tell them Mrs. Owen didn't do anything when I reported Jayden making jokes about me being Chinese."

"Yeah," chimed in Leon. "He only got two days' suspension when they did that investigation about you, Aaliyah, and the only reason it was that long was because we told Mr. Atkinson about the kind of stuff he does to us too. But he was allowed back in school and just carried on the same. He actually threw a chair at me on Friday afternoon, and guess what, he's still not been expelled—just suspended. My mum is furious!"

I tutted. "That's disgusting."

"Yeah, my dad said he wasn't happy a kid like that was still in school after all the stuff he gets caught doing," said Jonah.

Feifei spoke. "My mum's mentioned this so many times to Mrs. Owen, but she doesn't do anything."

"I heard it's because she's related to his parents somehow," said Leon. "They even have barbeques together in the holidays."

That makes sense, I thought. *Why else would he still be*

in school? But we couldn't talk about him right now, we had to stay focused.

"Okay, so we have to make the governors listen," I said. "If we're doing speeches, where do you think we should do them?" Furball rubbed her body against my legs. I leaned down and stroked her before continuing. "Where's the quietest part of the fete going to be—where they'll be able to hear us?"

"Ah, I know this," said Jonah. "So all the stalls are going to be at the top of the playground near the library like last year and all the rides will be further out on the field. The DJ is going to be round the corner outside the lunch hall. So the mobile classrooms on the far side near the staff car park will be away from most of the activities and should be the quietest if we get the music turned off."

I typed up this information. "Awesome! Thanks, Jonah!" I let out a sigh of relief. Everyone would be spaced out in the L-shaped playground; at least we wouldn't be crowded into one place.

"I've got a whistle we could use to get people's attention," said Sukhi.

"And I can round up the governors with Jonah to get them to the mobile area," Leon volunteered. "We can get all of them together before the music performance, when everyone is still outside."

I typed up each of our roles in my document.

"So we've got the governors in the quietest area, we've got a whistle to make them listen, what else?"

"I'll get the DJ to switch off the music!" shouted Sukhi, excited.

"How will you do that?" asked Jonah.

"I dunno. I'll bring him some food and tell him Mrs. Owen said he can have some lunch?"

We all laughed, but it was a good idea.

"Okay, so the music is off and everyone's in the right place," I said. "Now what?" I put my hands on my keyboard ready to type, when the doorbell rang. "Hang on, someone's at the door. Give me a sec." I jumped out of my chair and onto my bed to look out the window.

Sukhi's mum was walking up our driveway with a massive bouquet of white lilies in her arms. She was taking small steps, as if she was nervous. I leaned further to see who had rung the doorbell and saw Sukhi's dad. Why were they here? To talk about the fete? To say sorry? My insides relaxed. If they were talking again, things would definitely be back to normal soon.

"Yeah, we need to—"

Leon was saying something, so I got back in my chair.

"Sorry! I'm back," I said.

"What will you say in your speech, Aaliyah?" asked Jonah.

There was a silence. I felt as if the world's responsibilities were on my shoulders.

"I don't know. I have to write it up. I'll do it tomorrow, but I'm thinking I'll talk about how we are more than our clothes and the way we look?"

"Yeah, that would be good," said Jonah. "You should also talk about freedom of expression like you highlighted on your signs at the silent protest."

"Yeah, I will, thanks." I smiled, feeling like maybe I could do this thing. "Feifei, so you're going to talk about the school not doing enough?"

"Yeah," she replied. "I also want to talk about human rights."

"Oh, yeah! Good idea!" I said.

She continued, "I've been looking it up and I want to mention how we are all equal and if you discriminate against one person, then you have to discriminate equally . . . so they've already stopped some of us expressing our cultures and identity, like when they sent Leon home last year because of his braids and Simone in Year Ten because of her hair extensions; they made me take off my rainbow badge on my coat, and Jamie was sent home on the first day of term when they came in wearing a girls' uniform, and now they're going for religious expression, so why are kids in school wearing branded shoes and jackets when it specifically says on the uniform list you can't wear them, and why are the kids who wear long black coats, black eyeliner, and have black nails, dyed black hair, and ear piercings allowed to come to school like that and *you* can't wear what you want?"

I leaned back in my chair. "That's true, Feifei. If their look doesn't affect their learning, why does ours? In fact, if it makes us happier to be able to express our identities, then that's a good thing!"

"I'll tell you why," said Leon. "Because the people asking for the ban think they're better than us and they can get away with it."

"What do you mean?" Sukhi asked.

"Well, they see anyone who is brown or different as beneath them. And anything that feels wrong to them, they want to get rid of. The racists and far right think their identity and culture is better than ours. And just group us all together because of one bad experience."

"You sound like my dad!" Sukhi joked.

Leon laughed. "Actually, it's 'cause my dad teaches this stuff at the uni—his books are always lying around and he talks about it A LOT. What's happening at school is just the same as what's happened in history before. They said Black people were violent or uneducated and should be kept separate from them."

"That Jews were stingy and couldn't be trusted," Jonah chipped in.

"Yeah," Leon continued. "And now it's all Muslims

are violent and dangerous. So you can't express your-self the way you want because they think it's a threat. It's so unfair, but they'll keep doing it if we let them."

"Yeah, you're right," said Jonah. "They start off by making the people they hate or find threatening out to be evil. They're doing it to refugees too."

What Leon and Jonah said hit me in my gut. It was the same old story—make up hateful things about the people you don't like so you can attack their identities and create division and fear. And our head teacher and her husband were supporting them!

I knew there were only a few people who thought like this, but they were ruining so many lives. "And by creating this division and wanting white zones or whatever," I added, "they're making it look like all white people agree with this disgusting far-right stuff, when they don't and it affects them too!"

I didn't want to say it out loud but I was thinking of how Darren had changed in the last year and how it had affected his family. Maybe Lisa could talk about it. I'd email her later.

"Yeah," Sukhi said. "It's like when people think all Muslims believe all that ISIS rubbish—the racists try and make it look the same."

"Exactly! Leon, will you talk about this, please?" I asked.

"Uhh . . . yeah, sure. I could also back it up with

examples, like how every time there's an incident, the school always assumes I'm the threat, that it was me who started it because I'm Black. And it doesn't matter what Jayden does to me, I get in trouble too. As if we're anything like each other. If it wasn't for Mr. Wilkinson saving my butt, I'd have got suspended last Friday along with Jayden."

"And it's not good enough that we only have one teacher who would be willing to stand up to Mrs. Owen and do that for us," added Jonah.

"The power is definitely skewed at school," Leon added.

We all murmured in agreement.

It was true. Even Mrs. Alcock was half-heartedly implementing the ban because she felt she couldn't challenge Mrs. Owen. She'd even looked away when she'd seen me in my hijab in the playground last week after Mr. Wilkinson had chatted to her.

"Jonah, do you want to say something?" I asked.

There was a short silence before he spoke again. "I could talk about why suspending you two and Lisa for your peaceful protest was too harsh and wrong?"

"Oh my god, Jonah!" said Sukhi. "Yes, please!"

I laughed. "You're right, it was harsh, but my dad said it's because we deliberately broke a school rule and then didn't listen. He said his school would have suspended us for more than three days!"

"Yeah, but he's a teacher, so he would say that," Sukhi chimed in.

"Hmmm, okay. Well, maybe I could talk after Leon about the similarities of the way the far right work now to back in Nazi Germany and how the school are letting people divide us through this ban rather than doing anything constructive to bring us together?"

"That would be awesome," I said, stroking Furball as she nuzzled my calves.

"So who will speak first?" asked Sukhi.

"I think Aaliyah should," said Leon.

We continued brainstorming and discussing how we'd do things on the day, like how Jonah and Leon would convince the governors to go to the mobile classrooms. Forty-five minutes later, we had a plan. Everyone had a role, everyone knew what they were doing. Except Lisa. But we'd tell her what she had to do as soon as we got hold of her. It seemed Darren had got into her phone again and it might be better to try and chat to her when we were all back at school.

On Wednesday, we had another call after the others had got back from school. Feifei and I went through our draft speeches with the group, and they made suggestions of things to add. I'd spent all of Tuesday and

Wednesday on my speech, but it still needed work. I wanted to do some more research on how important identity was and how expressing it helps us to represent who we are — that was going to be the thing I'd focus on in my speech.

We'd all agreed to record our talks and share them to make sure they were good enough, and honestly for the first time since everything had gone *so* wrong, I felt accepted and supported.

And in that moment I relaxed, even though I knew when I went back to school tomorrow I'd be expected to not wear my hijab and express myself the way I wanted. And that was going to totally suck.

CHAPTER
38

Lockers slammed in the hallway, shoes squeaked past, kids huddled together, laughing. A typical Thursday in school. And it didn't feel any better to be back. I could see why some kids preferred homeschooling. I bet they didn't have to drag their sleepy selves out of bed at seven A.M. every morning. It was as if a few days away had made everyone forget the protest outside Mrs. Owen's office.

At least they weren't snickering about me today. To avoid any more trouble, I'd worn a wide black stretchy hairband to cover my hair. My hair was in a neat bun and tucked just under it—leaving only a small gap around the top, where you'd see my hair only if I dropped my head. It wasn't a scarf, so they couldn't say anything, but my hair *was* technically covered. I hadn't given in.

I rubbed my neck, which was bare above my shirt and blazer collars. It was as if a part of me was missing.

Sukhi stood at the lockers, cramming her books in, as I approached them at break time. She grabbed my arm, pulling me toward her.

"What's up?" I said.

"Look." She pulled out her phone and shoved the screen into my face. It was a photo online of a far-right poster—the same ones that had been circulating around Lambert—only this time instead of the sketched man, there was a headshot of a blonde girl on it.

It was Lisa.

I stood still. My throat was raw.

"Can you believe it?" said Sukhi somewhere near me. "Ali?"

"IS THIS FOR REAL?"

At first, I thought I'd only screamed that inside my head, but everyone jumped and turned to me, eyes wide.

Time stopped.

"Let's talk on the field." She yanked my elbow and dragged me out of the corridor.

"She wasn't in French first lesson—didn't you notice she wasn't in at form time?" said Sukhi once we were out of earshot near the school perimeter fence.

We were standing in the shade under the trees to avoid the scorching sun.

I hadn't even realized I was pacing until Sukhi clutched my arm to stop me. "Ali?"

"I don't understand. She came to the protest with us!"

"Look at her pic properly!" Sukhi shoved her phone in front of me.

I snatched it out of her hand. This time I noticed how pale Lisa looked. How forced her smile seemed. When Lisa was happy, she smiled with her eyes too, but here her lips were stretched into almost a grimace.

"He's forced her to do this, Sukhi," I said, my voice barely coming out, as it dawned on me that Lisa might be in bigger trouble than I realized. We hadn't heard from Lisa since the protest. I'd been that distracted by The Gamechanger calls, writing my speech, and Yusuf and his dumb plans. I hadn't bothered chasing her because I didn't want Darren to get any angrier. But he clearly wasn't angry at her. He was using her.

How could I have been so stupid? All this time I'd been trying my best to stop Yusuf from hurting Darren, scared that Lisa might get hurt too. Ugh. What an idiot I was. Her brother was *already* hurting her. "We have to go and talk to her." I handed Sukhi her phone.

"What? At her house? 'Cause she isn't answering her

phone or any messages, remember?" Sukhi raised her eyebrows to make her point.

"Yeah. Her house. We've got no choice." I swallowed hard.

I gazed out at the crowds of kids in the field and the playground, trying to erase the image of Darren that was making me feel as if I was suffocating.

CHAPTER
39

LATER THAT DAY, after last lesson, we met the Gamechangers in the library for an update on the PTA's plans for the fundraiser for Jo and the other Ratcliffe Academy concert victims. We had to change our speech timings to work around the activities to make sure it all went smoothly, but I found it hard to concentrate. I was too busy thinking about facing Darren.

Afterward, Sukhi and I went to the science block toilets. I pulled out my hijab from my bag and wrapped it around my head, keeping it loose because it felt as if it was a hundred degrees out there.

Sukhi glanced at her watch. "You wanna go back to the library and get some homework done before we head off?"

"Nah. I can't think straight," I said with my pin between my lips as I fastened the top of the scarf in place.

"True. Let's just walk slowly and make a proper plan, then. I mean, what if Darren doesn't leave the house? How long can we stay out?"

We'd have to watch the front door and pray Darren left.

I tried not to think about him catching us, but I couldn't help it. My muscles tensed and my ears rang just as they did after the concert when he'd screamed in my face.

"Ali?" Sukhi forced me out of my daze.

"Errr. I don't know. We can't stay out late. Mum'll panic."

We headed toward Lisa's, and even though I hadn't been there since the week after the bombing, I probably could've got there with my eyes closed, it felt so natural. As we got closer to Lisa's house, I stopped. I was rooted to the pavement, my body unwilling to carry on.

"Come on, Ali, you can do this. He might not even be there," said Sukhi, rubbing my arm. That girl could read my mind. My head buzzed. I squinted and shook my head as if it would physically throw Darren out of mind.

But it didn't work. I felt as if my chest was filled with smoke and I'd struggle to breathe if I moved any closer to their house.

"Okay, okay . . ." Sukhi put her hand on my

shoulder. "Let's come back later when Darren's more likely to be out. He's always showing off pics of his dinner or drinks on Snappo. If I keep an eye on it, we can come back after dinner, yeah?"

"Yeah." I let out a big breath.

"And we can sit and watch the house for a bit before we knock to make sure he's not in, if that helps?" Sukhi rubbed my arm and we turned toward my house.

I hung my head, feeling deflated. Would I always have to hide from Darren and people like him? Was I always going to be scared? Would he always have this power over me?

CHAPTER
40

A FEW HOURS LATER, I stood outside the chippy, my bag of chips steaming, the vinegary smell wafting up my nose and making me want to rip it open and eat one right there. Mum and Yusuf came out with the rest of our food, and we walked together toward the car.

As Mum pressed the key to open the door, someone shouted something, and we all turned toward the rough voice.

An older bald man standing outside the chippy with two younger guys yelled, "Go back to your own country! Go eat your curry somewhere else!"

Oh my god, one of the guys behind him was Darren! If we hadn't left her street, I could've spoken to Lisa, but now I was in front of the one person I really *didn't* want to be anywhere near.

My chest throbbed and my leg muscles tightened. I was just about to run to the car when Yusuf shoved the chips into Mum's arms and stomped back to the men, both fists clenched.

"WHAT DID YOU SAY?" he roared.

"Yusuf!" Mum screamed.

My body automatically started moving back to the car as if I was watching a scary scene in a horror movie.

Yusuf squared up to the men, all of their shoulders and legs wide, jaws clenched and hands fisted.

Any second now someone was going to throw a punch. I squeezed my eyes shut, hoping it would all be gone when I opened them, but no luck. They were all shouting even louder at each other and Yusuf was pushing one of them back.

"Stop!" Mum dropped the bag of fish and chips and ran toward them. She wedged her body between Yusuf and the group of men.

The burly chip shop owner ran out of the door and joined her, saying, "Leave my premises now, or I'll call the police."

A group of people from the convenience store next door had gathered to see the drama. I blew out and wiped my clammy hands on my jeans.

"Aaliyah—get in the car now!" Mum said, her voice shrill.

I jumped and rushed to the car, keeping my head down. I didn't want to look at him, breathe the same air as him, let alone think of him. He was going to affect my life forever and I had no voice or way to stand up to him or tell him what he'd done.

Mum and Yusuf followed behind me, picking up the dropped chips and slamming their doors as they got in.

How did I think the fete could be anything like last year's with those men there? Yusuf wouldn't be able to ignore them. Half the community was going to attack the other, ending up in the biggest disaster ever. At my school.

Yusuf had clenched his jaw all the way home from the chip shop. And I totally understood why he was angry, but I wished he could see that fighting would only make things worse. He'd either get hurt or in trouble. Or both. What if he didn't come with me to the fete on Saturday and went to the rally and fought with Darren instead? I'd seen how much they hated each other. What if he couldn't stay away from his new "man-gang"?

I cocked my head to see what Yusuf was looking at on his phone in the car, see if I could get a name or something, maybe even a far-right group name to tell Dad to search up, but he was surfing the Nike site, browsing trainers.

After we'd eaten at home, Mum told Yusuf to go and mow the lawn. She then got chatting to Sukhi's mum on the phone—they had made up properly now, and when I'd asked Mum why Sukhi's mum brought her flowers, she said it was because Sukhi's mum was "sorry for posting something offensive on Facebook" which had made Mum reconsider their friendship.

I decided it was the best time to go into Yusuf's room while I could hear Mum talking downstairs and Yusuf was still outside. But I couldn't find any more evidence about his plans for the rally and had to leave when Furball wandered into his room.

Even though I could hear the lawnmower churning, I didn't want to get caught in there, and especially not with Furball. I picked her up and took her back to my room.

Furball seemed to be more confident about leaving my room. She'd been so good for weeks and would only just come up to my door and then go back into my room when I'd enter, but now she was sleeping less and it seemed she wanted to explore more. And the calming plugs were not keeping her as calm as when she first came to stay. Maybe she'd been depressed or something and now she wasn't. Or maybe she was just more comfortable now that she'd been here a few weeks. I'd have to come clean about her once the fete was over and I could face the punishment I'd get for hiding her. Mr. Baldwin would be home from hospital soon, and I'd probably have to give her back . . . but I didn't want to think about that right now.

I rolled out my prayer mat and sat on it with Furball, sighing. Maybe I should pray and ask for help? What should I be doing? What was most important? And in what order? I needed to prepare myself to speak to the chair of governors to reverse the religious symbols ban on Saturday, assuming Mrs. Owen had already told them about it. It was just over a day away and my only chance before school broke up for the summer—but I also needed to stop Yusuf from getting hurt, and ALSO try and save Lisa from whatever hell Darren was putting her through.

Lisa's phone went to voicemail, so it'd either been switched off or her battery had died. Sukhi and I had wondered if we should just go to the police, but Lisa would get so angry with us if she wasn't really in trouble. And Darren would hate me even more if he found out I'd called the police on him. We had to find a way to speak to her. All we could do was keep an eye on what Darren posted online. There was no way I could go to his house and just knock on the door and risk him being home.

I hadn't slept more than four hours all week. Well, that's what my body and eyes felt like. I'd stayed up late doing my homework and recorded my speech on my laptop and watched it back, then watched Feifei's practice video. And by the time I'd fallen asleep, the pigeons were already cooing on the roof.

It was 6:15 A.M. on Friday. The sun streamed through my curtains and there was way too much to think about to sleep. So I gave up trying.

Furball sat in my lap, enjoying me scritching her head as I tried to read. My eyes drooped. I wasn't interested in what Katniss had to say to Peeta for what right now felt like the hundredth time. But I had to keep reading so I wouldn't think about Lisa, or the fete, or what Darren might do to Yusuf at the rally tomorrow if he didn't come to the fete with me.

My laptop pinged and lit up with a notification from Sukhi. She was up early too. Maybe she couldn't sleep either.

Look!

She messaged with a screenshot. It was a photo that Darren had shared ten minutes before. He was eating a donut in their kitchen, sugar all over his lips. Caption:

Fueling up before I hit the gym.

He was definitely going out! Oh my god.

I squeezed my eyes shut to get Darren's face out of my head. My laptop pinged again.

Sukhi: Round 2?
Me: What, to speak to Lisa?
Sukhi: Obviously!
Me: Right now?
Sukhi: Err yeh
Me: How we gonna get out tho?
Sukhi: Sneak out?

Sukhi added a shrugging emoji.

I thought about Yusuf sneaking out and getting away with it. Maybe I could, just this once. And if I got caught, surely Mum and Dad would understand because I was going to see if my best friend was okay and maybe get her away from her racist brother. I'd made my decision.

Me: Okay. Where shall we meet? I've gotta figure out how I'll get downstairs!
Sukhi: Let's say we want to go for a run before school?
Me: Yeah, good idea!

And we wouldn't be lying because we'd have to run there and back to get home in time for school.

I looked around my room for my joggers.

Sukhi: Be quick! We have to get there before he finishes his dumb gym session. I'll meet you round the corner on Tudor Road in 10 mins to save some time, yeah?

Me: OK!

Furball woke up as my weight came off the mattress and made her bounce. "Shh, don't move, go back to sleep," I told her. But she was already up and looking around.

It was 6:30 A.M. As I dressed, I looked out the window; the road was filled with morning light, still and quiet. My heart began to beat faster.

I tucked my keys into the pocket of my joggers.

Oh, flip. I had to go down. I closed my eyes and inhaled before letting out a big breath — I'd never done this before and I prayed to God I wouldn't get caught.

I put my finger between my door and the doorframe as I opened it. Thankfully it made no sound.

Dad was in the shower — he always went first — and I had no idea where Mum was. I crept down the stairs, my teeth gritted, staying as close to the middle as possible, where I was sure the boards didn't creak. I made it to the bottom step and trod on a loose board. CREAK.

"What are you doing up?" I stopped and turned to the kitchen. It was Mum in her pyjamas, holding a cup of coffee, the smell wafting up out of the cup.

"Uhhh . . . I couldn't sleep, so I thought I'd go for a run. I—I thought it might make me feel better and more ready for school." I tried to look convincing.

"Aaliyah! You can't just go for a run without telling us! Just wait a few minutes, I'll join you," she said, turning to the kitchen door.

Oh, no. She couldn't come. Sukhi would end up waiting for me for ages and Darren would see her and this would go horribly wrong. "Mum, I haven't got five minutes, I've got to get ready for school! Ever since I quit running club, I've missed it. I just want to go for a run and think some things through. I read that exercise can help when you're dealing with trauma."

"Oh, my baby. Yes, yes. It can. Okay, you go but stick to the streets and don't go too far."

"I will. Maybe we could go for a run together on Sunday?" I said, hoping that would make her feel better about me not waiting.

"Yeah, let's do that." She smiled and watched me leave.

I opened the door and stepped into the porch, gently pulling the door behind me. Pushing my feet into my school running shoes, I went outside.

A COOL SUMMER BREEZE filtered through the stuffy July morning. All the cars on my street were still parked. I stopped on our driveway and looked at the house. A wave of nausea passed through me. What if Darren caught me outside his house? I didn't want to go near him, breathe the same air as him, but I had to do this. For Lisa. *Come on, Aaliyah,* I told myself. *Go.*

I lifted the hood from my top over my scarf. I wasn't going to risk Darren yanking it off and attacking me if he saw me. I walked as fast as I could, taking long confident—well, what I thought looked confident—strides.

The shops on the main road were shut. Only a few cars passed by. I kept my head down, my shoulders hunched. The morning air was already warm, but I still had goosebumps all over my body.

I took a deep breath and jogged across the road,

trying to look as if I was a runner. My bladder twinged. I needed to go and soon. Oh god, not now. I just needed to make it one more block. I could do this.

As I approached Lisa's road, I saw Sukhi standing on the pavement outside a detached garage, which belonged to the house on the intersection. I stopped on that corner with her and stepped back, and I swear my heart skipped a beat when I remembered Darren might see us.

He's not there, he's gone to the gym, I told myself and forced my legs to walk toward Lisa's house with Sukhi, praying the whole way under my breath. *Allah, please help me get through this, make it easy for me, not hard.*

Lisa lived in a three-bedroom semi-detached house with a large bay window above the one on the ground floor and a smaller one upstairs at the front, which was her room.

"This is like being in a movie," Sukhi said, munching some breakfast biscuits she'd brought with her. We crouched on the curb between two parked cars opposite Lisa's, a few doors down the street, so if Darren did come out, he wouldn't see us straightaway. It was 6:45 A.M., and thankfully most people hadn't started leaving for work yet.

"Yeah, only it's real and we might actually get attacked," I said, carefully peeling off the foil wrapper of the biscuit packet Sukhi had given me.

A blonde curly-haired woman stepped out of her door a few houses along, balancing a small white cake box on her left arm as she locked the door with her key. She jumped into a cute red Mini and drove off, her exhaust so loud I glanced around to see if anyone was looking out their windows.

Sukhi sat up and looked at me. "Shall we go?"

"NO!" I said, a little too loud. "Not yet. We don't even know if he's in. What if he's coming back from a warm-up run and he sees us?" The thought had only just occurred to me and made goosebumps rise across my arms and neck.

"Well, we have to find out somehow, don't we?" Sukhi said, shoving her empty biscuit packet into her jogger pocket and pushing herself off the curb to stand.

"What if we call his number?" I said.

"The one on those posters?"

"Yeah, the photo will be in your messages," I said, gesturing for her to find the photo I'd taken and sent to her. It seemed I was getting better at using my brain first in stressful situations.

"Hey, Ali!" Sukhi's eyes sparkled with excitement through her glasses in the morning sun. "Why don't we make something up to get him out? Like an emergency or something?"

"Err . . . okay . . . why don't you do it in your Scottish accent?"

Sukhi laughed. "What, like: *therre's bin a faya at the gym, sun, ye need te leave hoooom naow. We need ye help.*"

"Was that: there's been a fire, son?" I couldn't help laughing out loud. The smile slid right off my face as a tall guy stepped out of Lisa's front door, his hands in his pockets.

It was Darren.

Sukhi saw my face and turned, quickly ducking behind a car, while I squatted backward to hide behind another.

We both peered around the cars, and my heart dropped to my socks when I saw Darren casually walking toward us.

I pulled my head back behind the car and closed my eyes, praying he wouldn't cross the road and see us. My heartbeat felt like it had tripled. My fingers tingled, and I felt as if I was trapped in a fishing net under a boat with no way out. I don't know how long I stayed frozen, my eyes squeezed tight. I jumped when Sukhi whispered, "Ali!"

"Huh?"

"He's passed us." She pointed behind me.

I didn't move for a moment. Then Sukhi pulled me by the arm, and I slowly stretched my aching knees from my squat position to peek above the car. Darren's back swayed rhythmically as he swaggered down the street away from us.

I let out a huge breath.

"He's going to the gym," Sukhi said. "So we've got ages."

As soon as he disappeared around the corner, I stood tall. Sukhi put her hand on my arm. "Now what?" she asked.

"Now we have to be quick and get Lisa's attention," I said, trying to fight the panic invading my body.

"That's if she's even there," said Sukhi. "What if she's in Wales again?"

I swallowed. I didn't know what we'd do if we didn't find her here.

Sukhi linked her arm into mine. *Thud. Thud. Thud.* My heart—that's all I could hear.

We stood in front of the brass knocker on Lisa's red wooden door. The doorbell was still covered in masking tape—it'd been like that for over a year. Lisa said that nothing ever got done at their house as neither of her parents were into DIY. They worked long hours, so they were never home, and when they were, they were catching up on sleep instead of sorting the house out. I glanced around to see if anyone was watching, picked up a small pebble from their driveway, and threw it at Lisa's window. And then another. Sukhi did the same so we wouldn't wake her mum or dad.

We waited. There was no response. No pulling back of the curtain or opening of the door. Nothing.

We shrugged at each other. I threw one last stone. Maybe Lisa wasn't here after all. Maybe we should just go home.

A slight movement in the window above caught my eye. I lunged forward, grabbing another stone. If it was Lisa, I hoped she'd open the door before someone reported us for throwing stones.

Sukhi kneeled down to pick up another and threw it harder. Nothing.

Maybe I'd imagined it. It was wishful thinking. Why did I even think we could talk to her? Maybe she didn't want to be found?

I turned and linked arms with Sukhi, crossing to the other side of the street. We traipsed away in silence. The hum of the cars on the main road becoming more apparent.

I glanced back at Lisa's window, a feeling of loss inside of me. The curtains had been pulled away a little. A sleepy pale face with blonde hair stood peeping out onto the road.

I gasped and tugged on Sukhi's arm, forcing her to spin. "She's there!" I shouted, followed with a shaky laugh. Relief washed over me like a wave over a sea wall.

Lisa quickly moved away from the window, releasing the curtain into its position.

"Lisa!"

I stepped forward, but Sukhi wrenched me back. "He's coming!"

I turned toward where Sukhi's eyes were focused. Darren was heading in our direction, smoke curling from his mouth, his phone to his ear. His familiar chuckle drilled through my ears. "Yeah, I won't be long, I'm just grabbing my lifting gloves."

Sukhi yanked my arm and dragged me down the street, away from the house, behind a parked car.

"We'll go as soon as he's in the door," she whispered. "Just breathe, Ali. It's okay. Breathe," she said, crouching next to me and clutching my hand.

CHAPTER
42

JUST AS I'D CAUGHT my breath and we'd stood to leave, Lisa's front door opened and Darren came back out with gloves in his hand.

I ducked down again and squeezed my eyes tight.

Sukhi put her hand on my shoulder. "He's jogging," she whispered. "He won't be back for a while now. He just wanted his gloves—look."

But I didn't want to open my eyes. I wanted to sink into the ground and never see his face again.

"He's turned the corner. Come on. We're safe," Sukhi declared.

Focusing on the cracks in the pavement—stepping between each one to slow my breaths—I stood in the driveway.

Sukhi picked up more tiny stones to throw at Lisa's window, checking for curtain twitches before she threw the first one.

Sukhi screeched, "Ali!"

It was Lisa's face at the window! I jumped onto the pavement outside their drive and strained my eyes to make absolutely sure it was her.

Lisa waved at us with a big grin.

Sukhi pulled me back into the driveway as a car approached. The exhaust smell filled up my lungs as I waved my arms, gesturing Lisa to come down.

And then the front door opened.

"What are you doing here, girls?" It was Lisa's mum. She had bed hair and wore pink pyjama bottoms and a white T-shirt. "Everything all right?"

"Umm . . ." I started. "Sorry we woke you, but . . . erm . . . is Lise . . . Lisa in?"

"Oh . . . she's probably asleep." She folded her arms to her chest. "We don't usually get visitors at seven A.M." Her eyes fell on my hood with my hair tucked under it neatly. She put a hand on her hip. "It's great you girls want to stand up for your right to wear your religious items, and I was pretty impressed that you all wanted to, but there are other ways of doing it. Not listening to your teachers and getting yourselves suspended isn't exactly the best approach, is it?"

I shuffled my feet. "Ummm . . . yeah, we didn't think—"

"—it through," Sukhi interrupted, as if she was

worried I'd say something like, *We didn't think Darren would find out.*

I gave Sukhi a short look and added, "You're right. Sorry."

"Anyway. Why don't you come back later when she's up?" she said sleepily, starting to push the door closed.

"Umm . . . we can't come later because we'll be late for school." Sukhi said, looking at me. It was clear she was trying to figure out a way of not saying we don't want to see Darren.

My stomach was in knots and I tried to ignore the panic rising inside my throat, imagining Darren finding us here any moment now.

"It is *so* good to see you!" said Lisa, popping up behind her mum in her checkered pyjamas.

"Oh, you're up," Lisa's mum said, turning to go back inside. "Well, I'll leave you to it. I'm just going in the shower." She looked at Lisa and said, "Don't take too long. You have to get ready for school." She gave us a small smile and left.

I pointed at Lisa's shoulder in a sling. "What did he do to you?"

"Who? You mean, Darren? Oh, he didn't do this," she said, rolling her eyes. "It happened when I was rollerblading in the garden. Can't believe you can dislocate a shoulder from falling down! Trust me, I'm not rollerblading for a while!"

"Are you sure?" I asked as I frantically searched the street, praying I wouldn't see Darren approaching again.

"Uhh, yeah! I think I'd know how I got hurt, Ali! Anyway it's much better now, I'll probably have this off in a couple of days." She pointed at the sling with her good hand.

"So why haven't you been in touch?" Sukhi asked, brushing her arm with mine so that we'd both fit in front of the door.

Lisa pulled the front door from behind her, so her mum wouldn't hear and sighed. "Darren was so angry that I'd taken part in the protest about the hijab ban that as soon as I got home, he took my phone and threw it across the kitchen, which smashed the screen on the tiles. Then he put it in his pocket and didn't give it back. He said while Dad was away at his conference, he's the man of the house and I needed to sit out my suspension with a proper punishment."

I stood gawping at her, not sure what to say.

"He's lost it," she continued. "He thinks he has to keep me safe so no one can 'hurt me.' He wouldn't even let me use our iPad because of my suspension—he told Mum he'd sent it off for repairs, so I had literally no way of getting in touch with you. And I don't even remember your numbers. You have to write them down for me!"

I knew Darren hated me, but it was hard to accept that he was so full of rage that he'd smash up his sister's phone and control all her devices. If he could do this to her, what might he do to Yusuf at the rally?

"Why didn't you tell your mum he did that?" Sukhi's mouth was wide open.

Lisa was quiet for a moment then lowered her voice. "He said if I did, Mum and Dad would fight even more than they do. And they've been arguing so much, I was worried they might divorce because of me. I thought I'd wait it out till I was back in school." Lisa shrugged as if it wasn't that important.

I couldn't believe she'd let Darren treat her like that. "You have to tell your mum, Lise," I said. "He can't get away with stuff like this."

Lisa chewed her lip then stared at us, as if she wanted to change the conversation.

"And why'd he keep you off school yesterday?" Sukhi raised one brow above her glasses, looking unimpressed.

"Oh, I had a hospital appointment to get my arm checked, and I got seen by the doctor so late Mum said there was no point me coming in for half an hour. Even though I begged her 'cause I was dying to see you!"

"You're coming today, right? I asked.

"Yeah! I am not staying in this stupid house with that doofus any longer. I'll just go get ready, then we can go together?"

"Uhhh . . ." I looked down at my clothes and then eyed Sukhi, who was also in her joggers.

"Okay, you guys go and get ready." Lisa laughed. "Hang on . . . why did you come in your joggers and so early?" She searched our faces.

"Long story! We just needed to see you were okay," Sukhi piped up. "All right, we'd better get home. See you at school!"

"See you soon!" Lisa beamed.

Sukhi knocked into my shoulder, making me turn and leave. As we strolled toward the main road, Sukhi said, "Darren is *so* nasty."

"He is the worst," I muttered. My eyes drifted to the moving cars. "It all feels wrong. We've got to get Lise to tell her parents."

I sprinted to the end of my road and stopped, bending over to catch my breath, my face near my knees. My ears throbbed so loudly, it felt as if the blood in them would burst out any moment. My head spun with a million questions—what if Darren did something worse the next time he caught Lisa talking to me?

What would he do to Yusuf tomorrow? What would he do to *me* if he saw me?

"Mum, I'm back!" I shouted, running up two stairs at a time. It felt as if I'd run a marathon for two days and I'd only been out forty-five minutes, most of which I hadn't actually spent running.

The faint sound of cutlery being put away made its way upstairs. Someone must be emptying the dishwasher.

When she saw me, Furball rolled on her back on my bed for a tummy rub. I rubbed her soft, warm belly, then quickly slipped out of my hoodie and joggers and got into my uniform. I sat on my bed and hung my head. The fete was tomorrow. All I wanted was to lie down and sleep but I'd agreed to meet the student council to finalize our plan for the fundraising activities. And there was no way I could skip the fete—I had to do this for Yusuf, to keep him away from the rally. I had to do this for me. And I had to do this for everyone else who wasn't able to express themselves the way they wanted.

CHAPTER 43

SATURDAY 9TH JULY. It was the day of the fete. My body ached and I felt groggy after another sleepless night, but I got dressed and went downstairs as if it was the most exciting day of my life. I just needed to get through today, and then I could relax and be sleep's new best friend.

We got to school a little after the fete opened at 11:30 A.M. Sukhi was wearing her new 3W T-shirt—I hadn't seen one since *that* night. When we'd discussed what we'd wear, I said I couldn't wear that, and had instead opted for a white shirtdress, navy jeggings and a printed navy-blue scarf with red poppies on. I finished off my look with the new All Star Low white leather Converse Dad had bought me to replace my favorite sequined high-tops. I'd had to give them to charity because I couldn't wear them after the concert—they brought back too many bad memories.

Yusuf traipsed behind us with his friend Shafique, hands in his pockets, making it clear he didn't want to be my "bodyguard." But it didn't matter if he wasn't happy that Dad had forced him to come, as long as he was nowhere near Darren.

To my relief there wasn't a big crowd yet. Just a few families with overexcited kids scattered across the sun-filled playground, scouting the stalls as they finished setting up. I didn't know how I'd feel when it got busier, but I stopped myself from thinking about it.

"Let's go and find your mum," I said to Sukhi, pulling my scarf into place around my neck. "Find out where they've put the stuff we need to set up the activities."

I had to wear a hijab today, especially as I was talking about it. I hoped no one would tell me off—though technically they couldn't, because it wasn't a school day and the fete was open to everyone, scarf or no scarf.

After I'd helped set up the hall for the music performance and put the leaflets the student council had designed to encourage people to donate toward the fundraiser on each of the chairs, I went to fill buckets of water for the "Teacher Target" activity. Lisa and Sukhi were at a table, squirting spray cans of whipped cream all over paper plates, all face up and ready to be splatted.

"Shall we get a drink?" asked Sukhi after we'd

finished our jobs and passed a stall serving tea, coffee, juices and fizzy drinks.

"Let's get one in a bit," I said. "I want to see what's what first. Find those governors."

Lisa scanned the grounds nervously, biting her lip.

I tapped her arm. "You okay, Lise?"

"Yeah."

"Darren won't be here. He's busy at that racist rally till later, remember?" Sukhi said.

My insides twisted. I hoped she was right and he had ignored Dad's message inviting him to the fete.

"Oh, look!" Lisa pointed at the archery area. It was as if she'd snapped out of a hypnotic state. "Don't let Aaliyah get hold of that, she might just point it right at Jayden's cold heart!"

I rolled my eyes. "Ha-ha, funny, Lise."

"We've SO got to go on the go-karts," she said, standing on her tiptoes to get a better view of the makeshift race circuit on the running track in the distance.

I gave her a look. I hated go-karting, but knew I'd probably get dragged into doing it.

A DJ had set up his decks on a table on the raised patio outside the lunch hall, his aviator sunglasses reflecting the sun. The smoke from the sizzling burgers on the barbeque rose behind him, plastic plates stacked high next to it. The smell of lamb, onions, and grilled cheese made my stomach groan. I didn't think I could eat because I was so worried about speaking today, but now I was wondering if I should try before I fainted or something. Or maybe food would just make me throw up.

"We're all set!" one of the PTA parents shouted.

Now people just had to roll in.

"Hey, Aaliyah!"

I turned to see Jonah with his dad and little sister. He was wearing his kippah. I'd never seen one up close before. It looked just like one of Yusuf's topis, only slightly smaller.

"Hey, Jonah," I said, pulling on Sukhi's top to get her to stop with me and Lisa.

"Dad, I'll see you in a bit. I've got more stuff to do. Mum's probably wondering where you are," said Jonah, before turning back to us. Once his dad and sister had walked off toward the stalls, he asked, "Are you ready?"

"Umm, yeah. I think so." I shuffled my shoes on the shimmering tarmac. I had to get this speech out of the way.

The lunch hall door opened and a man wearing a blue shirt and khakis came through. He had a red lanyard around his neck.

"That's the chair of governors," said Jonah, his voice high with excitement.

"Oh god," I said.

"Hi!" said Jonah, putting his hand out to him as he came down the steps.

My eyes locked with Sukhi and Lisa. He was so calm.

"We've prepared a few short speeches. We'd love it if you could come and listen," Jonah said.

I couldn't believe he was actually doing this. This was happening.

"It'd be my pleasure," said the governor, smiling warmly. "Where will you be delivering them?"

"Umm . . ." I pitched in. "By the mobile classrooms over there, where it's a bit quieter." I glanced at my phone. "In about half an hour."

"Great! I look forward to it," he said.

My cheeks warmed as I shook his hand.

"See you soon!" Sukhi said. She jerked her head as if to say "let's go" to me.

I looked around for Yusuf. He was chatting to the DJ with his friend. Maybe he'd forgotten about the rally, and Mum and Dad's chats had finally sunk in and he'd realized that neither Darren nor his rally were worth getting involved in. He knew that Mum and Dad would be here later for their shift on the raffle stall, so he *had* to stay with me. The relief I felt was as if I'd just singlehandedly saved the *Titanic*.

328

The school grounds were full of pockets of people. The buzz was electrifying. I stood on the ramp to the drama mobile classroom and swallowed. *You can do this*. If someone had said a year ago that I'd have come up with this idea, I'd have told them to stop being ridiculous. I'd only ever thought a fete was a fun day out with your friends, not a place we could actually make a difference. I guess being hated on had some benefits—it made you want to make change. My hands started sweating and the hair touching my neck felt damp under my scarf. *You can do this*, I told myself again.

People from the local area were scattered about enjoying their day. My insides glowed, seeing everyone getting along—there was even a man in a turban in the crowd. People had actually come together. Maybe everything would be okay.

Sukhi handed a burger to the DJ as the music thudded. She was telling him to stop playing for ten minutes while there was an "important speech," like we'd agreed. Of course Sukhi *had* to get a cheeky request in; she said earlier that she'd also ask him if he could play her favorite 3W track after his lunch. Yusuf and his mate were sitting on the grass next to the drama mobile dipping their chips in plastic ketchup tubs. Lisa was chatting to a couple of governors she'd recognized when we walked in. I spotted Jayden and his mates eating hot dogs in the Beat the Goalie queue behind the mobile. My stomach plunged, hoping they wouldn't ruin my speech. Mrs. Owen and our deputy head were at the activity next to them, watching kids throw wooden balls at a row of fake coconuts that were balanced on thin posts. I hoped they'd all stay there. I was glad Mum and Dad would go to the stall section round the corner when they got here and would be nowhere near us to hear our speeches.

Leon and Feifei came and stood with Sukhi a few meters in front of the mobile. They looked eagerly at me. Okay, this was it. I had to do it. For all the kids who'd had their rights taken away.

A smile instantly covered my face. Mum always said everything happened for a reason, and maybe this was it. Maybe I was supposed to be tested to my limits so that something good could come from it. I felt as if I had fireworks sparkling inside me. I didn't think I'd feel this way.

I took a deep breath, pulled Sukhi's whistle from my back pocket, and blew hard. And then again and again, until people noticed where the shrill noise was coming from.

Sukhi, Lisa, Leon, Feifei, and Jonah ushered people over. Mrs. Owen scanned the crowds, confusion on her face.

"I want to talk to you all today," I started. But from

the expressions on people's faces, I don't think they could hear me properly.

I eyed my surroundings to see if I could get to a higher position and noticed the picnic table on the grass next to the mobile classroom. I ran to the bench, leaping on the table like I was some sort of slow free runner. If I was going to do this, I might as well do it properly.

I stood tall, making sure I stepped away from the edge of the table. The growing crowd looked at me expectantly.

"I want to talk to all of you today," I shouted at the top of my voice. "About a human's right to express themselves." People murmured in the distance. *Carry on,* I told myself, as my eyes fell on Mrs. Owen, her arms folded across her chest. Her eyes closed, as if she wasn't breathing—and when she did, she would breathe fire.

"I didn't wear a hijab until this year. I never wanted to until I was older, but after the 3W bombing—" My voice cracked. My body juddered. *Don't cry, Aaliyah. Not now.* I took in some air, focusing on Sukhi and Lisa's faces telling me to go on. Jonah gnawed his nails as he watched.

"But after the bombing, I was targeted even more for being a Muslim. The terrorist that hurt my school friends and other children called himself a Muslim, but what he did was the opposite of the religion I know. I put on a hijab because I wanted people to look at me and be able to see straightaway that I am a Muslim, and that I'm a good person. I wanted everyone to know that Muslims aren't evil. That we aren't like the terrorists on the news and we don't want to hurt anyone, but just live peacefully like anyone else.

"I . . . I . . . want to be judged for my intelligence, my character, NOT for what I wear. And so today, I am asking you, the governors . . ." I scanned the bulging crowd, trying to spot the people wearing red lanyards. Some people had their phones up taking photos or recording. The chair of governors stood with Mrs. Owen, his arms folded, but his face was not angry, more surprised. She glared at me now, her lips pursed. I blinked and told myself to carry on.

" . . . to please think about the effect your recent ban on wearing religious symbols has had on people of faith, and the effect your rules on cultural expression have on us too. Instead of *helping* us, you have *divided* us and encouraged people to openly share their racist views, to openly attack us—for choosing to wear a religious or cultural symbol. I have been physically attacked at school. I didn't report it formally because after I mentioned it to a teacher, it seemed like it was more important I don't have this on my head than how I might feel." I left my hand on my head, pinching my scarf. "No one cared to ask *why* I put it on. Just like no one cared to ask Jonah why he hasn't felt confident to wear his kippah to school until today." I pointed at him and everyone's eyes followed. "The school should be making people feel included, not singling us out so that we're easier targets.

"So I'm asking you: how has this decision made us safer? How is this decision fair to all your students? If I *don't* wear my hijab, or Jonah *doesn't* wear his kippah, or Sukhi *doesn't* wear a turban, or Leon *doesn't* wear braids or a cross. HOW? Those of us who want to should be able to wear our religious clothing or express our cultures.

"It's really important for young people like us to be able to express our identities. It creates a good sense of self-esteem—if the school takes that away and controls how we express our differences, you're stripping us of our sense of belonging and confidence in ourselves." I blew out, relieved I'd remembered everything I'd practiced.

I pointed at Leon. "Leon said he felt that way when he was told he couldn't come to school with braids in Year Seven, and he'll talk more about that later . . . do you want us to leave school unsure about who we are and feeling confused and negative about ourselves?

"Through this hijab, I feel empowered. I don't have to worry about my hair in the morning, I don't have to worry about what I look like. Instead I can focus on my studies—isn't that what you want?" I stared straight at the chair of governors, who seemed to be interested in what I was saying. "Wearing *this* makes me a better person—when I'm upset with someone for insulting me, it helps me to remind myself it's better to walk away, when before I might have dealt with it by attacking them right back. When Sukhi's cousins wear their dastaar, they're showing they're ready and willing to serve and help. When Jonah and Leon wear their kippah and cross, they're expressing their commitment to their religion. When I'm wearing *this*, I make sure I work hard to be the best I can be. HOW can that be a bad thing?"

Sukhi, Lisa, Jonah, Feifei, and Leon burst into applause. Other adults and kids in the still-growing crowd started to clap too. I noticed a few Year Tens and Elevens and some teachers looking impressed, even Mr. Atkinson. The smattering of applause became a loud steady clap.

I spotted Yusuf on his phone, his face red and jaw clenched. He put it in his pocket and started pacing in front of the mobile classroom next to the one my table was in front of, looking for someone, possibly his friend. Something had happened.

"Aaliyah!" I looked down to see Mrs. Owen glaring up at me. "That's enough. You've had your say. Get down. Now."

Something scraped the table. I spun round. Feifei had climbed onto the table too. Brilliant! She was up next.

"Hey," I said and smiled. "Ready?"

"Yup," she said, and stepped forward.

I scanned the crowd to check if Yusuf was still there. He was on his phone again. His eyes had a weird faraway look, and he was wading through people as if he didn't see them, knocking them aside as he pushed past.

"Feifei would like to tell you about how her identity being questioned has affected—"

My leg was dragged backward, forcing me to fly forward. Before I knew it, I landed hard on my chest, my head and arms hanging off the edge of the table.

A collective gasp arose before someone screamed, "GET DOWN, TOWELHEAD! WHO DO YOU THINK YOU ARE, TELLIN' US WHAT TO DO?"

It was Sasha. Going for me. Oh god. I had to get up.

"SASHA WILLIAMS!" a teacher screamed.

I spun onto my back, but before I could sit up, Sasha had grabbed my shoes and dragged me toward her. I kicked out of her clutches and pushed on the table, crouching to leap up. She gripped my scarf and yanked my head.

That was it. I clasped her wrists and dug my nails into them, trying to get her to release her fingers from my scarf before she ripped it right off.

"SASHA WILLIAMS!" a teacher screamed again.

"OW!" she screamed, jolting her arms back and looking at her wrists. I took the opportunity and turned to the side of the table.

"COME BACK, YOU COW!" she screamed.

I rolled off the table, trying to land on my feet. My foot slipped, and I lost my balance.

"COME BAAAACK!!!" Sasha screamed as I thumped onto my side on the dry grass.

I turned over and got up. UGH. Everything hurt.

"Ali! Are you okay?" Sukhi and Lisa came running, their eyes wide, shock all over their faces.

"Urr. Yeah." I pulled my scarf back into place. "I'm good."

"Mrs. Owen's just dragged Sasha off to the side!" Lisa grinned.

"NO WAY!" I said, hobbling around to find a horde of people pushing to get closer to the mobile classroom, and Mr. Atkinson frantically trying to unlock the classroom door, probably so he and Mrs. Owen could tell Sasha off inside.

I scanned the crowd, even the DJ area, to find Yusuf. He would've jumped onto the table if he'd seen Sasha pounce on me.

But he was nowhere to be seen.

CHAPTER 44

MR. ATKINSON asked everyone to move away. People backed off. The DJ put on a new track. The teacher standing with him must've asked him to. Bass thumped from the speakers and immediately drew the crowd away, like rats to the Pied Piper's magic pipe. I shifted my neck to loosen the fabric around it. My heart raced faster by the second. I stood in the middle of the playground, unsure if I should stay and speak to a teacher or find Yusuf.

I eyed the playground to see where his friend was and noticed he was talking to someone in the crowd. My stomach lurched. Could he be round the corner at Mum and Dad's stall? He was annoyed with Dad for making him come, so that was unlikely. It must've been at least five minutes since he'd gone missing.

My eyes scanned the playground again. Nothing.

Everyone was heading back to the stalls to enjoy

the rest of their Saturday while Mrs. Owen and Mr. Atkinson focused on Sasha. All I could think of was Yusuf. He was out there somewhere getting into trouble.

"Ali!" Someone tapped me on my shoulder. It was Sukhi. "You okay?" she asked, searching my face.

"Huh? Uhh . . . No . . ." I said.

"Aaliyah?" It was Lisa.

"Come over here," I said, nodding toward the car park behind the lunch hall where no one could see us. My throat was dry, and I could barely speak.

As soon as we got onto quieter ground, I welled up. "It's Yusuf," I said. "He's gone and I think he's in trouble."

Sukhi yanked out her phone from her bag and glared at it.

Lisa held me by the shoulders. "Ali, I saw him run off up the drive. He was fuming."

I blinked, and a tear rolled down my cheek. My breathing got faster.

"The rally," said Sukhi, staring at her phone. "He must be going there."

"Give me that," I said, snatching Sukhi's phone from her. She was staring at a photo Darren had posted of a group of guys standing in a street on Snappo.

Whose country is it? Who's gonna win?

338

The caption was followed by a thinking emoji.

"Darren," said Lisa.

I looked at Sukhi and Lisa, and without a word we sprinted up the long drive to the school exit.

It felt like it took forever to get to the street, and all I could imagine was Yusuf at the rally getting hurt. As we approached the open car park gates, I turned to see if anyone had seen us leaving, but no one was there. The bass from the music at the fete was now a distant thumping.

An old red car was parked in front of us on the quiet, empty street. The passenger door was wide open, and a man was adjusting the placards sticking out of its back passenger window.

The placards were white, all with different messages painted in black:

STOP ISLAM

GET OUT

WHITE ZONE

GO BACK TO YOUR OWN COUNTRY AND TAKE YOUR HIJAB WITH YOU

One had the Nazi symbol painted on it. I gulped.

The rally people had come, but not to support the fundraiser.

A spit of rain dropped on my nose. The gray sky hung heavy and low. It was early afternoon, but the color of the sky made it feel closer to sunset. It was hard to tell if it was the wind or the ugly words on those signs that was giving me shivers.

"Darren . . ." said Lisa from somewhere.

Sukhi and I locked eyes.

"AALIYAH!"

I looked behind me and then around, which is when I saw Lisa gesturing from a few meters away on my right, her face ashen. Sukhi pulled her phone out and swiped to video. Behind Lisa, I saw two guys wrestling each other on the ground.

It was Yusuf.

And Darren.

CHAPTER
45

LISA RAN OVER TO THEM. "Darren! STOP!" She grabbed Darren's shoulder as he rolled on top of Yusuf. Darren pushed her hard, sending her flying.

Darren did a double-take. "YOU STUPID IDIOT." He jumped off Yusuf as soon as he clocked Lisa had fallen and thundered toward her, his shoulders hunched forward. "I've been looking for you. YOU TAKING THE TERRORISTS' SIDE AGAIN? You think no one tells me you're supporting pro-Muslim speeches! Stop wasting my time and get in! I've gotta get back to the rally!"

Darren clinched Lisa's good arm and hauled her toward the car. "WHAT'D I TELL YOU LAST TIME? EH?"

"LEAVE ME ALONE!" Lisa screamed as she tried to get out of his grip. "IF YOU DON'T, I SWEAR I'M GOING TO SHOW THE POLICE YOUR

WEAPONS AND ALL THE PLACARDS YOU'VE BEEN MAKING. I'VE HAD ENOUGH!" She pointed at me and shouted, "She's my best friend, and not ONE Muslim has ever done anything to you—ever. No one YOU know has done anything wrong. Darren, you're WRONG! GET OFF ME!"

He'd started shoving her head into the car and then her body. It all happened so quickly, Sukhi and I hadn't even looked at each other until now. Her mouth hung low, as shocked as I was.

How were we going to get Lisa away from him?

A big burly man who lived across from the school stepped into his front garden, talking on his phone, watching the commotion.

A bus hissed past.

"LISA!" I cried.

I leaped onto the canopied grass verge where the car was parked. My Converse crunched the dry twigs and bark beneath me.

Darren and Lisa turned. Relief overcame Lisa's teary face, and a snarl appeared on Darren's.

"STAY AWAY FROM MY SISTER, YOU TERRORIST!" he shouted, continuing to push Lisa as she struggled.

Sukhi caught up with me, her brown ponytail swinging from side to side. I tried to gulp in air to slow my breathing.

"What, you're picking on little girls now?" Yusuf shouted. "Can't handle someone your own size?"

Darren spun around, his eyes bulging and spit flying from his lips. "NOW YOU'VE ASKED FOR IT!"

I eased back out of his way.

A couple holding hands had mooched in our direction; now they were staring and slowly edging away as if they didn't want to get hurt.

"Pipe down or I'll—" Yusuf marched toward Darren, his hands in fists.

"Or you'll WHAT?" Darren sneered.

Darren put his face into Yusuf's, rolling his shoulders into him. He still wasn't done.

The blood hammered through my body.

Speak up. Speak up, I told myself. I'd spent all of this time planning to speak at the fete, because I thought speaking up about my right to wear my hijab would fix everything, but now I realized that it didn't matter that the speech had gone well, because what I needed to do was to stand up to Darren. That was the only thing that would free me.

I'd spent every day since the concert being scared of Darren and trying to avoid him. But I hadn't actually thought about what I should *say* to him. I didn't think I'd ever have to. Up close. In the flesh. In front of my brother and best friends. I'd focused on avoiding him and keeping Yusuf away from him, but now I needed to show him that his hate had no control or power over me. I had to find my voice in front of *him*.

If I didn't, I'd never shake off what he'd done to me.

To us.

I had to fight back.

I took a breath and closed my eyes for a beat. An icy sensation ran up and down my spine. My hands quivered as I looked straight at him.

"Look at you!" I screamed. "Do you think THIS is going to change anything?!"

He stopped and glanced at me. Yusuf too.

Then Darren grimaced and shoved Yusuf hard.

I took a step and swallowed. "LOOK AT LISA!"

Darren turned.

"You keep saying Muslims, brown people and refugees are ruining your country and your life? Well, you're *actually* ruining lives, and one of them is your own sister's. You're so blind with rage, you'd even hurt *her*! Look what you're doing to her!"

Darren blinked, as if he didn't know I had a voice . . . or a brain.

Yusuf looked just as surprised.

Then Darren sneered. "You don't know nothing! Shut up!"

Lisa walked to me and stood by my side. She'd got out of the car. Phew. But I had to finish what I'd started.

"*YOU'RE* AN EMBARRASSMENT TO THIS COUNTRY!" My face felt as if it might explode. "*YOU* SHOULD LEAVE!"

Lisa put her hand on my shoulder as if to say, "Well done."

Darren snarled, his red face raging as he moved toward me. Yusuf put his arm out to stop him.

Darren turned back, his nose almost touching my brother's. Darren's eyes bulged, his chest out.

My throat felt scratchy. My chest ached. It had taken everything to speak up. I couldn't just stand here.

"DARREN, DON'T!" screamed Lisa, as he raised his fist toward Yusuf's face.

I swallowed. He was going to hit him. My spine tingled. My stomach churned. I was going to be sick.

The big man with tattooed arms from across the road marched up to them, his shoulders hunched and jaw clenched. At the same time, a police car screeched to a halt, and two police officers in black uniforms jumped out, leaving their car doors open, their walkie-talkies screeching.

Darren's friend reversed his car a few meters to get distance from the police car and drove off.

A police officer with a ginger moustache sprinted to get between Darren and Yusuf and pushed them apart. He turned to Yusuf, but the burly man pointed at Darren. "It's him! He's been attacking this guy and also that girl," he said, pointing at Lisa.

I released my breath. The man who lived across from the school must've called the police. I wanted to hug him for it.

Darren backed away with his hands up. "I didn't do nothing!"

"We just stopped you from punching him," said the other officer with black curly hair. "And we've got witnesses. Now get in the car." He grabbed Darren's arm and pushed him to the police car.

The officer with the moustache pulled the burly man and Yusuf to one side and took some notes.

I shared a look with Sukhi and Lisa, then glanced at the police car, where Darren slouched in the back seat with his head in his hands.

CHAPTER
46

MY FINGERS TINGLED as Sukhi flicked a persistent fly away from my face, then hugged me. "OH MY GOD!" Sukhi laughed nervously. "I can't believe you stood up to Darren like that!" She turned to Lisa, who looked exhausted. "You too, Lise!"

"Let's get back to the fete," Yusuf said, rubbing his neck. He had a cut on his lip and his T-shirt was creased, with a speck of blood on it.

"Hang on, Yusuf." I gestured that I needed a moment with my friends.

He stepped back and pulled out his phone and started typing something.

"Lisa, you have to call your dad," I said. "Look, you can't wait till your mum comes off shift or wakes up. And if they do divorce, it's not gonna be because of you. It's probably because they don't get on or something."

Sukhi chimed in. "And if they do divorce because

they fight about this, then it's 'cause they didn't keep an eye on Darren—that's hardly your fault and you can't avoid it if it's gonna happen. I mean, if either of them would rather let Darren treat you like this, then you're better off with one parent anyway!"

"Please, Lisa." I put my hand on her good shoulder. "You have to tell on him. He's getting worse. He might have been shocked when the police got him, but he's not gonna let you off at home, is he?"

Lisa shuddered. "You're right." She sighed deeply. "Let me use your phone?"

"Thank you!" I said, pulling it out of my pocket and handing it to her. Thank god Dad had given it back to me this morning.

"Can I log you out of your Gmail? His number's on one of the emails he sent me from work."

"Yes, 'course."

Lisa stepped away from us and started thumbing the phone.

"What's the time?" I asked Sukhi as she pressed Send on her phone. All the photos and videos Sukhi had taken of Darren attacking Lisa and Yusuf swooshed over to Feifei.

"Umm . . ." Sukhi said, eyeing her phone. "1:21 P.M." She pushed her glasses up her nose.

"Oh, phew!" I said, letting my head fall back. "I have to find Mrs. Owen and the governors and say sorry about what Sasha did and for ruining the fete."

"Err, no, you don't," said Sukhi, eyeing me from head to toe as if I was stupid. "Mrs. Owen saw you running away from Sasha. She took Sasha into the mobile with Mr. Atkinson. *Sasha's* the one who's in trouble. By the way, you look a mess." She was focusing on the scuff marks on my white top from where Sasha had dragged me.

"Well, *he* looks worse," I said, staring at Yusuf's lip.

"Feifei said she's gonna put the photos and videos on her anonymous photo blog and Snappo account as soon as she gets home," said Sukhi.

"I can't wait to see him shamed publicly. If the police pick them up, even better. He might think that big man with the tattoos who called the police took them. Anyone who passed by could've taken them."

My pulse throbbed thinking about Darren.

"Hey!" It was Lisa, red-eyed, my mobile in her hand.

It was such a relief to have everyone together and safe. Sukhi wrapped her arms around Lisa. I pounced on both my friends and squeezed them.

"Lise. You okay?" I said, inhaling the drifting smell of burgers and chips, my stomach growling.

"Yeah, I'm fine. Stop worrying! I told Dad . . . Are *you* okay?" she asked, picking some dry grass off my scarf.

"Yeah, I'm good," I said, not really interested in talking about me. "What did your dad say?"

"I'm so glad I told him. He didn't have a clue because he's been away with work for so long. He was angry at Mum for not telling him, but I told him it's not her fault. She's been working long shifts and had no way of knowing what Darren was up to because I never told her. I was crying that much, Dad sounded like he's going to kill Darren himself when he sees him. He said he's going to the police station as soon as he gets off the train from London in an hour. I can't wait to see him." Lisa's eyes started filling up.

"THANK GOD!" Both Sukhi and I chimed, our faces showing Lisa we were proud of her.

"I'll meet you in the Year Eight toilets, yeah?" I said to both of them. "Just wait for me, in case I get stopped by a teacher or something."

"You want us to come?" asked Lisa.

"Nah. I won't be long. You guys go ahead," I said, making eyes toward Yusuf texting on his phone, so that Lisa and Sukhi would get the hint and leave.

"So, umm . . ." I said to Yusuf as we stepped onto the long drive leading to the school car park. "Aren't you gonna thank me?"

"For what?" he said.

"Oh. My. God. Could you be any denser?" I rolled my eyes. "You'd have broken something by now or be arrested, if we hadn't stepped in."

Yusuf stopped. "What do you want me to do? Nominate you for the Nobel Peace Prize?"

I jabbed my elbow into his arm. Twice.

"Okay, okay . . . Thanks for saving my butt." He smirked. "Never knew you could be so loud, or brave—or kinda scary."

I grinned and pushed my hands into my pockets.

"Oh my god, that was unbelievable," I said a few minutes later, knotting the two fabric ends of my scarf around the back of my neck after I'd reset it in the toilets.

"*Unbelievable* isn't the word, Ali," said Sukhi, applying some lipstick. "I can't believe you told Darren he's an embarrassment!" She side-eyed me and continued, "I think you're my superhero now!" She laughed.

"I *know* you are," said Lisa, putting her uninjured arm around me. "Aaliyah Girl."

"Erm, no," Sukhi and I said together.

I smiled, still not quite able to grasp any of the last day had happened. This wasn't my life. I didn't do any of this . . . stuff.

In the playground people were engrossed in happy conversations, unaware of the chaos that had taken place just outside the school. I scanned the grounds to find Yusuf. He was chatting to the DJ, who was licking his whippy ice cream as they spoke.

I stood taking in the noise and the scene around me, and took a beat.

"Let's get out of here," I said. "I'm so tired. Let's go back to mine and listen to some 3W. This DJ's got the worst taste in music."

"What about the governors and Mrs. Owen?" asked Lisa. "You wanted to speak to them about the ban."

"I said what I had to say before Sasha jumped me, I guess." I shrugged. "I don't think we're going to get the ban reversed easily, you know. Look what happened in the middle of our speeches." My stomach flipped. "And even if we do manage it, there are so many people outside of school, like Darren, who will never accept us or our beliefs." I linked arms with both Lisa and Sukhi and straightened my shoulders. "This isn't over—we're going to have to make a proper plan. I might sit down with my dad tonight and see what he suggests—maybe we could see if we can work with other high schools in Lambert if any have a similar ban. Really put the pressure on the school."

"That's a good idea," said Lisa.

"Yeah, it is," Sukhi said as we walked. "Sasha's racist attack was probably a good thing, actually. She's only made herself look like a total sickburger."

"That's true," I said. "And the best thing is *she*

provided the evidence to Mrs. Owen, who didn't even bother dealing with her when I went to her before."

"But this time Mrs. Owen can't deny it happened," said Lisa, flicking her hair off her face. "And the governors saw that it's the racists that make the school look bad, not religious symbols."

"Hey!" Jonah waved as he made his way toward us.

"Hi!" I awkwardly waved back with both my hands, which remained linked with Lisa and Sukhi's.

"You okay?" he asked. "We were worried. Mr. Atkinson's been looking for you, but we couldn't find you anywhere." He smiled at Lisa and looked down at his shoes, his cheeks flushed.

Sukhi and I raised our brows at each other.

"What happened after? Did Feifei get to finish her speech?" I asked.

"No. It was chaos after Sasha jumped you. Mrs. Owen dragged her away, her parents were called in, and everyone was asked to move on."

Oh, yeah. I saw that. How could I forget? It felt as if it happened days ago.

"But we spoke to the chair of governors. I told him everything that we discussed and how you inspired us all to speak up, and how so many of us felt it was unfair that the school had banned our right to express ourselves and not focused on the hate speech or bullying."

"Oh, wow. Thanks, Jonah," I said.

"You would've done a better job. What you said on the picnic table—it was brilliant. Brave." His honest eyes made me blush. "But I said what I could after you'd gone, and he said he hadn't looked at it from this perspective and he was going to see what the other governors thought about discussing the ban again and maybe taking another vote." He put his hands in his pockets.

"NO WAY!" I turned to Lisa then Sukhi and grinned. "So it might actually get reversed?"

"Yeah, it might." Jonah said.

The DJ put on another track. Something old. Sukhi tutted and led us all away from it.

"Where are you going?" Jonah joined us. "What about the PTA charity collection announcement?"

"We've raised the money—we can find out how much we raised later. I want to go home now. Don't want to bump into Sasha or her parents—god knows what she'll do—and I can't let my mum and dad see me like this," I said, looking down at my filthy top.

He looked at me as if he agreed. "What are we gonna do next, then?" he asked as he spotted his little sister skipping toward him with a giant bubble-wand in her hand.

"We're gonna figure that out." I smiled as I locked eyes with Lisa and Sukhi.

EPILOGUE

"Aaliyah!" Lisa squealed, throwing her arms wide open. "Feels like ages since I saw you."

"It's only been a week, Lise!" I laughed, entering into a tight bear hug and taking in the smell of washing detergent from her fresh new uniform. It was the first day of school in September, and we were all sparkling and clean, ready for Year Nine.

"How was the trip to drop Darren at the airport?" Sukhi asked Lisa, linking my arm and dragging us all ahead to start walking. I was glad she asked—I wanted to know if Darren had gone.

"Ugh. It got cancelled, THANK GOD. I told Mum I didn't want to go, but she said I had to. Then the police told Dad that Darren can't leave the country even if it's only for a few weeks because of his court case. So Dad said if he can't go and volunteer at the hospital in Zimbabwe, Darren has to volunteer at his office. He's taken him to London to get him away from me."

"So what's he actually gonna do there?" I asked.

"Do we have to talk about Darren?" said Lisa, flicking her hair off her shoulders.

"Not after this—just tell us what he's doing in London!" said Sukhi, giving me a look that said, *I'm doing this for you.*

"Well, Dad's got him volunteering on some project that maps all their work across the world, and he has to attend appointments in London for that program for terrorists . . . I think it prevents angry people from becoming terrorists? And Dad said he does seem a bit different. Anyway, guess what? I get his TV in *my* room!" Lisa grinned as if she'd won the lottery.

I couldn't help but smile. Oh, the irony. The guy who had spent months calling Muslims terrorists had to be on a terrorist program wherever he lived in the country. Ha! "When's your dad back?" I asked as I adjusted my stretchy hairband. Hijabs were still banned in school, so I planned to cover my hair the best I could until we could convince the governors.

"He'll stay with him a week, settle him in his friend's apartment and show him around the hospital he used to work in . . . Anyway," she asked, looking at me, "how was *your* London trip?"

We stopped at the pedestrian crossing, all our eyes on the flashing amber traffic light.

"It was all right, actually. The journey was rubbish—I had a duvet pushed up against my head the whole way—but once we dropped Yusuf at his student halls, Mum and Dad took me to Oxford Street."

"Yeah, I saw your Snaps! I'm so borrowing that top!" said Sukhi, her eyes lighting up.

"I can't believe you bought another pair of Converse!" Lisa rolled her eyes.

"Had to!" I said. "Got to make the most of Mum and Dad in an emotional mood! Mum would've bought me anything, she's so grateful she still has one kid left at home."

Lisa giggled. "Where did you leave Fluffball?"

"It's Furball!" I laughed. "Mum let her out for the day. She might have even visited Mr. Baldwin. I've been taking her over to cuddle him every evening since he got home—he can't look after her anymore because he keeps forgetting things and can't walk properly. We're getting a cat flap put in so Furball will be able to do that herself whenever she wants." We walked across the road once the green man flashed up. "Mum's fine because of her allergy tablets. I can't believe I went through all of that stress hiding her, when all I had to do was come clean! I am so stupid."

"Yep!" said Sukhi, and I elbowed her.

We got to the other side of the road and I looked at both Sukhi and Lisa and smiled. The September morning sun lit up their faces. We were in Year Nine. We'd got through the summer and managed to keep Yusuf and Darren apart. Darren had been sent off to volunteer in London to sort himself out and get away from the "wrong crowd." He would hopefully get punished for his racist behavior when his case eventually got to court, and he was now on a far-right terrorist watch list himself.

Dad had introduced Yusuf to his police-detective friend, who told him the men he was hanging around with were on a police watch list and some had been in prison, and thankfully Yusuf stopped seeing them. He'd come to his senses and realized that being violent at rallies wasn't going to change anything, but would probably ruin his own life. He'd even helped me with my notes on why the ban at school was wrong. He was finally starting university, and it was just me, Mum, and Dad at home.

Sasha was expelled after the fete. Lisa said Sasha's mum had stormed in and shouted at Mrs. Owen and told her she was taking Jayden out too. If that was true, then Jayden was probably not going to be in school today, which was the best thing ever.

Before the summer holidays, I met the school counselor because I'd promised Mum, and it went a lot better than I thought it would. I was going to meet her this term too, to help me figure out how to handle people like Jayden, Sasha, and Darren. Those three might be gone from my life—I hoped forever—but I knew there would always be people like them I'd have to deal with.

The chair of governors had written to me after the fete, and I would hopefully be meeting him with the Gamechangers next week once we'd settled back into school. He said he would ask the governors to reconsider the ban. I'd heard Dad telling Mum there were rumors that some governors felt there was a "failure of leadership" and they'd also be discussing Mrs. Owen's actions at the next meeting.

Jonah, Leon, Feifei, Sukhi, Lisa, and me had chatted online over the summer. We discussed how to tackle the bullying in school and show that the religious symbols ban wasn't the answer. We thought talking more positively about our differences and identities might be a better way to approach it. Some older kids in Year Ten and Eleven, who had heard our speeches and conversations with the governors at the fete, had approached us in the last week of school and told us they'd join us in the new school year to maybe set up a committee. So we were looking forward to sharing our ideas with the governors—and hopefully bringing Mrs. Owen round.

The last few months hadn't been easy, but we were alive. There had been no more attacks in Lambert. Jo was out of hospital and a portion of the money raised at the summer fete went toward getting an accessible bathroom built for her downstairs in her house. She'd even replied properly to my message after she'd left the hospital telling me she'd like to meet up once she felt better. Everyone was getting on again—even our neighbor, Mr. Grimshaw, was managing to ignore us and not scowl at us . . . as much.

I'd realized that I wasn't alone after all. There were lots of people who were judged for who they were and struggling to express themselves, just like me, and it was only *together* that we could fight back against anyone who thought we shouldn't be ourselves. I knew now, despite all my fears, I could still have a voice and stand up to hatred. And there were so many ways to stand up to it.

Best of all, I had my two best friends on either side of me, and I felt whole again.

If it weren't for all of the challenges we'd had to get through, we wouldn't *ever* be as strong as we were now.

COMING TOGETHER AND SPEAKING UP FOR OTHERS

AN ALLY IS SOMEONE from one group who stands up to support another group of people who are being treated unjustly. An ally realizes there are people who are disadvantaged and stands up for them against injustice and for what is right. They show empathy and compassion for people who are targeted, by allowing them to be heard and feel supported.

There are many ways to be an ally. Sometimes it is being part of a bigger fight, showing up at protests, marches, writing to politicians, and supporting a larger community, like when white people supported the Civil Rights Movement against racial segregation, and when men asked for equal rights for women in the suffrage movement.

But you can also be an ally by putting yourself in someone else's shoes and understanding that when you see injustice, you can make a difference by stepping in and speaking up, like Lisa, Sukhi, Jonah, Leon, and Feifei did, simply by being good friends.

Being a good ally is:

- Using your privilege (be it wealth, education, social standing, or influence) to help empower others
- Asking questions when you see something unfair or unjust
- Recognizing we are never too young to be an ally
- Understanding we all have a voice and using it to uplift the voices of people who are being treated badly
- Giving support to others who need your help
- Being there for that person but allowing them to speak up—standing *with* them, not in front of them!
- Talking to others about how to be a good ally and what is just
- Learning the history about your community and the advances made by activists that came before
- Remembering it may be lonely to stand up/be an ally/fight injustice, but you are not alone
- Seeking out groups working together to amplify your voice

Workshops exploring identity, allyship, human rights, and freedom of expression are available with A.M. Dassu.

GLOSSARY

Alhamdulillah: praise be to God (Allah)

asr salat: the afternoon prayer (one of the compulsory Islamic daily prayers)

As-salaamu alaikum: peace be upon you (a Muslim greeting)

baitay: "child" in Urdu

behen (Savita Behen): "sister" in Urdu

beta: "son" in Urdu

beti: "daughter" in Urdu

chips: French fries

chippy: a shop that sells chips/French fries

daadi: grandma on father's side (Dad's mother)

dada: granddad on father's side (Dad's father)

dastaar: the turban worn by amritdhari/keshdhari Sikhs (those who have taken amrit, a commitment to be faithful, and maintain uncut hair). It is normally worn by men, but women can wear it too. Some women wear the smaller version called kesgi. Through the practice of wearing a freshly-tied dastaar every day, Sikhs keep themselves reminded of their solemn duty of standing up for equality, justice, self-respect, and selfless service toward all of mankind.

diamante: glass that is cut to look like diamonds

haldi doodh: turmeric milk

high school: in the UK students join high school aged eleven and leave at sixteen. It is the equivalent of starting junior high school in the US.

hijab: commonly used to describe a head covering or scarf worn by some Muslim women, especially in the English-speaking world and South Asian countries. It is an Arabic word that means *barrier* or *partition*. In Islam, hijab is a moral code that includes speech, behavior, and attitude, in addition to clothes for men and women.

holiday: vacation

ice lolly/lollies: popsicles

in shaa Allah: God willing (hopefully)

kurta: a loose collarless shirt, usually worn by South Asian people

kippah: or yarmulke, the traditional small head covering worn by Jewish men

lehenga: an ankle-length skirt, usually embroidered

marking: grading

ma shaa Allah: as God willed

mehndi: temporary henna tattoos usually drawn on hands or legs

naana: granddad on mother's side (Mum's father)

naani: grandma on mother's side (Mum's mother)

nappy: diaper

Nafl shukar: an optional prayer to give thanks

pastoral head: a senior position in a school to ensure the physical and emotional welfare of pupils

register: attendance record at school taken in the mornings and afternoons when students are in their form (home) rooms

revising: studying for a test/exam

salwar kameez: a long tunic worn over loose pleated trousers which taper around the ankles, usually worn by South Asian women

sari: a long garment wrapped and draped around the body, usually worn by South Asian women

topi: the traditional hat/skullcap Muslim men wear

trainers: sneakers

Walaikum as-salaam: peace be upon you too (in response to the Muslim greeting: "As-salaamu alaikum")

zuhr: the noon prayer (one of the compulsory Islamic daily prayers)

AUTHOR'S NOTE

EVERY TIME there is a terrorist attack, the first thing I think after praying that people haven't been hurt is that I hope the attacker is not a Muslim. I know what will follow if they are. Young people are affected by global news; it seeps into perceptions, conversations, and then sometimes actions. Growing up, I didn't encounter animosity the way that my children do now. When my eldest son started high school, an innocent eleven-year-old boy asked him "Is Islam a terrorist religion?" and "Is your god a terrorist?" That boy wasn't being vicious—it's what he'd heard at home and had been exposed to in the news.

My son responded in a mature and polite manner and told him that it wasn't the case. When he got home and told me, I had to explain why the boy and his parents might think like that.

The conversations that I have with my children—about the political climate, the language being used, the need for them to be exemplary so that no one will put them on a "terror list"—are sadly wholly different to the conversations I had aged eleven about music, reading, arts and crafts. But I have no choice as I try to help them navigate an increasingly prejudiced world.

Fight Back was inspired by recent terrorist events and the subsequent rise of the far right, and my desire to put a spotlight on a community that is vilified in the media. Islamophobia and prejudice are a sad reality for people from Muslim backgrounds. Hate crime is on the rise, and anti-Muslim attacks have risen year on year. *Fight Back* challenges the stereotype constantly depicted in the news and in films that Muslims aren't peaceful and a Muslim woman can only be empowered if she doesn't wear a headscarf, or if she is not religious. This story seeks to authentically represent the true lives of Muslims, particularly independent women who are free to make their own decisions.

Through *Fight Back* I wanted to show a different side to a story the world thinks it knows. I wanted to show how Islamist terrorism affects Muslims and also how far-right beliefs not only affect Muslims, Jews, and people of color but equally the families of far-right ideologists. I also wanted to show that it is not only a white working-class problem; in *Fight Back* we see how the negative media narrative affects Sukhi's mum, Mr. Kumar, Mrs. Owen, Darren, and even Yusuf.

We've seen the rise of the far right and division of communities across the world in recent years. Far-right politicians have emboldened those with previously hidden racist, xenophobic, antisemitic, and Islamophobic ideologies to come forward and act on their beliefs. Research shows the far right have engaged with young people online during the pandemic, and it is becoming a bigger problem than we once thought. To stamp these ideologies out, we need to start discussing what's happening at home and at school early. Stories are a vital tool for this—showing that there is nothing to fear, that there is another side to the narrative we might have been told. It is only through such stories that we can learn about—and from—different lives and cultures, and hopefully bring people together. And this is what drove me to write this book—the hope that Aaliyah's and Lisa's story will do just that.

Like Aaliyah and so many children who will read this book, I bridge two cultures, not completely fitting into one or the other. They are intertwined. I am privileged to be able to enjoy and understand both East and West, and so this book was driven by my desire to show that people from minority communities aren't that different; we share the same hopes and fears that others do. And I wanted to write characters who are compelled by their Muslim faith to do good, just like the thousands of other people of faith I know. But they are also flawed—because they're human.

The research for this book was harrowing. The most difficult: articles and footage of young people fleeing a concert bombing, seeing far-right posters—just like the ones depicted in this story—displayed in the UK as recently as 2017, and speaking to girls who were Aaliyah's age who have faced the same anxiety and prejudice. I spoke to people with the diverse lived experiences featured in this book about being judged and their identities stereotyped. Aaliyah's parents are inspired by people I know, and Aaliyah's initial experiences are very similar to those of my own children. Some of the conversations in the story are true to life, including those of Mrs. Owen, which were based on reported conversations between teachers and their Muslim students in France, where wearing a hijab is banned in school. In July 2021, France introduced an "anti-separatism" bill to battle Islamist terrorism, which included aggressive policing of Muslims and a ban on Muslim women under the age of eighteen wearing a hijab in public. And although we haven't seen a ban in schools in the UK or a widespread ban in the US yet, I wanted to explore a mismanaged school environment (which thankfully most schools reading this will not have!) and the impact racism and far-right ideology has on family and friendships, and the strength that comes from working together to stand up to it.

Like *Boy, Everywhere*, this novel aims to reflect the experiences of those who have faced discrimination, and for readers to experience and understand the impact of prejudice. Stereotypes are hurtful and they usually emphasize and belittle a part of a young person's identity they can't control. Recent revelations in sports news have highlighted the importance of words and how comments or "banter" about an individual's identity can be immensely harmful. Aaliyah's story seeks to build empathy, and helps to challenge stereotypes and break down barriers in our society.

This story about family, friendship, identity, freedom of expression, bullying, resistance, and belonging shows readers that awful things do happen, but with hope and courage and by working together, we can empower ourselves and turn things around. It enables us to walk in others' shoes and encourages discussion to combat the negative narrative embedded in our society through media and political positioning.

My hope is that through this book readers will see a happy, hard-working family that faces down challenges because of the actions of someone and something that has nothing to do with them, and understand how that family might feel in the face of those challenges.

Aaliyah's lived experience is individual and her journey uniquely her own, but through it she learns that others are going through similar experiences, and even though they are different to her, they have a lot in common that can lead to solidarity.

Some adults may feel this subject is too challenging, but it's a sad reality that Aaliyah's experiences are reflected in society and that many young people—of all backgrounds—struggle to express their identity and feel alone, scared, and judged. My hope is for anyone who hasn't been able to express themselves the way they want, or has been excluded, or doesn't feel like they belong, to see themselves in this story. Many people experience such struggles, but one thing is true: we are stronger when we support each other.

I hope that anyone reading this will see that though bad things happen, together we can get through them, and no matter how awful things get for you, you're never alone—there will always be someone who can empathize and who is willing to work beside you to make things better.

Growing up and finding your identity is never easy. If you're struggling, I hope you will see your own story through Aaliyah's. Not everyone is accepted for who they are or who they want to be. But please know that you're not alone.

ACKNOWLEDGMENTS

I COULDN'T HAVE WRITTEN this book without the village of gorgeous people who have wholeheartedly supported me these last few years.

A huge thanks must go to my critique group, Critterati, who read some of the first draft back in 2018 and encouraged me to finish it. Nicky Browne, thank you for also reading the later version when you were so busy, and encouraging me to develop it, you are awesome.

I cannot go on without thanking my confidant and dear friend, Catherine Coe, who told me all those years back that I had to get rid of the auction and add an exciting subplot. It's been a difficult year but you brought me so much joy throughout it. Thankful for you and for all of the things we do together!

Thank you to my agent, Jennifer Laughran, who loved the premise. It wouldn't be the book it is if you hadn't pushed me to go back and write it better! Thank you also to Christine Hepperman for helping me see how it could be.

The biggest thanks to my US publisher Lee and Low and my incredible editor Stacy Whitman, who snapped the book up before they'd finished reading it and before anyone else could! Thank you for believing in my storytelling and for working so closely with me and for pushing me to do my best.

A mahoosive thanks to my UK publisher Scholastic and Lauren Fortune, Ruth Bennett, Sophie Cashell, Arub Ahmed, Sarah Dutton, Harriet Dunlea, and Jenny Glencross for the beautiful offer letter (I want to frame it), the fastest contract and on-signing advance in history, for a supportive and wonderful editorial experience, and for making this book a hero title. I am truly honored.

Zainab "Daby" Faidhi, the award-winning illustrator who worked on the films *The Breadwinner* and *Shaun the Sheep*, chose to work on my second cover too, despite being busy in her new senior role in LA and not taking on any freelance work. Thank you, your support means the world and I *love* it SO much!

A huge thanks to Emma Roberts for rescuing me when I was lost and in despair and for giving me the confidence and support to see what needed to go. It meant a lot to me. Thanks to Dr. Philippa East for all of your advice on trauma psychology and anxiety and for telling me this book is stunning and honest.

Kaye Tew, you're a beautiful human being. Thank you for wholeheartedly supporting my work, giving feedback and connecting me with teachers in

Manchester who had worked with children around the time of the Manchester concert bombing. This book is better because of you.

Thank you to Bilal J, for sharing your experience of the Manchester Arena bombing with me and for fact-checking the book and telling me it was brilliant and true to your experience.

A mahoosive thanks must go to Sajeda Amir who taught girls who were Aaliyah's age in Manchester when the Arena was bombed. Her incredible support and feedback on the interactions of teachers inspired me to make Mrs. Owen take the rap! I also can't thank you enough for connecting me with your wonderful English class. Thank you, Class, for reading the book and for your written feedback. It was truly wonderful to meet you and hear how you connected with the characters and how realistic they felt to you. Rahma Yennoune, I loved your reactions to each chapter. Juily Zamal, I'm so glad it inspired you to do more. Zunairah Afzaal, I'm delighted you couldn't put it down, and Saleha Bilal, that you thought it was incredible!

A giant thank you to dear Joanna de Guia for your sincerity and honesty, your guidance about Jewish representation, for helping me fix that "particular conversation" and fact-checking the tiny details. It is so much better now! And Sita Brahmachari for your heartfelt suggestions—Mrs. Owen went rogue thanks to you!

A huge thanks also to Alex Wheatle for reading it early and for supporting me. You are such an inspiration, and I can't thank you enough for that mind-blowing quote. Heartfelt thanks to Liz Kessler for reading it when you weren't well—you are a wonder and I adore you. Thank you for telling me this book is important and relevant, and giving me confidence to go with Jonah.

Thank you to Caroline Fielding for your encouragement and feedback and to Rumena Aktar for yours; Aaliyah is off the roof because of you! And to Guntaas K. Chugh for telling me you loved the book and that Sukhi had been depicted accurately and well. And to Liz Flanagan for reading it early and for the cat advice. Kathryn Evans, you are a warm hug and the love I need always, thank you for saying this book really matters. Patrice Lawrence—I made Leon a nerdy Black boy with a father who is a professor for you. Representation matters!

Thank you to all my friends who have cheered me on and celebrated each tiny and big step I've taken, Sarah Broadley, Louie Stowell, Bob Stone, Kate Mallinder, Alex Shepherd, Lucy Coats, Hamida Seedat, Saima Ahsan, Louise Cliffe-Minns, Julie Sullivan, Jo Franklin, Louisa Glancy, Kate Walker, Dawn Finch, Nina Wadcock, Sophie Wills, Nizrana Farook, Eiman Munro, Alexandros Plasatis, Rashmi

Sirdeshpande, Catherine Emmett, Swapna Haddow, Claire Watts, Maisie Chan, Vanessa Harbour, Mo O'Hara, Kirsty Applebaum, Marie Bastings, Lu Fraser, Emma Reynolds, Anna Orenstein, Savita Kalhan, Nicky Schmidt, Catherine Johnson, and so many more I can't fit here that are in my SCBWI group and in the SWAGGERS.

And now my darling family: my husband Imran and children Mustafa, Ahmed, and Hana. I couldn't have done any of this without your beautiful, whole-hearted support. Thank you for your patience when I was stressed, for reading the book and celebrating every success. Mustafa, thank you for being my first child beta reader and for giving me invaluable insights into a thirteen-year-old's mind. You said this was my best book; hope you still like the final now that Aaliyah doesn't whack Darren with a stick! Hana, you read the book, aged ten, because you're "my biggest fan" and I was so impressed you understood all of the concepts! Ahmed, thank you for being my resident graphic designer and for all of your techy support!

Thank you to Ma and Dad Dassu and the Dassus Up North for all of your support, for sending hot chocolate and gifts to sustain me, for understanding when I couldn't visit you because I had to work to deadlines, and appreciating how much energy this work takes.

And finally, my mum. Thank you for telling the world to buy my books, for your patience and for giving me space to write when I needed it. Thank you for sending chicken soup when I was ill. If it weren't for you, I wouldn't be where I am today.

And of course God for everything; thank you for blessing me with a supportive family, friends, a writing community, wonderful publishers, librarians, book-sellers and amazing teachers, multiple awards, a com-puter, time, energy, and dedication to do something I not only enjoy, but also means the world to me.

This is a tribute to all of you.   ♡